I0769976

THE SENATOR'S WIDOW

Aoibh Wood

This book is dedicated to the good people of Appalachia who struggle every day for a fair shake. And to my mother, Eva, the anchor of my life. Both she and my father, Calvin, gave me the acceptance and love that I needed to make my life the lovely experience it is today.

A Carson Press LLC Publication

CHAPTER ONE
Sarah

"Fuck me," I muttered under my breath, glaring at Miranda and running a hand through my short black hair. It was three-thirty, and she was still at it. We hadn't even stopped for lunch. My stomach growled in commiseration over my meager breakfast of cornflakes. *One of those creamy thighs that Miranda strutted around on would be pretty tasty right now,* I thought with a devilish smirk. *Maybe with barbecue sauce.*

The lone guard beside me outside Tiffany's looked empathetic as my stomach growled again. I nodded and rolled my eyes. He snorted a laugh.

I sighed once more in exasperation and looked around, wondering for about the thousandth time today how a senator from Iowa who owned a middle-of-the-road construction company could keep pace with Miranda's spending habits, which included places like this and Bulgari and Louboutin and Alexander McQueen. Miranda had blithely spent seventeen thousand dollars so far on this trip, and all she'd bought were some shoes, earrings, and a watch. It blew my mind. For a man who supposedly started poor and was a self-professed 'splinter-head construction guy,' Mitchell Reichert supported Miranda in a way that defied belief. But then again, they could afford my fee, so I couldn't bitch too much.

I swept the passers-by outside the store once more and spotted a fellow I'd seen a few times. He was paying way too much attention to the senator's wife. Of course, it could be that Miranda was gorgeous and grabbed the eye, which she was and did with her Greek column legs, raven black hair, and deep brown, almond-shaped eyes. But this was the fourth time I'd seen him today paying special attention to Miranda, and he didn't fit in well at the upscale mall, sauntering around in a nondescript dirty brown hoodie, heavily worn Lee jeans, and cheap, ragged sneakers.

As soon as he saw me looking at him, he tucked his mid-length, unkempt beard and dark brown eyes further into his hoodie and moved on. *Yeah, that's right,* I thought. *Just keep on truckin', fella.*

"Friend of yours?" The Tiffany's guard asked.

I shook my head, lips pursed in irritation. "Nope. And if he doesn't stop eyeballing my client, he's going to be looking for his teeth. That's the fourth time he's scoped her today."

"Want me to call Security?"

"No. He hasn't done nothin' but look at a pretty woman. I don't want to harass him for that."

"Suit yourself," the guard said and resumed watching the rest of the mall walkers.

Truth was, though, the guy was really setting off my spidey-sense, almost to distraction. Everything about the man had been wrong, from his clothing to the fact that he wasn't carrying any parcels or bags. He hadn't bought so much as a soda since I'd first seen him hours ago. It was like he was waiting for something.

I'd tried to convince Miranda to leave after the second time we'd seen him, but she'd ignored me, as usual. She swept relentlessly through CityCenter in her Versace outfit and Jimmy Choo heels like a whirlwind, moving too quickly and not paying a bit of attention to her surroundings. As a result, I'd had to keep myself alert and pretty much taut as an overtuned piano wire the entire time.

I could be overreacting, which was why I didn't ask the guard to call security. There were all kinds of creepy men out there who liked to leer at women but were otherwise harmless. I did my fair share of looking, too. Besides, all I wanted to do at that point was go home.

I gave a silent cheer when Miranda finally stalked out of Tiffany's, one of their trademark robin's-egg bags in hand, and signaled she was ready to leave. I did have the good sense to wait until Miranda passed me to shake my head and roll my eyes at the guard, who snorted and gave me a knowing smirk.

"So," Miranda asked casually over one shoulder as we started strolling toward the parking elevators. "Are you free tonight?"

No, I thought. *I'm fucking beat after you dragged me around without listening to a word I said.* But I didn't say that and certainly didn't mention that there wouldn't be a repeat of our last foray here when she'd coaxed me into a hotel room. I opted for a diplomatic answer—a lie. "Unfortunately, ma'am, I'm not. I have some work that can't wait. Running your own business means being your own accountant at some point."

"You can quit calling me ma'am, Sarah. We've been intimate. I think we're past the ma'am point."

I suppose you could call that intimacy, I thought, glancing around to see if anyone had heard. We'd only spent an hour in the hotel room, barely enough time to work up a good sweat, let alone do something I'd have called intimate. It had been nothing, just emotionless, quick sex.

Bullshit, the voice in my head said. It had been mind-blowing, passionate, hot-as-hell sex, and I couldn't deny that I'd wanted more of it, but I wasn't going to go down that road again. It had already distracted me enough today. Setting aside hoodie-man, I'd caught myself admiring Miranda more times than I could count rather than keeping my head on a swivel like I should have.

"Not when I'm working," I said flatly as I spotted hoodie-man again, this time hovering near the elevators. I pressed my lips into a thin line and pulled Miranda to a stop. "We should take the stairs, ma'am."

Miranda shot me an icy glare. "Absolutely not. I'm not walking down a set of concrete stairs. I'll bust my ass in these heels."

I suppressed an eye roll, then the corner of my mouth crooked up. "I could carry you if your feet hurt too much. Though that'll cost extra."

"Not that it doesn't have a certain appeal," Miranda

responded, raising a cool eyebrow and looking me up and down. "But no. I'm perfectly capable of walking on my own. I prefer it, actually."

Incredulous, I glanced down into those deep brown eyes and shook my head. Why didn't the woman ever listen?

Not that I made it a habit to hook up with the wives of ultra-right-wing congressmen and senators—well, sometimes, no strings attached and all—but this was Miranda Reichert, and her husband was about to announce his run for President. She could pull more strings than Gepetto at a puppet party. If Miranda had any mind to at all, I could find myself struggling to do business despite my prior experience at the Secret Service. Keeping it professional was the only way to keep things safe.

Besides, I had a strict one-time rule when it came to relationships—a couple of dates, one night of good sex, no games, no bullshit, and out. If I didn't play with fire, I couldn't get burned. Of course, I also had a rule about getting involved with clients, and well—

"Understood," I replied curtly, rapidly dousing my musings before they went someplace even more distracting. Looking up again, I noticed that hoodie-man had vanished, so I pushed my worries aside and we continued on toward the elevators, where Miranda pressed the down button.

Distracted as I was by my thoughts and the day's fatigue, I was out of position when the elevator opened. I should have been between Miranda and the doors, not a foot to her left.

Hoodie-man stood in the elevator, yanking his hands from his pockets.

"Get down," I yelled, stepping in front of Miranda, going for my weapon, and hoping to God that my vest would take the bullet, but I was too slow, and I knew it.

The man threw his hand forward, dousing us both with red liquid from a fat mason jar. "That's for all the miners your husband's gonna kill with that new law!" he yelled.

I had him down on the ground and cuffed in seconds, my knee in his back. I dug out my phone to call the cops. Then, I glanced up to see Miranda Reichert, wife to the most powerful senator in Washington, shaking in a mixture of mortification and rage, her face and chest covered in a thick layer of blood.

Shit.

Fortunately, it had turned out just to be pig's blood. The man was a former miner from Harlan County who'd lost his son in a mine accident just a few miles from my hometown. Sad really. Worse, though, Miranda was now in a sour mood, which didn't bode well for me or my business.

"I'm sorry, ma'am. Are you alright?" I asked, breaking the frosty silence as we pulled onto 495 toward Silver Spring.

Miranda didn't answer, instead just staring out the window.

Fuck, I thought. *I'm screwed.*

"I thought I paid you to protect me from these creeps," Miranda scolded finally from the backseat. "Where was your head, Rogers?"

Somehow, I didn't think 'up your skirt' would endear me to Miranda at this particular moment, so I just mumbled another apology and kept driving.

When we arrived at Miranda's house in Silver Spring, I stepped out, eyes sweeping the area for threats. But the Reichert house was on a flat stretch of land with few trees and no real places to hide. A sniper might be able to get her, but one security guard wasn't going to stop that, so I stalked around to the passenger side and opened the rear door of the SUV.

Miranda exited with her bags without a word and began marching toward the house.

"Would you like me to recommend an alternate firm?" I asked Miranda before she got too far up the walkway.

Miranda's steps stuttered to a stop for a moment. "No," she said without turning and then continued inside.

I closed the door and dropped back in behind the driver's seat. "Son of a bitch!" I shouted at the windshield and backed out, feeling a mixture of relief and total mortification. If Mr. Carter, a.k.a. hoodie-man, had been carrying a pistol instead of pig's blood, Miranda would have been dead. We both would have.

"See," I chastised myself. "This is why you don't fuck around with clients. It's bad for your business and their safety, you idiot."

I didn't stop berating myself until I arrived back home in Fairfax.

CHAPTER TWO
Miranda

Stepping from the shower, I heard the Imperial March from Star Wars play on my phone. I closed my eyes for a moment and steeled myself, trying to push down the panic and fatigue that threatened to overwhelm me. I'd been cool and collected at the time, but the incident at the mall had frightened me badly, and all I wanted to do now was go to bed and forget about everything, especially Sarah Rogers.

"What do you want, Mitch?" I said coldly into the phone as I answered it.

"Well, that's a nice hello," he responded in his irritatingly scratchy baritone.

I pressed my lips into a thin line and rolled my eyes.

Mitch continued. "The plane will be at Dulles JetPort to fly you to the Quad Cities tomorrow. Don't be late, and don't screw this up."

"Oh, fuck you, darling. Of course, I'll be there. One big happy family." I said sarcastically. "I know what's at stake. I'll be fine. I'll even be bringing my own security."

"I don't care what you do. Just be there." Mitchell hung up.

I slammed the phone down on the bathroom counter. "Bastard," I hissed.

A knock came at the door. "Is something wrong, Miss?"

I straightened up and steadied my voice. "No, Gina, everything's fine. I'm fine." I didn't want Gina reporting to Mitch how upset he'd made me. I felt like a prisoner in my own home.

"Very good, Miss."

Besides, as much of a bastard as Mitchell was, I was Miranda Danbury long before I met Mitchell, and the Danbury's kept a stiff upper lip. But I really was so fucking tired of all this.

I placed the flat of my palms on the counter and gazed back into the mirror, examining my face. Dark circles, formerly hidden by the day's makeup, lingered under my eyes. The reflection staring back at me looked drawn and old.

"I'm only thirty-four," I murmured, but the last twelve years married to that malignant narcissist had taken their toll, like fucking dog years.

Bending forward, I laid my forehead against the cool faucet as my thoughts drifted. All I'd wanted to do was get it out of my system—see what it was like. I'd done that alright—well, the seeing what it was like bit, the rest, not so much.

My thoughts spiraled back to that afternoon in the hotel room. Her striking blue eyes had bored into mine as my body pressed into her rippling muscles, and she held me up against the wall with one arm. I'd felt helpless when she'd pinned my wrists with the other. *God*, I thought, remembering wishing that I could spend all day with my hands wandering over Sarah's body.

"No," I whispered, shoving the vivid reminiscence aside. "There's no future there. No happy ending. Not for me." I was the wife of the most powerful senator in Washington and stuck right where he wanted me.

Looking away, I finished washing and moisturizing my face for all the good it would do. But when I dropped the towel to put lotion on my arms and legs, I looked in the mirror again. My body wasn't bad; I was still fit from cycling and cardio.

It would only be five more years if Mitchell won the election or nine if he were re-elected. Then I could go. No one cared if an ex-president got divorced. It was newsworthy for all of five minutes. Mitchell would certainly let me go then, wouldn't he?

Of course, it would be with nothing. I didn't even have a college degree, and he'd demanded a prenup after his first marriage had fallen apart. If I left, my life would be over, penniless and broke, starting from zero again. I'd have to slink back to my parents and live with them.

I shook my head. That wasn't going to happen.

"I'd rather be on the street," I whispered to myself.

With an attempt at a deep, cleansing breath, I snatched up my phone and left the bathroom.

Five minutes later, dressed in a set of warm flannel pajamas, I sat down on the bed to type out a message to Sarah, only to find my phone screen shattered and dark.

"Shit."

I got up and headed for Mitchell's office. I'd replace the phone at some point tomorrow. For now, I needed to make a call, and there was only one landline in the house.

Paranoid as ever, Mitchell kept his office door locked, but I dug into the liquor cabinet and found the spare key. He kept it sitting underneath an ancient bottle of scotch so old that the label was worn away—a stupid place to hide it. Once inside, I dropped into his ugly, ostentatious leather chair and dialed Sarah's number.

"Rogers," Sarah answered on the first ring. She sounded tired.

"Ms. Rogers, it's Miranda Reichert. I need you for a few days."

There was a pause. "A few days? I have another client I have to tend to, Miranda. What is it exactly you're asking for?"

I rolled my eyes in irritation. Why couldn't anything be easy with this woman? "As you know, Mitchell is announcing his bid the day after tomorrow, and I'd like you to accompany me." Then, as a short silence ensued, I added. "In a professional capacity, of course."

"Let me see what I can do. Can I call you back in an hour?"

"You can't just check your calendar now?" I really was in no mood and just wanted to go to bed.

"Well, you caught me coming out of the shower. Hang on."

The thought of Sarah in the shower niggled at my insides, and a flush ran up my cheeks. *No, no. That's all over now.*

"I'm committed for a few hours tomorrow evening, but if I move a few things around, I'm free for the four days following."

I pursed my lips. *Whatever.* "Fine. My flight leaves tomorrow at eleven a.m. sharp. So, if you could escort me to Dulles and see me off, that'd be great, and then I can book you a ticket for Sunday morning."

"I'll drive," Sarah replied.

"Drive?" *What the fuck for?*

"I don't like to fly," Sarah said, sounding almost embarrassed. "So, after I'm done tomorrow evening, I'll drive. It's thirteen hours. I should get there Sunday morning around nine. A few hours of sleep, and I'll be ready to go. The announcement is on Monday afternoon, right?"

"Why don't you fly?"

"It's a long story and not worth telling." Again Sarah's tone was professional and flat, holding none of her earlier glibness. For some reason, that bothered me. Maybe I'd been too hard on her. *No,* I thought. *She fucked up. Of course, Miranda, if you hadn't slept with her—*I let that thought die.

"Is everything alright?" Sarah prodded, pulling me from my musings.

"Perfectly," I answered.

"Okay, I'll see you in Davenport on Sunday morning. I appreciate your business."

I blinked at the perfunctory response. *So that's the way it's going to be. Fine by me, better, in fact.* I shouldn't have crossed the line with her anyway. "Sounds perfect, Ms. Rogers. Pick me up at 9 am. I'll make sure your room is waiting in Davenport. We're at the Riverside Imperial."

A pause. "You're not staying at your home there?"

I hesitated for a second. Apparently, Sarah had researched more about Mitch and me than I'd thought. "No, I'm not," I said impassively. "The campaign staff will be at the hotel, and it's just easier." It was a lie, but a small one.

"Sounds good. Is there anything else?"

"No. That'll be all. Thank you." I hung up. Then I stared at the phone for a moment, dumbfounded, not by Sarah's impersonal response but by my own irritation at it.

As I stood, I bumped the keyboard of Mitchell's computer, and the screen lit up. He'd forgotten to lock it. The broad monitor displayed a strategy map of the US with four states marked in red: Wisconsin, North Carolina, Michigan, and Arizona. The four biggest swing states outside Florida.

It was the usual crap I'd seen a dozen times, and I dismissed it.

But as I reached down to lock the computer, I noticed the edge of another window. I frowned and sat back in the chair, pushing the map window aside.

Behind it glowed an email screen. My brow furrowed, and I bit my lip as I stared at it. It wasn't his normal Senate email account. It was something else. I read through the message currently displayed on the screen, my lips silently following the words. My chest sank, and my stomach clinched.

"Holy shit," I whispered in horror.

"Miss?" Gina said from the doorway.

Shit. I thought, startled, nearly jumping and clutching at my collar. I hadn't even heard her come in. I turned off the monitor and quickly stood. "Yes?"

"I'm sorry. I saw the door open."

I held up my cracked phone, desperately trying to keep my voice level. "I dropped this thing earlier and broke the screen. Mitch has the only landline, and I had a call to make. I was just leaving."

"Very good, Miss," Gina said.

I stood and stalked to the door, closed it, and handed Gina the key. "You know where this goes?"

"I do, ma'am."

I could feel Gina's cold eyes burning into my back as I walked to my room. As soon as I closed the door, I gave a sigh of relief, but then a flush of panic ran through me. "Good God," I whispered. "What did I just see? And how long had Gina been standing there?"

I set my alarm and went to bed, though I found myself unable to sleep, my head churning with what I'd seen in that one email. At three in the morning, I finally made a decision, rolled over, and rubbed the sleep out of my eyes. Taking a few minutes to grab the micro-SD card from my camera and the USB adapter that went with it, I padded back to Mitchell's office as quietly as I could.

With a last look around, I slipped into Mitchell's office and closed the door behind me.

CHAPTER THREE
Sarah

Saturday morning, I opened the SUV and then immediately closed it. "Well, that'll have to be detailed." It smelled awful, like rotting blood. Miranda had left a bloody towel in the back floorboard, and it had stunk up the entire car. I opened the door again and pulled out the stinking towel. This thing would have to be aired out and the rugs in the back shampooed. I didn't have time for that.

With a sigh, I walked around to the other side of the garage, where sat my baby. A 2022 metallic blue Mustang Mach-1. I had bought it just last year.

When I was a kid, I'd always wanted one, but Mom and Dad hadn't been able to afford anything like it when I was growing up, so on a whim, for my last birthday, I got it. I'd even paid cash for it. Despite the shame of it, in some ways, being tossed from the Secret Service had probably been the best thing that had happened to me. I'd been allowed to resign quietly, and while I'd never made pension, my experience had brought me a host of well-paying clients. I wasn't rich by any means, but I did just fine.

"Well, Miranda, I guess you'll have to just suffer today," I said to myself and slid behind the wheel. As always, I closed my eyes as I pushed the start button and listened to the purr of four-hundred-seventy-eight horses. I did feel a little guilty about owning a gas guzzler, but it wasn't my daily driver. The Chevy was a plug-in hybrid, so as far as I was concerned, I was doing my part for the planet. A few minutes later, I was well on my way to Silver Spring.

Miranda raised a delicately arched eyebrow when I rumbled up the driveway and got out.

"You can't be serious," she said as she glared at me.

I smirked and waggled my eyebrows. "Well, someone who shall remain nameless left a blood-soaked towel in the back of my SUV. I naturally assumed you wouldn't want to arrive at Dulles smelling of rotted pork."

"If you had been in proper position and paying attention instead of dilly-dallying like you were, you would have seen that man and stopped him before I was covered in that repulsive substance," Miranda shot back. "At least they arrested that idiot hillbilly."

I did my best not to scowl at the epithet, but Miranda might as well have been talking about my father. The guy was just an angry coal miner. It wasn't the right way to protest, but it wasn't like anyone listened to Appalachia. Neither did I point out that Miranda was about to be escorted to the airport by one of those 'idiot hillbillies.' Instead, I just smiled and opened the car door.

The fingers of Miranda's loose right hand fidgeted as she dragged her suitcase down the walk to the car. "Nevermind. It just surprises me that with what we pay you, you'd have a white-trash Ferrari as your personal vehicle."

I forced myself not to react, but a flush of rage tinted by a long-standing embarrassment colored my cheeks. I hoisted Miranda's bag into the trunk and then opened the door, offering her a hand. Miranda ignored it and slid into the passenger seat, bringing her long legs in behind her.

I nearly slammed the passenger door shut before stalking around and dropping into the driver's seat next to her. "Do you need to make any stops beforehand?" *Maybe to pick up a broom for your flight?* I finished in my head.

Miranda shook her head and stared straight out the windshield, making no more scathing remarks or giving any harsh looks. Instead, I caught what I thought was a tremble in her lips.

"Are you alright, ma'am?" I asked, shifting my tone and trying to be as gentle as I could.

Miranda barely acknowledged me. "Perfectly fine. Straight to Dulles, please. The executive jet center. Mitchell's plane is waiting."

A little bewildered, I fired up the car, and we headed out.

Like the evening before, the ride was silent as the dead, except for the rumble of the engine and road noise.

"Would you like some music, ma'am?" I asked, expecting Miranda to ask for her usual classical, but instead, she turned a cold eye my way.

"No, I don't want any music," she snapped. "If I'd wanted music, I would have asked. Why do you always insist on asking me that?"

I gave her a wide-eyed look and turned back to the road. "Sorry, ma'am, just offering out of politeness." *What the hell?* I thought. Miranda was always frosty, but she was also always controlled. Now I knew something was wrong, but I didn't dare ask again. I was obviously on thin ice as it was. Maybe I'd been a little too businesslike the night before, and that had set Miranda off. "Look, about last night, I'd just gotten out of the shower and wasn't—"

Miranda's face was pale, but the edge in her voice was unmistakable. "Ms. Rogers, all of my thoughts don't revolve around you. Let's just get to the airport with a minimum of discourse."

I snapped my jaws shut and continued to drive without another word, keeping my face neutral, but real worry began to eat at me.

We pulled into the Dulles Jet Center, a private aviation hub, at ten.

"What time is wheels up, ma'am?" I asked as I handed over her suitcase from the trunk.

Miranda's hand, cold and clammy, brushed mine as she took the bag. "I told you last night, eleven sharp. Were you not paying attention?"

As she went to turn away, I decided to risk it and reached out, taking her arm gently. "Miranda? What is it?"

Miranda spun around, looking about to snap, but whatever

retort lay on her lips died there as she stared at me slightly wild-eyed, desperation coloring her voice. "Nothing, I'll be fine. Just make sure you are there tomorrow morning."

She was terrified. Something had happened last night. "What is it?" I asked, pausing briefly in scanning the surroundings to look her in the eye.

"Just be there," Miranda replied with finality, then, after a moment, she added a quiet, "Please."

I had never seen Miranda Reichert anything but in strict control of herself, certainly never like this, so vulnerable, so unnerved. But I suppressed the urge to give Miranda the hug she obviously needed. Instead, I released her arm, and it was as if someone had snatched up her puppet strings, drawing her straight and tall, the mask of the confident, unflappable Mrs. Reichert finally returning.

"I'll be fine, Sarah. Just make sure you're there."

I nodded. "I'll be there."

Miranda turned and clacked away in her heels, the wheels of her bag rumbling across the pavement, my eyes following her until she entered the Jet Center. I sat against the car like that for a few minutes more, still staring after her with my brows knitted and eyes narrowed. Then I sighed and got back in the car, but it was long moments before I drove away, still disturbed. Finally, I huffed out a breath and started the car. "I have a bad feeling about this."

Back on the highway, after cogitating on it for a few minutes, I hit the phone button on the steering wheel.

"Who would you like to call," the voice assistant asked.

"Call Eye in the Sky."

"Calling Eye in the Sky," it responded cheerily.

Yeah, go fuck yourself, I thought irritably.

A deep bass, flowing like chocolate, answered a few seconds later. "Well, hello, stranger. World War III hasn't broken out, so I assume this is a casual call."

I smiled. Despite all the training, warfare, and everything he'd been through, Mike was just a big old teddy bear. A lethal teddy bear, but still. "Hi, Mike. Nope, sorry. I'm calling in that favor you offered."

There was a long pause, but I just waited, then Mike's voice dropped as he finally answered me. "You sure? You must be in a world of shit to make this call. Are you okay?"

I didn't answer immediately. *Why was I doing this?* Mike had promised me a favor, just one, anything, anytime, anywhere. I could call for a bomb strike on the University of Louisville Basketball Team, and Mike probably would find a way to make it happen, but I was going to use it on something that might be nothing. Then I thought about the look on Miranda's face, the fear, the terror, and the misery. I couldn't shake it. Something was going on, and it involved the man who would most likely be the next President of the United States. If there was something wrong with him, now was the time to find out.

"I'm about to be, I think," I answered finally. "I need an agency quality workup on Senator Mitchell Reichert in my hands by tomorrow in Davenport, IA. I also need three pre-paid credit cards for $5000.00 each with it, no trace. I'll drop the cash to pay for them by the house later today. I also need four burner phones."

Mike scoffed. "Is that it? That's nothing, Sarah. I told you to save this for when you really needed it. You could do that workup yourself, probably, except maybe bank records. And you can buy credit cards and phones."

"I know, but this is *that* important and I don't have the time. Make sure you check for shell corporations, affiliations, secret accounts, the works. If this man has farted at someone wrong, I want to know about it. Also, I don't want those phones or cards traced to me."

"Tell you what," Mike said quietly. "Why don't you think about it and call me back in an hour? You could pay for that kind of intel. You don't need me for that."

"Mike," I said, my voice gaining a bit of an edge. "I don't need to think about it. Just do it." Then, losing the edge, I added. "Please. I know you don't think it's big enough of an ask, given what I did. But my gut says otherwise."

There was a long pause. A sigh. Then Mike said, "Where do you want it all delivered?"

"Have it left for Ellen Carter at the Riverside Imperial."

"Will do. Is there anything else?"

"No, that's it. How are Jamal and Jessica?"

Mike perked up at the mention of his kids. "Jamal's great. He just started fifth grade, and Jessica blew the roof off her SATs. She's applying to MIT. The Agency's already approached her. She's mulling it over."

"Good for her. Maybe soon, we can have a cookout."

Mike laughed. "Sure. I'll tell Maria to put on some of her carne asada for you. Jamal wouldn't be here without you, so you're welcome anytime. You know that."

I chuckled. "I just did what anyone would. Thanks, Mike."

"Sure. I'll get it done." He hung up, and he would—get it done, that I knew.

I raced home to add some things to my go bag and make a few more calls.

CHAPTER FOUR
Miranda

Sitting quietly on the plane alone, I felt the Lear's leather seat sticking to the backs of my lower thighs, making them sweat as I panicked. Had Gina seen what I'd been doing? Had she told Mitchell? If he knew what I had, what would he do? *He'd probably kill me*, I thought, *If he found it on me.*

I tried to think of nothing to quell the anxiety, but then thoughts of that one hot afternoon with Sarah intruded. I'd been bored and horny and had only intended for it to be a fling, a one-time thing. But now I couldn't stop thinking about it. So far, I'd resisted the urge to ask her again—well, almost, but it had been hard. And that annoyed me. What bothered me more, though, was that, now, I needed Sarah, needed her protection. I couldn't trust anyone else. Sarah was independent, not tied to a larger company, and she had no business with Mitchell of any kind. I'd checked. And I thought I had a good read on her.

I had made one realization in the last hour of fretting over Mitchell's insane and, arguably, seditious plans: I had no one. Not a single soul could I depend on. Not my parents, who thought that Mitch hung the moon. Once, in confidence, I'd told my mother that I'd thought Mitch was overbearing and bordering on abusive. Instead of being supportive, Mom and Dad had reported it back to him, suggesting that I had made up the tale because I had cold feet about our engagement. That had resulted in the first bruise.

I touched my cheek, trying to remember which lie I had told the doctor about how it happened, but I couldn't. There were just too many of them. The human mind can juggle only so much before it gets full. Of course, each one, no matter which, was followed by the standard "Yes, don't be ridiculous. Of course, I'm safe at home."

"Gods, how did I get here?" I mumbled beneath the roar of the engines.

After a few sips of wine from the wet bar, my nerves calmed slightly, and I began to think more clearly. "Okay, I just need to hire Sarah for a longer term. I also need to keep her in her space."

I had spotted the slip at the mall. I wasn't stupid. And I knew it was my fault. I'd seduced Sarah, dragged her into that hotel room, and it led her to distraction later—could have gotten us killed if that idiot had been carrying a gun instead of pig blood.

Gods, what must the woman be thinking of me now? I thought. The married icon of supposedly pure, Christian devotion who moonlit in dark corners for lesbian trysts—a total self-loathing hypocrite. I'd been trying to settle the matter once and for all, and all I'd done was open up a flood of need that I'd never known I had.

At least I wasn't kidding myself about it. I took a long drink of my wine, finishing the first glass and fetching another. And I wasn't a self-loather either. I just hadn't known.

Liar, my head barked at me. *You've been eyeballing women for years.*

I sighed and started on the second glass, looking out the window.

If I get caught, I mused. *I'll probably end up missing or dead on my morning jog.* Everyone would rally around the grieving senator. Poor Mitch lost his wife even after he'd forgiven her for her lesbian affair with some disgraced dyke Secret Service Agent. I could see the headlines.

No. That wasn't going to happen.

I would just need Sarah to help me. She would keep me safe while I twisted my way out of this mess and, hopefully, convinced Mitchell to abandon his insanity. He had as much chance of tearing the country apart or putting himself in jail as winning The White House. It wasn't a flattering title, but I wasn't known as the Webspinner of the Senate for nothing. I'd get through this. The irony that, of all the people I knew, both powerful and rich, the only person I could depend on was the person I paid wasn't lost on me.

Two hours after wheels-up, the jet dropped to the tarmac at the Quad-Cities Airport with a bump and a short hop. By then, I had sucked down three glasses of wine and was feeling much better and, perhaps, a little drunk.

I decided Mitch was clueless. Gina didn't know what I'd been doing on the computer, even if the little tattler had even seen me using it. And there was no way Mitch would give the housekeeper his password. *I'd locked the computer, hadn't I?* It didn't matter; Gina was a housekeeper, not a computer guru.

I would follow through with today's schedule and then appear with him Monday at his announcement with Sarah on hand, assuming Sarah showed up and didn't have car trouble. *Who drives fourteen hours after working all evening?* I thought derisively. The woman was insane. Yet another reason not to be cuddling up to her.

The plane finally parked near the main terminal, and I snatched up my bag. Mitchell's driver, Thomas, gave me a curt nod. "Mrs. Reichert."

"Where's Mitchell?" I asked when I realized we were alone.

"Working on his speech. He'll meet you at the hotel." He opened the doors of the armored SUV and waited for me to step inside before stowing my bag. I watched him nervously as he got in, but he seemed fine. Maybe it was okay.

"I have to stop at Sheldon's Jewelers before we meet up with Mitchell," I barked. "I also need to stop at the phone store."

Thomas didn't turn around. He simply nodded and put the vehicle in gear.

I sat quietly in the back as we drove away from the airport toward Davenport—and my husband. My hands turned clammy again before we even reached the bridge, and fear squeezed at my chest as we crossed the river. It was unbearable, the feeling of being trapped.

I was sick of Mitchell and his overbearing bullshit. I had been for years. It's why we slept in separate bedrooms, separate hotel rooms, and even separate cities.

I needed Sarah here, I decided, and just the thought that she'd be here soon quelled some of my shaking and worry.

At Sheldon's Jewelry, I was relieved they still had the locket I'd seen on my last visit a few months before. It was a little strange but beautiful, embossed with three stags, a chevron, and a trefoil rather than a silhouette or floral imprint. It was a perfect fit for Sarah, who wasn't the flower type. With a few words to the salesman, I paid for it on Mitchell's credit card rather than on my own and left the store. Gina would simply pay the bill, assuming the charge to be for one of Mitchell's paramours.

A few minutes later, I arrived at the phone store. Thomas, per usual, waited in the SUV while I went inside.

"Hi there, ma'am. Welcome to Bertie's Mobile. How can I help you?" A perky blond woman with pink and blue hair said as I walked in.

I held out my phone with the cracked screen. "I need this replaced and the data moved."

CHAPTER FIVE
Sarah

"Huh?" I grunted, realizing someone was speaking to me as I watched the dining guests.

"I said," Denise repeated with a wry laugh. "You seem distracted." She owned the security firm that had hired me to help at tonight's fundraiser.

I pursed my lips at my own inattentiveness. This was becoming a problem. "A little bit, but I'm fine. Congressman Whitman is with a different woman this time, I noticed."

Eyes scraping the tabletops, Denise spotted the balding fifty-year-old sitting with a beautiful, classy-looking blond about half his age. She chuckled. "That's his daughter. Have you never met her? I could introduce you after we're done. She's just your type, queer and into one-night stands."

I smirked. "Cute. No. Normally, I'd say yes, but I'm not in the mood."

Denise gave me a puzzled look but said nothing else as we continued our vigil, bored out of our gourds.

This was a cake detail. There were no high-profile targets at this fundraiser, and Denise's men were scattered around the room in various places. It wasn't exactly a high-threat situation. Unless, of course, you counted some of the less scrupulous lobbyists and donors.

I wasn't a necessary addition to the security detail; Denise was giving me a little extra business and trying to convince me to close my LLC and join hers. I'd known Denise since my Secret Service days when we'd bumped into each other, quite literally, at the White House Correspondents Dinner. The chance meeting had led to drinks, and we'd ended up in bed together. Denise had only been curious, though, and I didn't do relationships, so it kind of worked out for the best. Regardless, we'd become good friends, and our relationship was easygoing.

"So, what gives? What's on your mind?" Denise asked after a while.

"Miranda Reichert," I whispered, keeping my voice low.

She raised an eyebrow and hissed, "The senator's wife? Please don't tell me—"

My cheeks flamed, but I kept my lips wisely closed.

"Well, she must not be as cold as everyone says. I don't see any frostbite on your lips."

I bit my bottom lip to suppress the ensuing grin, but I couldn't keep the corners of my lips from turning up at the joke. "No, but they might be a little burnt. It was, um, intense. But that's not what's got me bothered. She asked me to provide security for her in Davenport tomorrow for the announcement, and when I picked her up at her place to take her to Dulles this morning, she was white as a sheet. I mean, terrified. Something's up."

Denise snorted. "I'm sure she's just afraid of breaking a nail." Then she turned a doubtful eye to me and lowered her voice to a whisper. "You're serious? You had sex with the reigning queen of evangelical purity?"

A plate clattered behind us, and I turned to look over her shoulder, glaring at the clumsy waiter. Then I caught Denise's eye and nodded before facing the crowd again.

"What is that even like?" Denise hissed.

I didn't answer immediately, but the suppressed smirk returned, and my face flushed again. "Hot," I said finally. "Very, very hot."

"You got a death wish or something? Mitchell's a bastard, and for better or worse, he's likely to be the next president. I've done work for him before. He's definitely the jealous type—and creepy."

I tapped my foot, still seeing Miranda's terrified face as I dropped her off. "What do you mean, creepy?"

"He's a snake," Denise answered. "So, how did you end up in this predicament? And since when do you care if some conservative politician's wife is having kittens over something? Weren't you the one who said they're someone else's problem once you're off duty?"

I caught sight of a waiter I didn't recognize and leaned around a column to get a better look at him. "You know that guy?"

Denise glanced over, following my gaze. "That's Paul Cambert. He was late for work. Car trouble. That's why he wasn't at the afternoon meeting. And you're dodging my question."

"Which one?" I asked.

Denise gave a low, superior-sounding chuckle. "All of them."

"She got a room and dragged me inside."

She laughed again. "Oh, yeah, the five-foot-two half-Korean senator's wife just 'dragged' you into a hotel room. I assume it was at gunpoint."

I snorted a quiet laugh. "Not exactly."

"But why do you care if—" Denise's eyes widened. "Ooh, the ice queen got behind Sarah Rogers's legendary defenses? Say it ain't so?"

Irritated at the comment, I snapped my gaze back to Denise. "Leave it be. She's in trouble. I can feel it."

"Follow me," Denise ordered, and we headed toward the side door that led to the staff hallway. Once inside, she pressed me. "Are you really this twisted up about one of *them*? We've known each other for a long time. This isn't like you."

I frowned. "You think I don't know that. But it's bothering me. You should have seen her, Denise. She's usually unflappable, but damn, she was terrified. She's in serious shit, I can feel it."

With a sigh, Denise placed a hand on my forearm. "Look, if you're that worried and have to be in Davenport tomorrow, you should leave. I know you don't fly, and it's a long drive."

My eyes went wide. "You're firing me?"

Denise's face screwed up in disbelief. "No, of course not. I'm giving you the rest of the night off. I'll pay you, don't worry. Go do what you need to do."

I kissed the older black woman on the cheek. "Thanks. I owe

you one. Remind me why we never got together?"

"Because I'm straight. We figured that out. I'm also married now. Besides, you only do one-night stands. No complications, remember?"

"Yeah," I muttered, nodding. "So I keep telling myself."

"And yes, you owe me one, but I want details," she whispered. Denise let the team know over comms that they were now a person down, but then, as I walked away, she called out, "And be careful."

CHAPTER SIX
Miranda

After four fruitless calls to the desk, I started breathing a little easier when I heard the door in the adjoining suite open. Sarah's trademark grunt sounded as she dropped something heavy to the floor. I stood from the little desk chair and marched to the connecting door, opening my side and knocking.

There was a moment of rustling, a bump, and some cursing, and finally, the other door opened. Sarah stood there rubbing her elbow.

"Fucking desk. Someone moved it in front of the door, and I had to slide it out of the way. How are you?"

I kept my face and tone cold and impassive. "I'm fine. What took you so long?"

Sarah snorted and stepped back as she started to strip. "Wow. I just drove thirteen hours for this, and that's how you greet me? Nice to see you, too."

I scoffed. "Well, I am paying you for your time, including travel. That gives me the right to ask."

Sarah continued undressing, turning her back to me. "I got stuck in construction traffic a few times, including almost an hour delay outside Cleveland. Now, if you don't mind, I'd like to rest for a couple of hours before we do whatever you intend to do."

I turned my back, heading into my room rather than trying to cover the flush rapidly heating my face. "I have no plans today. There is a meeting at seven this evening to review tomorrow's events. After that, I'm staying in, eating room service, and keeping a low profile. This is Mitchell's shit, not mine."

I looked up from relaxing on the bed in front of the TV as Sarah peeked around the doorframe, eyebrows raised.

"Is everything alright, ma'am?" She asked.

"Yes, perfectly fine," I lied. Sarah looked skeptical but disappeared from view.

I heard her unzip something, probably her duffel, and she said, "You want me to leave the door open?"

I didn't bother rolling my eyes; she couldn't see me. "Yes. It'll be hard for you to protect me properly if you have to open the door."

There was a long pause of unsettling quiet.

"What?" I asked irritably, pushing the button on the remote and turning off the television.

"Nothing. If you need me, just holler."

I was about to close my eyes and try to relax when I heard the tearing of paper a few moments later from the other room. Curious, I got up and peeked around the frame. My breath caught. Sarah had drawn the blinds and was standing completely nude, her back to me, a large manila envelope in her hands.

I couldn't help but admire her physique, and an almost irresistible urge came over me to reach out and run my hands over the woman's muscular backside. Instead, I crept back to the bed, head spinning and breathing heavily. And for a moment, I couldn't keep my thoughts together. Finally, I realized Sarah had said something.

"What did you say?" I called back. "I couldn't hear you."

Sarah chuckled. "I said, can you close the drapes on that side? I'd prefer to have less light."

I drew the drapes, returned to the bed, and turned the television back on.

The news was all about Mitchell. Instead of the usual fair of Fox News that Mitchell insisted on having on all the time at home, I flipped over to MSNBC and listened to the commentators prattle on about Mitchell and his racist viewpoints. They weren't kind, but neither were they wrong. Mitchell was a bigot, plain and simple. I'd tried desperately to temper his nasty streak in the first few years, but it had been useless. All it had gotten me was abuse, so I'd abandoned that idea long ago. Mitchell pretty much hated anyone who wasn't cisgender, white, straight, and male. Women he only tolerated if he thought he could fuck them. He was a fucking cliché.

The discussion turned to me, and I had to close my eyes and breathe to keep from yelling at the TV. Not that I didn't deserve some of the vitriol spewed my way, or even all of it. I'd worked hard to get Mitchell to this point. And I'd used every trick I knew short of sleeping with people or breaking the law to push his shitty agenda of white grievance and anti-wokeness, whatever that was supposed to mean. Mitchell could never define it, but I could. It was just anti-everything progressive: gay rights, women's rights, minority equality, good healthcare for the poor and middle class. Whatever he could use to make ignorant white people angry landed in that bucket.

All of that I could handle, but then one of the commentators referred to me as the would-be future First Racist. *Ouch*, I thought. *That one stung.* I usually didn't care what people said about me. They hadn't lived my life, didn't know what I'd been through with Mitchell, how trapped I was. But that excuse had started to ring hollow of late, and if anyone found out about Sarah and me, I'd end up being vilified as the next Ken Mehlman.

After a few minutes of listening, I felt a profound fatigue and turned off the television. I'd made my bed, I realized, and now I had to lie in it—alone.

I must have dozed off because a knock at the door jerked me from sleep sometime later. Before I'd cleared the sleep from my eyes, Sarah was already in my room and looking through the peephole.

"Did you order room service?" Sarah asked.

I gawked at the naked woman for a moment, then pulled myself together and looked at the clock. "Yes, I ordered a two-thirty lunch of sandwiches and sodas."

"Just a second," Sarah called through the door and returned to her room. Moments later, she returned to the door in a pair of shorts and a t-shirt, her gun behind her back. She opened the door and said, "Come right in," in that sweet Appalachian drawl that made me shiver.

As the waiter entered, Sarah continued facing the man as he moved around the room and set the tray on the small dining table in the corner.

"Go ahead and just leave the check. We'll sign it when we're done," Sarah said and shot the man a knowing smirk. He smiled back and nodded.

My unease settled a bit as I watched her. Sarah kept her eyes on the man and stayed between the waiter and me. He wasn't an obvious threat, but she clearly wasn't taking any chances. It reminded me that I'd made the right choice in asking her along despite our complications. And for just a split second, I felt safe.

The waiter spoke with a hint of a Latin accent. "Just place the tray outside when you are done. Do you need anything else?"

"No, we're good. Thank you," Sarah said perfunctorily, ushering the man out before closing and bolting the door. She set her weapon on the table next to the tray and opened the dishes. Inside were two well-presented club sandwiches accompanied by two Cokes and two glasses of ice.

"You gonna eat?" Sarah asked, but I was stuck firm, suddenly feeling very warm. The attraction to Sarah sexually was something I'd had expected, but this other thing, this weird comfort; I hadn't expected it at all, and it bothered me.

I frowned, pulled myself from the bed, still a little tired, and sat in the other chair. I looked at Sarah, already digging into her sandwich, her silverware still rolled in the napkin. Had no one ever taught her how to eat?

"Sarah," I said, then paused momentarily, trying to figure out how best to put this. "The fork goes on the left of the plate. The napkin should be tri-folded to the left of the fork. The spoon and knife go on the right, the knife edge toward the plate, and the spoon on the outside."

Sarah blinked and froze, one cheek full of sandwich. Then she chewed it and swallowed it down loudly. "Umm. . . what?"

I carefully arranged my silverware properly and made a sort of voila gesture. Sarah rolled her eyes, but, to my surprise, she rearranged her silverware, placed the napkin across her lap, and continued eating.

"So, what's this all about?" Sarah said around a mouthful of her sandwich, hiding her mouth behind one hand.

I glared at her in irritation. "Ms. Rogers, didn't anyone ever teach you not to speak with your mouth full? The worst sound in the world is the smacking of someone's lips."

Sarah snorted a laugh. "Jesus, you sound like my mother. But seriously. What is going on? Mitchell has more than enough protection around here, so why do you need me?"

I finished chewing a bite of my sandwich and swallowed, wiping mayonnaise from the corner of my lips with the napkin before answering. "Mitch's team is for Mitch, not me. If someone comes after us, they'll save him and leave me to die or whatever." I waved a hand dismissively. "What with all the attention around him, his policies, and now his announcement, I felt I needed my own protection. That's all."

"Mitchell doesn't know." It wasn't a question.

"Yes, he knows. He does not know that it's you. Not yet, anyway. And not that it matters. That reminds me. I bought you something."

Sarah raised an eyebrow. "You did what?"

I drew out the little white box from the nightstand. "Call it a gift. Something to remember me by."

Sarah screwed up her face. "You make it sound like you're dying or something."

It took all my self-control to keep a straight face and not break down. Instead, I forced a laugh. "No, nothing like that. We had a nice time once, and I thought we might close out that part of our —" I struggled for a word, finally settling on "relationship."

Sarah frowned, clearly skeptical. "Uh-huh. I see. Do you get gifts like this for all the women you drag to bed?"

My neck burned with embarrassment and irritation. "Ms. Rogers, you are the only woman I have ever taken to bed. What do you take me for? On second thought, don't answer that. Just take the fucking thing." I shoved the box at Sarah, who finally took it and opened it.

"Wow, this is beautiful, but I can't accept it. It's—um—too much."

"You can, and you will. I insist," I demanded sharply.

Sarah's eyes widened, probably at my tone, but she pulled out the locket and opened it, finding the small photo of me inside before closing it again and setting it back in the box.

I rolled my eyes then stood and walked behind Sarah, snatching up the locket. "Here," I said as I drew it around her neck. For a moment, I thought about choking her with it. The woman could be so infuriating.

Sarah inclined her head, and I watched the gooseflesh rise as my fingers brushed her skin. I felt a shiver of my own, knowing I affected her that way. I tried to force myself to breathe normally, but my pulse thudded as the backs of my knuckles rested against the nape of Sarah's neck. I closed my eyes and swallowed, the sound loud in my ears. I had lingered too long. Quickly, I locked the clasp, almost, but not quite, brushing against her short hair. My hands were trembling as I released the gold chain.

Clearing my throat, I returned to my seat and gave Sarah a carefully controlled smile. "It looks very nice on you, I think."

Sarah fingered the locket. "I don't know what to say."

I lifted one eyebrow, pretending not to notice the settling goosebumps on Sarah's arms. "'Thank you' is the usual pleasantry."

Sarah rolled her eyes. "Thank you, ma'am."

"You're welcome." I kept my expression neutral, then had to look away—anything to keep her from seeing.

The rest of the meal passed in silence, and before long, Sarah stood and left for her room. Before leaving, though, Sarah turned back and opened her mouth to say something, but she seemed to think better of it and disappeared through the door.

I partially closed the door between rooms to afford myself some privacy. I was tired, and my heart was pounding against my ribs. I pulled my knees up to my chest, nestling them against it. Then, I rested my forehead on my knees. The flesh of my legs felt cool against the flush of my face, and after a few slow breaths, the panicky feeling faded.

I turned on the TV again and muted the sound, then stared at the door between the suites, wondering if Sarah had noticed how I flushed constantly around her. I couldn't help it.

But I needed to keep this professional. I certainly didn't dare get close to her, not with Mitchell watching my every move. All that would do is put a target on Sarah's back. It was one thing to use Sarah as protection. I paid her for that. It was Sarah's job, and Sarah knew the risks. But to let anyone get close to me? That would be a recipe for disaster, and I knew it.

No. I was alone in this.

CHAPTER SEVEN
Sarah

Despite needing more sleep, I took an hour to glance through the dossier I'd picked up at the front desk. It seemed that Senator Mitchell had been busy in the last few years. He'd acquired several hotels, mostly non-franchised small hotels, though one of them caught my attention, the Adirondack Bayline up at Lake George in New York.

It was a larger hotel, but the old hotels in Lake George weren't terribly popular anymore, not by the standards of their heyday. Strangely though, Mitchell's hotel seemed to be doing exceptionally well, ridiculously better than any others nearby. I put a pin in that, narrowing my eyes. "Hmm," I muttered to myself. "What do you have going on up there, Senator?"

Mitchell also made six trips to Louisville in the last year. The Senate Majority Leader, Jeffery Copeland, lived there, so it wasn't unusual at first glance, but six trips within a year seemed excessive, and each trip lasted almost a week. Three of the trips were when the Senate had been in session, so he definitely wasn't meeting with Copeland, at least not those times. He'd also taken his son with him.

"So," I mused. "Daddy's little boy is following in his father's footsteps. Interesting."

Mike had been true to his word, collecting every bit of intel he could find on the senator. Given the thorough file, I had a funny feeling that Mike had been looking into him for someone else before I'd asked, probably opposition research for another presidential contender.

"What are you reading?" Miranda asked from the doorways, and I about jumped out of my skin. I had been so engrossed in the dossier that I hadn't heard her creep to the door.

"Good God, woman, do you have to sneak up on me?"

Miranda just gave me a cold look and raised an eyebrow. "I asked you a question."

"Not that it's any of your business, but it's a dossier on your husband."

Miranda's eyes went wide. "Mitchell? Why?"

"Just homework," I lied, my voice impassive.

"Uh-huh." Miranda narrowed her eyes.

"Miranda," I said. "I don't know much about him besides his public face, so I decided to see what kind of man he is and learn more about his business interests. Nothing underhanded. It's not like you've been forthcoming about him these last few months."

Miranda gave me a sour look, appearing not at all pleased that I had pulled a file on Mitchell, though it was hard to tell. Miranda always looked mildly disdainful, making her hard to read sometimes. Rather than continue and start an argument, Miranda turned around to walk out.

Before she could get through the door, I poked the bear. "What is it? I mean, *if* you want to tell the girl with the redneck Ferrari."

Miranda spun around, fixing me with a glare. "I already told you I'm fine." Then her voice rose, turning shrill, the tone giving the lie to her words. "Will you please quit asking? It's getting old."

I waited, my features twisted in sympathy. I could see her fragile state, but Miranda just gave me a stony expression and left, gently closing the connecting door behind her. Despite the distance and closed door, I could hear the sniffle and muffled sobs from the other room.

I pursed my lips. I could do nothing if Miranda wouldn't tell me what was wrong. So, with three hours still before I needed to get up and showered, I put the dossier in my duffel, rolled over, and sacked out.

I woke to the beeping of my watch. The door between the rooms was open again, and I peeked in to see Miranda sleeping quietly.

I stretched, ran in place for a few minutes, and did a few pushups, burpees, and jumping jacks before entering the bathroom to shower.

Standing in the hot water, I quietly reviewed everything I had learned so far. Miranda was scared—scratch that—she was terrified. Something had happened the night before last that had set all of this off. Nothing in Mitchell's file explicitly suggested he was dirty, but I knew how much money Miranda spent on her expensive shopping trips. That kind of money had to come from somewhere, and Mitchell Construction wasn't exactly a household name. Nor was Caravan Property Investment Group, his shell company for the hotels he'd bought.

I thought about how Miranda had expressed herself regarding the announcement. "This is Mitchell's shit," I whispered to myself.

Miranda certainly didn't seem to have much respect or love for her husband. Maybe he'd threatened to cut her off. But if that was the case, why had she gone out of her way to arrange this entire affair? It certainly didn't explain Miranda's perceived need for personal protection beyond Mitchell's team. I just didn't have enough information. But it was undoubtedly clear that Miranda felt threatened. And that was enough for me.

After showering, I grabbed one of the burner phones Mike had sent me from my duffel and made two calls, arranging a room at two different ratty motels along different routes out of the city under the name Carolyn Fry—single king-sized beds in both cases. One was west of town and one east. Then I pulled out the body armor I hadn't expected to need until tomorrow and fingered it. I hated wearing it, but I wasn't taking any chances.

Finally dressed, I examined myself in the mirror. My collarless suit jacket sat neatly over the banded collar shirt. The crease of my black pants was neat and clean, making a straight gig-line with the edge of my jacket pockets. I tugged momentarily at the vest beneath my shirt to get it comfortable and then brushed myself down. I looked good, maybe even a little on the badass side. Finally, I holstered my weapon and knocked on the adjoining doorframe.

"Come in. I'm almost ready." Miranda was still in the bathroom, and I waited patiently for her to emerge. When she did, I almost fell over. Miranda looked spectacular in her business attire: a black pencil skirt, silk stockings, four-inch heels, a white blouse, and a black jacket. Her long hair was neatly braided and pulled down one shoulder. She was stunning.

"You. . . uh. . . You look very nice, ma'am," I stuttered, suppressing a smile.

Miranda waved away the compliment. "This won't take long, but I expect there will be press in the hotel, so we must look our best."

Miranda took a moment to look me up and down, then she stepped back, indicating the door.

I looked through the peephole, opened it, checked the hallways, then escorted Miranda outside. I wasn't about to make the same mistake twice, so I kept my eyes watching every corner for threats. At the elevator, I stayed between Miranda and the opening doors as we rose to the top floor and the presidential suite where the prep meeting for tomorrow's announcement would be held.

The doors opened, and we were greeted by two armed guards from Mitchell's security detail. They both nodded to me. I didn't know them personally, but I'd seen them at a couple of social events Miranda had hired me for.

Mitchell's suite was huge. It had three rooms, including a small conference room where the essentials were assembled.

I entered first, and Miranda followed behind. Inside, Mitchell stood on the opposite side of the round conference table. To his right sat Mitch Jr., looking very much like his father, though younger, more fit, and with less gray in his hair. Next to him sat Amanda Cross, Mitchell's campaign manager, and to Mitchell's left sat Will Berringer, Mitchell's head of security. I nodded to Will, who nodded back professionally.

"Ms. Rogers, can you wait outside?" Mitchell said, flashing me his trademark smile.

"No sir," I said flatly and probably with just a little hint of self-satisfaction. Then I stood behind Miranda as she sat at the conference table in the chair farthest from her husband.

Mitchell continued to smile, but I could see the burning rage shining in his eyes. People didn't often tell him no, I figured, certainly not women. Well, too fucking bad. The exchange gave me some measure of Miranda's situation. It was clear that this man was dangerous and had anger problems; I could feel it in my bones. I decided then to have Mike look into Miranda's public appearances for any sudden cancellations and maybe taxi rides to the hospital or her doctor on the same days.

Once Miranda was seated, I squared my shoulders, my eyes still on Mitchell, whose jaw worked furiously. He was pissed and fighting to get himself under control. I didn't care one whit. I'd been hired by Miranda. He could go fuck himself, senator or not. I wasn't Secret Service anymore. I didn't have to give this asshole one bit of deference.

"Suit yourself, but you'll be bored," he said nonchalantly, finally plastering a charming smile across his face. Then he turned back toward his campaign manager.

I placed a surreptitious hand on Miranda's shoulder and squeezed it briefly. She seemed to lower her shoulders a fraction. She'd gotten the message. No one was going to hurt her while I was there, and I wasn't leaving, not without her.

The first forty minutes of the meeting were spent discussing Mitchell's atrocious speech, and it was all I could do not to glare at the man. It was a doozy full of veiled threats against minorities, LGBTQ persons, woke culture, whatever that was, and anyone else not cisgender, white, and heterosexual. I wondered briefly if he understood that included his wife. Probably not.

"So," Amanda said, turning toward Miranda. "That's when you'll come in and move to Mitchell's right side. Mitch Jr. will be on his left. The security detail is to be off stage."

I frowned. "That won't be possible."

"I'm sorry?" Amanda said, raising an eyebrow. "Who are you?"

"Sarah Rogers, I'm Miranda's security escort for the event. I will be here." I pointed at an area to the right of the stage, largely out of view of the audience but still on the stage proper. "Honestly, that's further than I'd like, but I will not be off-stage or unable to reach Ms. Reichert at any time. Assuming you want her to attend the announcement, that is."

Berringer barked a laugh but turned it into a cough at the last minute, then he looked at Cross as if to say, 'I told you.'

Cross looked at Miranda, and I noted the slight bunching of Miranda's shoulders, but to her credit, Miranda didn't flinch away. Unable to see her face, I had to imagine Miranda's delicately raised eyebrow of disdain, not hard, given how many times I'd been on the other end of it. Cross looked at Mitchell, who shook his head in some unspoken sign.

"It doesn't matter, that's fine," he said, shooting both of us an angry glance.

Cross pursed her lips as if she'd just sucked on a lemon but nodded her assent. "Fine."

I nodded, and I paid close attention to the rest of the meeting, which was filled with who goes where and what they would do once Mitchell left the stage. Thirty minutes later, Miranda and I were dismissed, and I escorted Miranda back to her room.

Once inside, Miranda turned to me and gave me an enigmatic look. "You know," she said finally. "I don't think I've ever seen Mitchell that angry at anyone but me before. You really pushed his buttons."

I raised a non-plussed eyebrow and let my Kentucky drawl slip out. "That don't seem hard. That man's a turd, Miranda, and a bully. You deserve better." I was fucking fuming and didn't mind letting it show at that point.

At Miranda's gape-mouthed expression, I stalked through the connecting door and into my own room and changed into sweatpants and a t-shirt. "What's for dinner?" I called back as I set my weapon on the nightstand.

CHAPTER EIGHT
Miranda

The next morning began early. Sarah and I spent most of the day standing or sitting around while Mitchell met with the press, his campaign staff, and his security. Mitch Jr. followed his father, watching everything with interest.

A few times, 'Daddy's Little Boy' glanced over at us as we sat nearby, gazing at the entire spectacle. Finally, after a few hours, he stopped at the table we'd taken in the hotel restaurant. Sarah was sitting ramrod straight and watching the doors when he walked up.

"So, after this is all over, do you want to grab a drink?" he asked her, flashing what he probably thought was a dazzling smile. And, maybe, to anyone else, it might have been charming, but to me, it was oily, just like his father's.

I had to stifle a laugh as Sarah glanced at Mitch Jr.'s wedding ring, then back up at him and said simply, "No." She clearly knew how to handle men like Mitch and his son. I watched Mitch slink away back through the door and into the hotel lobby, and then I turned to Sarah.

"You don't like him very much either, do you?" I asked, twirling around an empty glass.

"No, ma'am," Sarah said, again her voice was stiff and flat.

"My, we're professional today."

She turned her eyes toward me, hawkish and penetrating. "This entire affair stinks. I don't like the setup or the arrangements for security around the stage. It's why I picked this table and this seat. It gives me a full view of all the entrances and exits."

I swallowed. I'd spent the last few hours trying to forget my predicament. But now, the things I'd seen on Mitch's computer came back with a vengeance, and I felt the blood drain from my face. Sarah clearly saw it, too, as she uncapped the bottle of sparkling water on the table, poured a glass, and slid it to me.

"I don't like being in the dark, Miranda," Sarah said as I took a sip of the water. "Something's going on here. I don't know exactly what, but I'm not pleased with how coy you're being. You know something." It wasn't a question.

I looked back at Sarah, my expression flat, but I could feel the tremble in my lips, and I gripped the water tightly to keep my hands from shaking. "I'm sure everything's fine. I—" Then I stopped. I'd been about to say something stupid, so I changed the subject. "Nevermind. I notice you're wearing the locket I gave you."

Sarah raised an eyebrow. "Yeah, as long as Mitchell doesn't know where I got it, I'm sure it's fine."

I snorted a nervous laugh. "No, of course he doesn't. How could he? Besides, I'm allowed to give gifts to friends. It's not exactly illegal."

"Is that what we are? Friends?" Sarah asked, her voice rife with sarcasm.

"Well, no, not exactly. But I think, once things calm down, we could be."

Sarah glanced around at the empty restaurant again, then lowered her voice. "Let's get something straight. You're nice enough and certainly not the worst client I've had. But in no way, shape, or form are we friends. You support a man whose agenda includes vilifying people like me—and you," she added a moment later. "You're a hypocrite and a liar. And while we slept together once, that doesn't mean that I want to do it again or that I want to be your pal. Your politics disgust me. It's that simple. I'm here because you hired me."

I pressed my lips into a thin line. The dagger of scorn in Sarah's voice and harsh words had hurt. "It's not what you think," I said a little defensively, then caught myself. *Why do I care what this woman thinks? She doesn't know my life.* "Besides, don't flatter yourself. I'm not inviting you to sleep with me again. Period."

"Perfect," Sarah whispered. "Honestly, I don't know why you asked me to come here other than to protect you from your husband."

I sat back in the chair and folded my arms across my chest, then spoke in a harsh hiss, "How dare you judge me. You know nothing about me, not the first thing. Before you jump up on your soapbox, you should probably know what the actual fuck you're talking about."

Sarah scowled back. "Miranda Danbury, age thirty-four. Born in New Haven, Connecticut, to Robert Danbury, an old money real estate mogul, and his socialite wife from Seoul, South Korea, Bora Jeong, a.k.a. Beatrice. Skipped college. Went on to marry Senator Mitchell Reichert twelve years ago after his first wife left him. From there, well, it gets a little murky. You're well known in political circles as the 'Webspin—"

"Stop!" I hissed. "That's enough. Just because you know some basic facts doesn't mean you know the first thing about how I grew up, what my parents were like, or what was expected of me." Then I lowered my voice even further, looking around. "Or how I feel."

Sarah continued to glare at me for a moment, then resumed her vigilance, watching the doors. "Drink your water. You look white as a sheet."

I did as she asked, then took a deep cleansing breath, but nothing seemed to take the sting out of Sarah's words. I didn't believe in any of the crap Mitchell spewed as red-meat to his base. I'd initially supported him because I thought he'd change and soften with age. *No,* I thought. *I believed I could change him.* But over the years, he'd only grown worse, more demanding, more threatening. And now I was stuck.

I glanced back at Sarah, who was watching Mitch Jr.'s back just outside the main doors of the restaurant. I couldn't decide if I wanted to rail at the woman or throw myself at her mercy and beg forgiveness. It was maddening. No one had ever gotten under my skin like this, and it was pissing me off.

I would have liked to say it was a mistake to hire her then send her away, but I couldn't. I could have hired another firm, but it hadn't even occurred to me. Despite the incident at the Mall, which I knew was my own fault, I trusted Sarah. *And she was honest*, I thought bitterly.

I sat like that for an excruciating period, excoriating myself internally about the entire mess, specifically my support of Mitchell and, oddly, what Sarah must think of me. The pall that fell over us seemed dark and cloying, so I was thrilled when Amanda walked in to tell us it was time to leave.

"Thank God," I said and got up. "Let's get this over with." I hoped no one could hear the shaking in my voice.

Despite her protests, Sarah was forced to ride in one of the following SUVs to the Mississippi Valley Fairgrounds, where the event had been staged. I rode with Mitchell and Mitch Jr.

As soon as I got into the car, I could feel Mitchell's cruel blue eyes burning into me. I sat as far from Mitchell as I could get, which wasn't more than a few feet. It was just me, Mitchell, and Mitch Jr., and I'd never felt more alone than I did at that moment —or as vulnerable.

I looked out the window and kept my hands clasped in my lap. As it was, a shiver of fear ran down my back as we pulled away from the hotel. This was it.

"So, Miranda, don't forget to smile," Mitchell said from the other side of the car. His ooze-ridden voice felt like a wriggling thing in my ears.

I turned toward him, eyes narrowed. "Don't worry. You'll get exactly what you expect from me: nothing more. When have I ever embarrassed you? In public, anyway."

Mitchell's face darkened at that, but he recovered quickly, a thin, evil smile sliding across his features. "Gina says all is in order at the house. Though, I really wish you'd ask before you enter my office—" then he added ominously, "or use my computer. No one likes nosey people, Miranda."

I raised an eyebrow and kept my face carefully neutral. But when I looked at Mitchell, I swallowed hard before speaking. "I don't use your computer, Mitch. We've had that discussion before. Why would you suggest otherwise?"

He didn't answer. He just kept watching me, that thin curl of a smile still resting on his lips. I turned away and looked back out the window.

"Well, perhaps after the event today, we'll discuss that. But then again—" he trailed off.

I squeezed my hands together and shifted in my seat as the blood drained from my face. I felt a touch faint. *He knew,* I thought. *He knew what I'd seen.* I'd been wrong. Gina must have been standing there longer than I'd realized. It was all I could do not to panic. I took a deep breath and remembered that Sarah was right behind us. She'd be with me the whole time. And it was at that moment I made up my mind. I would leave Mitchell, money or no. No one could live like this. No one.

I turned to him and gave him a hard stare, mustering up every ounce of courage I had. "I want a divorce," I said, my voice harsh but even. "I'm done with your bullying and abuse, Mitch. It's over. Go fuck one of your adoring floozies, but we're through. You can enjoy your run for the presidency without me."

I expected Mitch to rant or rave or lose his temper, which would be perfect. But he didn't. He just smiled in malicious glee. "We'll talk about that after the announcement. I'm sure you'll have a change of heart. A move like that could ruin a lot of lives. You seem to think I don't know what you've been up to."

I rolled my eyes and looked out the window, but inside, I was terrified and shaking. *Did he know about my tryst with Sarah? How could he?*

Fortunately, the ride ended just a few minutes later, and I exited the limousine to flashing cameras and a press of people on the northern side of the speedway where the stage had been erected. Throngs of reporters hoping to catch Mitchell's attention called out. Guards surrounded him, and for just a second, Mitchell had ahold of my arm. My heart raced, and I felt faint again until I felt a soft feminine hand peel away Mitchell's fingers with surprising strength and replace them with its own. I looked over and straight into the eyes of Sarah Rogers, standing right up against me and guiding me gently away from the cameras.

"You don't need to be in this crap," she whispered as we backed away slowly. All eyes were on Mitchell anyway. He turned back toward us and shot us a baleful glare before plastering on his trademark smile and turning back to the press.

Once we were away from the cameras, the campaign staff hurried us to the edge of the stage, where we both waited at the stairs. Sarah had a hand on my shoulder, her eyes scanning the crowd for threats. I realized I felt safe for the first time in two days, even if it was only for a moment. If someone *were* coming for me, they'd have to get through Sarah first. That much was certain, and I allowed myself a minute of calm and a relieved breath.

It was almost an hour later, after a couple of the local GOP politicians had warmed up the entire gathered crowd that Mitchell took the stage. I waited in the wings as he gave his speech. This was my last appearance with him. I just had to get through the next few minutes alive.

CHAPTER NINE
Sarah

I had to hand it to Mitchell. He could get a crowd going. His voice resonated through the amplifiers spread around the raceway. Crowds of his followers, or as I liked to call them, 'The Third Reich-ers,' were clapping at damn near every pause.

"We shall instill our values into the very fabric of this great nation. In every home, let the presence of traditional family structure and wholesomeness protect our children from the insanity of 'woke' influences. So we can guide our children to a better America."

His words were greeted with the resonant, thunderous cheers of his supporters.

"Not a bad speech, Senator," I muttered. "But most of us think being a little 'woke' is a good thing, you pompous asshole."

Miranda stiffened slightly.

"I'm not going to apologize for hating him and his politics," I whispered. "He's a prick. Another cynical creep pushing a bigoted agenda for votes. It's all he's ever been, but given the state of things in the country, I'm pretty sure he'll win next year's election. So, not to worry."

Miranda looked down, her cheeks flushing. And for the first time, I saw it, scrawled across her face as if I'd written the word myself. Shame.

She tilted her head in my direction but didn't quite look at me, whispering, "I know. I'm sorry."

Stunned and at a loss for something to say, I just stared blankly. The urge to reach out and comfort Miranda was almost overwhelming, but I squelched it. Swallowing hard, I stepped a little closer—into Miranda's personal space. "That was uncalled for. You were right. I have no right to judge you."

"Yes, you do," she whispered back. "But it doesn't matter anymore."

I frowned, and my brows knitted at the finality and somber hopelessness in Miranda's tone. Then I tore my gaze away from her and back to the crowd. I didn't know what was going on, but come hell or high water, Miranda Reichert was going to survive the night.

The senator's voice continued to rise and fall in pitch as he spoke, drawing his audience through wave after wave of his inane prattle until they finally clapped and cheered. He held his arm out toward stage left, the signal for Mitch Jr. and Miranda to join him.

Still a little dumbfounded at our exchange, I watched in silence as Miranda plastered on a genuine-looking smile and stepped up onto the stage, walking across and waving as if she and Mitchell were the perfect couple.

As I continued to scan across the heads in the crowd, now perched on the edge of the stage, cameras flashed from every direction, the Reich-ers getting their jollies in selfies with Mitchell in the background, press cameras, campaign shots. But something caught my eye, far in the distance to the south, opposite the stage, a flicker of light. It disappeared, and then a little later, in the cacophony of bursting fireworks, the finale of the event, it appeared once more, much more clearly this time, along with something else—a muzzle flash. A cold shot, the noise squelched by the fireworks. I squinted, and my stomach dropped.

I didn't bother screaming; no one would be able to hear me in the noise. Instead, I launched myself across the stage, pushing past Mitch's two security guards. Time seemed to slow to a crawl as I charged across the platform at a sprint.

Mitch Jr. turned and stared wide-eyed. Senator Reichert shot me a nasty questioning glare or had begun to when I knocked him aside and dove for Miranda. I wasn't going to make it. A splatter of hot liquid and gore sprayed across my face, neck, and shoulder. The crack of the shot echoed in my ears a half second later. I fell forward, dragging Miranda's limp body in my arms as we rolled away from the podium and off the stage into the crowd.

A stampede ensued. The crowd surged in all directions. People screamed. It was absolute chaos, and I couldn't see Miranda's body. I'd lost her somehow. I took multiple blows to the head from the stampeding guests trampling over me.

I tried to rise, but someone barreled into me and knocked me flat once more. I felt another kick to my head and a bootheel land on my ear. It was absolute pandemonium. All I could do was curl up into a ball and try desperately to protect my head, but boot after boot whacked me from every direction as the crowd bolted over me. And through it all, all I could think was that I'd failed Miranda, until finally, blissfully, darkness enfolded me.

CHAPTER TEN
Sarah

I opened my eyes to the soft noise of a heart monitor. My head felt like it had been sitting inside the engine block of a Chevy 328 running full tilt. My left arm hung bandaged and aching in a sling. As I took stock of my body, I felt a twinge in my right ankle, swollen and angry. I was in the ER—at Genesis East Medical Center, by the look of it. I reached up and touched my forehead, finding a neat row of stitches over my right eye.

The memories of the event came storming back, clouding over my thoughts and emotions. Miranda was dead. I'd seen him. I'd seen the sniper. I'd just been too slow. I sniffed as fat tears fell over my lashes and washed across my cheeks. "Fuck," I muttered to myself dejectedly.

All I could do was mourn, and I didn't even understand why I was this upset. I felt heartbroken. *I didn't even like her,* I thought, but a deeper part of me knew that was a lie. We'd bonded in some way in the last couple of months. It hadn't been the sex. It had been something else, something I couldn't put my finger on. And now, it was gone, and that loss hurt more than I ever thought it could. So lost in my own misery was I that the sudden whoosh of the curtains startled me and made me jerk, drawing a sharp stab of pain from my left shoulder.

"Oh, good, you're awake. I'm Doctor Lanesmith."

I looked up to find a young black woman in her early thirties with long brown hair and dark mocha skin staring down at me.

"How are you feeling?" She asked, her tone professional. "Any blurry vision, aversion to light?"

I wiped the tears from my face with my good hand. "No, just a headache."

Lanesmith shined a pen light in each eye. "Your pupils are fine. You might have a mild concussion."

"Where is she? Can I see her?"

The doctor looked puzzled. "Can you see who?"

"Miranda Reichert. I'm her security detail. I'd like to see the body."

Doctor Lanesmith blinked in obvious confusion. "What body?"

I raised my voice as if volume might reach this lady. "Miranda's body. What part of what I'm saying isn't getting through to you?"

A sudden realization crossed the young Doctor's face, and she smiled with genuine compassion. "Ms. Rogers, Miranda Reichert is alive and well, a few bumps and bruises, but she left almost an hour ago. I wanted her to stay, but she said she'd rather go home. She did ask about you, though."

"And the others?"

Her face turned dark. "Senator Reichert is dead. Shot through the neck. Fortunately, he died instantly—a severed spinal column. His son is a few beds over. Would you like to talk to him?"

It was my turn to blink. *Miranda was alive? Miranda was alive!* "No. Help me up. I need something to wear, and where are my things?"

"Ms. Rogers, you've taken quite a few blows to the head, and you're in no condition to—"

I glared at her, stifling the argument. "I said, help me up. I can't be here right now. Please, it's a matter of life and death." I'd made that last part up, sort of, but Lanesmith didn't need to know that.

The doctor crossed her arms, turning stolid and unyielding. "You came in with three fractured ribs, a dislocated left shoulder, and a nasty sprain in your left ankle. On top of that, you likely have a mild concussion. You need to stay put."

I continued to glare at her. "I'm signing out AMA right now. Now, where's my stuff?"

Lanesmith gave me a disappointed look. "Hold on, I'll be right back."

Apparently, in a hospital, 'I'll be right back' means something different than the rest of the world because it was almost a half hour before she returned with some scrubs and a large bag with my belongings. She also had my firearm and holster.

"The FBI are here, Ms. Rogers. They took your clothing as evidence. They want to take a statement. If you're fit to leave, then I'm sure—"

I waved at her to let them in as I pulled on the scrub pants and dragged the top painfully over my head.

"Ms. Rogers?" One of the agents asked as they replaced the doctor.

I stood bolt upright and turned as I recognized the gruff Chicago accent. It was Phillip Cameron, the Chicago SAC. I'd met him exactly twice. Once, years ago, during a lecture at FLETC. But it was the second time that I recalled most vividly when I'd resigned from the Secret Service under a cloud. A fan of Sarah Lou Rogers, he was not. As a matter of fact, he didn't like me in the slightest, as far as I knew. And the feeling was mutual.

"You've got five minutes, Phil," I said brusquely as I gathered the remainder of my belongings together and began putting on my shoes.

"We're gonna need longer than that," Phil responded with a sigh. "This is Special Agent Walters." He pointed at a younger man to his right.

I looked up from tying my shoe and snorted in amusement at the snot-nosed brat hugging Phil's coattails. "You look like you graduated from BYU just last year, son."

"Three years ago, ma'am," he answered briskly, accompanied by a warm, genuine smile.

I smiled back before finishing tying my shoes. "I'm on my way out, Phil. Like I said, five minutes. If that's not enough, then call my secretary."

The big man scowled. "Fine, just tell us what happened, and we can take a longer statement tomorrow."

"Sure, that's easy. I was stage left. That's the right side for non-theater folks. Miranda, uh, Mrs. Reichert, had just joined her husband on stage. Amid the camera flash, I caught the glare of something in the distance. It looked to me like a sniper scope. Then I saw a muzzle flash when the fireworks started, so I ran up on stage and pulled Mrs. Reichert to the ground. From what I hear, I saved her life."

Phillip scowled. "And knocked the senator straight into the path of the shot."

I froze. "What?"

"I said you knocked the senator into the path of the bullet." Phil's eyes were hard and narrow, his jaw tight. He had an accusing look on his face.

I crossed my arms in defiance and stared back at him just as hard, irritation filling my voice. "What the fuck do you want me to say, Phil? Oops? My bad? I was protecting my client."

"Why did Mrs. Reichert think she needed protection?" Walters asked as he sat on the little round stool, taking notes on a legal pad.

"Because she was afraid of her husband," I replied, my tone flat. No point in keeping that a secret now. The man was dead. "He terrified her. Something happened between them on Friday night. She called me and asked me to provide security for her while she was here."

"Were you fucking her, too?" Phil asked loudly, holding up the locket she'd given me only that morning.

"Special Agent Cameron!" Walters exclaimed, his eyes wide. "Really?"

I snatched the locket away and put it over my neck. Then I glared at Phillip with disdain before turning to Walters. "Relax, kid, he's just trying to rile me up." I looked back at Phillip. "Phil, I told you what happened. Now, if you'll excuse me, I have things to do. Unless you'd like to arrest me without a warrant for saving my client. I'm sure that'll play really well on MSNBC. Hero security guard and former Secret Service Agent arrested for accidentally pushing bigoted senator into the path of a bullet meant for his wife."

"Disgraced former Secret Service Agent," Phil shot back, a bruisingly sadistic smile splitting his bearded face.

An angry flush ran up my neck, and I squeezed my hands into fists. I wanted nothing better than to beat the snot out of the old bastard right then, but there was nothing for it. I snatched up my holster and the shitty plastic bag they'd given me for my things. "Let me remind you, Phil, that I resigned to keep bigots like you from trying to embarrass the Secret Service. Tell the D.C. office I'll come in on Wednesday to give a formal statement. In the meantime, go take a flying fuck at a rolling donut." On my way out, I shot Walters a stiff nod. "Sorry, kid. Your boss and I have history. Give me your card, though."

Walters did as I asked, and I left them there to ponder what just happened. Fuck that guy, I thought scornfully as I walked out.

I peeked out the window of the ER doors and saw the mob of reporters in the waiting room. "Can't go that way," I muttered wryly to myself.

"So, since you're leaving AMA," Lanesmith said behind me, voice low. "I didn't tell you that there's a back exit through the rehabilitation wing through there." `She pointed through a back set of double doors. "I also couldn't suggest that there's a taxi stand where you can usually find one hanging around about now."

I turned around, and Lanesmith handed me a clipboard.

"How much did you hear?" I asked as I signed the medical release form and handed back the clipboard. I probably looked a little sheepish.

The doctor grinned at me. "Hard not to hear all of it. Go get her."

Without thought, I gave Lanesmith a quick hug and took off in the direction she had indicated, nursing my arm and broken ribs all the way.

CHAPTER ELEVEN
Sarah

Back at the hotel, the door to Miranda's room was propped open, and the entire room had been turned upside down. Someone had been looking for something. From the destruction, it was clear they'd been desperate to find whatever it was. The mattress was even cut open, with bits strewn everywhere. There was also a dent in the drywall about the size of a big, meaty hand, which smacked of frustration. They almost certainly hadn't found what they were looking for.

Shaking my head, I opened the door to my own room, finding it thankfully untouched. I wondered at that briefly, then decided it was probably just sloppy work on someone's part, or maybe they hadn't known which room was mine. Could it have been that neither Mitchell nor Berringer had known I was staying in the hotel at all? My jaw worked as I considered that.

I snatched up my duffel, making sure the dossier was still inside. I wanted to split, but I still had bits of Mitchell's blood on me, so I showered and dressed quickly in casual clothes before taking the back stairs to the busy lobby.

Now in a nondescript gray hoodie and jeans and carrying my ball cap, I stopped by the front desk. "Checking out before it gets any crazier around here."

"How was your stay, Mr., sorry, Ms. Rogers?"

I smirked and mussed my hair. "It's the short hair and the name. Happens all the time. Family's from the mountains, you know?"

"Is it short for Louise?" The clerk asked.

"Nope, just Lou. That's Appalachia for ya." I smiled and took the guest receipt, then left through the rear of the hotel.

I had my answer. Miranda had reserved the room for Mr. Lou Rogers, and the clerk who had checked me in had probably thought someone had just put in the wrong salutation. I felt a stab of worry. Miranda knew she was in real danger and that her life was threatened, and she wanted anyone coming for her at the hotel to get a nasty surprise. And they had, hadn't they—not at the hotel, but still.

I sat in the car and thought about just leaving this craziness behind and abandoning Miranda to her grief, assuming there was any; she clearly hated Mitchell. But it was a fleeting thought, and something was still niggling at my insides, the state of Miranda's hotel room. Miranda had something, or someone thought she had something, something that they wanted very badly. Their next stop would likely be Miranda's home. This wasn't over.

I hadn't thought Mitchell was the kind of man cut out for murder, but I'd been wrong before—plenty. But why target his wife? He had her very much under control, or at least it seemed so. In any event, there was only one person who knew the answer to that question, and given that I'd almost taken a bullet for her and that I'd have to sit through an FBI interview, I wanted answers.

I fired up the Mustang and pulled out of the hotel parking lot right past the gaggles of reporters hanging around outside. They were probably waiting for Mitch Jr. to return so they could pester him with questions. *Later, you vultures,* I thought as I pulled out of the parking lot.

Once I hit the first red light, I punched up the GPS on the dash and entered Miranda's address in Bettendorf. I was going to find out what the fuck was going on.

I paused at the end of Rosewood Lane, watching as protesters and mourners shouted at each other in the middle of the street, separated by a single police car. There weren't many of them, but they might come to blows at any moment.

I frowned. *Good riddance to Mitchell Reichert, but who protests a dead man?* These people were no better than folks protesting the funerals of dead soldiers like those Westboro numbnuts, I decided as I watched briefly. Of course, the signs they carried were a lot less inflammatory than Westboro's trademark 'God Hates Fags,' paraphernalia.

I sighed and turned the Mustang down Oak Street, quietly driving past the side of the house. I pulled off just past a small copse of trees in a vacant green space behind it. Exiting the car, I closed the car door as quietly as possible and looked around. Despite the insanity in front, the side street was empty. People here were probably used to this, keeping out of sight until it was over. I briefly considered grabbing my spare vest from the back, but considering my shoulder, I decided against it.

As I approached the back wall of the property, I smelled the sweet earthiness of tilled soil, which reminded me of home. Stepping from the treeline, I realized I missed it. Home, that was. If I lived through this night, I'd have to get back there sooner rather than later. I paused, the thought rattling around my head into the nugget of an idea.

"Huh," I muttered absently, then looked up at the property wall, thinking of my aching arm and ribs. "You fucking better be here, Miranda Reichert."

I leaped up and grabbed the edge with both hands, my shoulder screaming in protest as I hoisted myself, praising the wonders of the one-arm pull-ups I'd done about a million of in the gym. Then, dropping to the ground on the other side, I said a silent prayer. *No dogs. Please, no fucking dogs.* I had no desire to get all this way and be mauled by a pit bull or German shepherd or something. That would be just Mitchell's style. He'd definitely seemed like a dog person. A mean dog person.

As it turned out, there weren't any dogs, but an adorable little calico cat meowed at me from a small kitchen window at the back. The cry was gentle, almost like a whisper, and the cat's green eyes followed me as I crossed through the expertly manicured garden.

I silently approached a set of broad sliding glass doors revealing a sprawling master bedroom. Miranda was inside the dimly lit room, packing in a panic, throwing clothes into a suitcase haphazardly. *Oh, yeah,* I thought. *She knew. And she's still afraid. This is bigger than Mitchell.*

I paused and watched for a moment. Miranda looked so different from the woman I'd stood beside only hours ago. She'd ditched her elegant, conservative attire for a t-shirt, jeans, and an old pair of Reeboks. But it wasn't just her clothes. The not-so-subtle resignation that I'd had seen as she stepped onto the stage, as if she knew for sure she was going to die in a few minutes, was gone, replaced by a mixture of determination and fear. Miranda Reichert was ready to run for her life.

I tapped on the glass and watched as Miranda spun, eyes wide and terrified. Her gaze locked onto mine, and her expression softened slightly as she breathed a sigh of relief.

I tapped on the glass again, "Open the door. Please."

Miranda hesitated, then slid the glass back. "What are you doing here?"

"Isn't that obvious? I'm doing my job," I replied, crossing my arms, wincing in pain, then letting my left dangle.

Miranda glanced over her shoulder before speaking in a hissed whisper. "You've done your job. Besides, I can't pay you anymore. I don't have any money except a little bit I've squirreled away. It's all Mitch Jr's now."

I gave her a puzzled look. "What do you mean?"

"He left everything to Mitch Jr., and I signed a prenup with Mitchell that said I wouldn't contest the will." She looked down, clearly embarrassed. "I was young and didn't realize he just wanted to ensure his idiot son got it all."

"So what's your plan?" I asked, still standing in the doorway, my right arm moving a little haphazardly as if I didn't know what to do with it.

Miranda put a hand on her hip and rubbed the back of her neck. "I don't have one. I just need to leave. Like now."

"No shit. Did you know they were aiming for you?"

She just nodded and turned back to her insane packing

attempt.

I stepped through the door and gently touched Miranda's forearm. "Slow down. You're just making a mess." I pushed the clothes in the suitcase around. "You haven't even packed any underwear. Let me show you how you do this."

"You've done this before?"

I snorted a laugh and emptied the suitcase. "Gone on the run? No. But I *do* know how to prepare someone to get the hell out of dodge—the right way. I used to be Secret Service, remember? You learn things from the older agents. Stuff they don't teach you at FLETC. Now, here, let's get all this out and start over. Pack only rugged, nondescript clothing, gray, brown, that sort of thing. Nothing eye-catching or fancy. Got it."

Miranda still stood there, staring. "Why do you care? You made what you think of me pretty plain."

"Maybe I just have a soft spot for women in need," I joked as I took a black t-shirt and folded it, then rolled it into a tight cylinder before placing it in the now empty suitcase.

"I'm not helpless. I can handle myself."

I didn't look up from packing. "Not this, you can't. And if you think you can, then you're an idiot, and somehow, I don't think Miranda Danbury was raised to be a fool for anyone."

Miranda didn't respond, but she jolted into motion and followed my lead, rolling the clothes up before placing them in the suitcase.

"No more than you can carry with one arm," I said as I placed a long-sleeved shirt in the suitcase. "Now, where are your underwear?"

Miranda raised an eyebrow at that. "I'll handle my own dainties, thank you very much."

"My mamaw used to say that many hands make light work. Now, where?" I demanded, looking at the chest of drawers.

Miranda walked over, opened the top left drawer, and started rifling through it.

"Only plain underwear and comfortable bras. Simple. Easy. Comfortable. Remember. You're going to be running from—" I paused. "Who are we running from anyway?"

"It's a long story," Miranda sighed as she grabbed a half dozen pairs of plain cotton panties from her drawer and started rolling them up just like everything else. "And we," she motioned between us, "are not running from anyone. I'm running, and you're going home."

I smiled then. "Nope. There are two hotels outside of town set up with aliases and under a prepaid debit card, all ready to go."

Miranda spun around. "What?"

I just kept smiling. "Given how absolutely fucking terrified you've been the last forty-eight hours, I took precautions. I'm not stupid, Miranda. I was a good agent. That's why Mitchell is dead, and you're still alive." The truth was, it had been luck. I had just happened to be looking in the right direction at the right time, but I needed her to have confidence in me. "My job in the Secret Service was to keep people safe. That was all I did, all day, every day."

I watched as Miranda seemed to size me up. Her icy stare gave nothing away, but I knew that look. Miranda was assessing my worth—was I an asset or a liability?

Finally, Miranda spoke a single word, one I didn't have an answer to. "Why?"

My jaw worked as I tried to answer that question for myself. Eventually, I settled on, "No clue. But it's me or nothing right now, and I have resources, experience, and training. You don't. So you can take your chances alone or let me do what you hired me for." Then, as a joke, I added, "I'll put it on your tab."

A flicker of something passed behind Miranda's frosty expression, but then it was gone, and she turned flat. "Okay. I was planning to go to my parents."

I shook my head. "Nope. Just trust me. Right now, I want you to focus on staying calm and keeping cool. Family is the first place anyone would look for you when they realize you're not here anymore. And until you tell me what's going on, I'm calling the shots because it's my ass on the line with you."

Miranda stalled out for a moment, her lips pressed into a thin line as if she were rethinking going with me.

I gently placed my hands on Miranda's shoulders and felt the woman tense. It clearly made her uncomfortable. *That's good,* I thought. *I have her attention.* I spoke quietly but firmly, looking

Miranda straight into her beautiful eyes. "I just saved your life and nearly lost my own. You can trust me. I've got you."

That seemed to settle the issue for Miranda. "Do I need anything else?"

"Bring your phone," I said as she zipped up the suitcase. "And grab a jacket. It's cold out. Something simple and dark colored."

Miranda balked. "Won't they be able to trace my phone?"

I shrugged. "It would help if I knew who *they* were. But, as it turns out, I'm counting on that. But keep it off until I tell you otherwise. Come on."

Miranda turned off her phone as we slipped out the back door into the garden and the heady scent of the late-blooming flowers. The pitiful calico was still meowing from the window.

"Shit," Miranda swore. "I can't leave Remington."

"The cat?" I said incredulously. "Leave it. Someone will take care of it, call the ASPCA or something."

"No," Miranda whispered, and then added, almost to herself, "she's all I've got," as she dropped the suitcase and dashed back inside.

I rolled my eyes and followed swiftly after.

All holy hell exploded. Screams sounded out front as the staccato sound of gunfire ripped through the night. Bullets tore through the front of the house, throwing splinters across the bedroom and into the living room beyond.

I recognized the pop-pop of M4s in full auto, military gear, and, for a second, I worried about the people out front, if a bit half-heartedly. I reached Miranda just as the sliding glass door shattered in front of us, and we narrowly avoided being cut to ribbons. A layer of clear thermal insulation on the outside had kept it from exploding outward in a hail of shards. I dropped down on top of Miranda, covering her body. *Fuck,* I thought, *I wish I'd grabbed my vest?*

The cat meowed again, and Miranda tried to rise.

"Stay down!" I repeated, shouting over the racket.

We could both hear the cat wailing from the kitchen window like a tormented soul when the shooting stopped as abruptly as it started.

"They're reloading," I hissed. "We can't stay here." I grabbed

Miranda's arm and pulled her up just to have her break away. "Damnit."

I caught up in the living room as she reached the sprinting cat, scooping him into her arms and holding him against her chest. The front door splintered open, and two masked men barged in. I experienced that same slowing of time I'd felt on the stage, adrenaline, fear, and training. The deafening ring of their shots resonated in my ears, banging at my headache, but my muscles reacted faster than my brain, my arms wrapping around Miranda's waist as I dragged her back behind a wall and tossed her to the floor.

Glass and porcelain everywhere shattered as bullets rained through the living room, tearing into the family photos, vases, and whatever memories Miranda had made here. The acrid scent of gunpowder filled the air, and the entire house was once again engulfed in absolute chaos.

My emotions flattened as I drew my weapon with a practiced hand. I'd never been in a shoot-out, and it felt like an out-of-body experience, seeing myself moving with the kind of controlled urgency that comes with expert training. I stepped out, aimed, and fired three shots, taking one man down with two center mass and one in the head. Then, I dove back behind the wall, staying low to avoid the return fire from the second gunman.

Miranda was still on the floor with the cat in her arms. I rose once more and fired at the second gunman, but the bullets pancaked in a shower of drywall as he ducked back into a side room.

I grabbed Miranda and pulled her up, feeling the shooting pain in my shoulder again. "Come on."

I pushed Miranda in front of me and put a hand on her back, then thanked my lucky stars that the woman was trained to work with a security detail. We moved back into the bedroom and out through the shattered door into the backyard, where I holstered my gun and grabbed the suitcase with my good arm, lobbing it over the wall. Then I bent down to let Miranda climb over with the cat.

Finally, I jumped up and hoisted myself painfully over the wall just as a bullet shattered the stone perilously close to my head.

But we didn't stop running, not yet. I grabbed Miranda's arm again and half-led, half-dragged her through the cops of trees, not stopping until we reached the Mustang, where I opened the door and shoved Miranda inside, still shielding her body with my own.

I heard the screams and shouts of people in front of the Reichert home, some of them sounding injured, but that wasn't my problem. Throwing the suitcase into the hatch with my duffel, I took the driver's side and mashed the start button before flooring it and peeling out in a haze of burnt rubber and the squeal of tires. I hazarded a swift glance in the rearview; it was clear.

"Fuck that was close," I whispered before reaching over and patting all over Miranda's body.

"What are you doing?" Miranda protested, slapping at my hands.

I snatched my hand back and put it on the wheel, slowing down to the speed limit. "Are you hit? Are you hurt?"

"No," Miranda answered, then more firmly as if she hadn't actually been sure. "No. I'm not injured."

I hazarded a glance at the cat curled up in Miranda's lap in a tight ball. "You, little cat, have just used up all eight of your extra lives, so don't be fucking around. Jesus. Fucking cat people. This is why I don't have a pet."

CHAPTER TWELVE
Miranda

I clutched Remington in my lap, running the backs of my knuckles along her cheeks the way she liked, even as my hands trembled. Slowly, over the course of twenty or so miles outside of Davenport, my heartbeat finally dropped into the mid-hundreds, or so it felt, and my shoulders slumped.

Quietly, I stared out the window as we drove. This was exactly why I'd left Sarah at the hospital and gone home. I hadn't wanted to put Sarah in any more danger. *But, Gods*, I thought. *The woman is stubborn.*

I just couldn't understand why someone who had likely privately hated me the entire time she'd been employed would do this. In my world, it didn't make any sense. In politics, the kind I'd had to play with Mitchell, friends weren't real. The minute they became a liability, you jettisoned them like so much dead weight.

That brought my thoughts back around to Sarah's damning judgment of my character, and I blinked back tears, trying to focus for a moment on Remington's soft purring in my lap. It had stung. No, it had hurt me—deeply. Not just because Sarah was right. But for some reason, hearing it from her had stirred something inside me, a deep shame I'd never let myself feel. I hadn't wanted to feel it. I'd never wanted to feel it. But now, it had somehow become a part of me, burning me from the inside, making me want to wail about—about what? How unfair my life had been? How I'd been trapped by Mitchell or dragged through a horrid childhood by my ramrod-straight and more than mildly racist parents? Those were the whining complaints of a child, not a thirty-four-year-old woman who had conquered entire cadres of senators and congresspersons with her wit and style and charm, but still.

I'd had enough of searching my withered and exhausted soul when I turned my attention back to the present. "Where are we going?"

"We're almost there," Sarah answered. "We're about fifty miles west of Davenport. There's a small motel. We'll be staying there, but not all night."

"Huh? I'm exhausted, Sarah. I can barely keep my eyes open."

"It's important. I need a measure of what we're dealing with. Is there anything you can tell me?"

I turned and looked back at the window but didn't answer.

"Damnit, Miranda. I need something here."

I sighed and put my hand to my forehead. "This is something you can't even imagine. Please, let's just go to the hotel. I'll explain everything in the morning."

"Fine," Sarah grumbled.

Five minutes later, Sarah pulled into a small Hilton property just off the highway.

"What are we doing? I thought you said we were going to a motel."

Sarah chuckled. "We're not staying here. We're staying over there," she pointed to what looked to be a hooker hangout next door, "but probably not more than an hour. And leave the bags. We won't need them. Bring your phone. And leave the cat, we won't be long enough, and he'll create a problem if he gets loose."

"You have got to be kidding me," I said as we got out of the car. I looked across the small grassy embankment to the motel on the other side. "The Bug Inn? It's more like the infested inn. I'm not staying there." I shushed Remington and then locked her inside the car.

Sarah laughed and gave me a genuine smile. "I told you we're not staying there for more than an hour."

I stopped. *Is she suggesting? No, that isn't going to happen.*

Sarah had apparently read my expression. "No, we're not going to get laid in some fleabag motel. I crossed that off my list at sixteen. Now, come on, girl. Get a move on. We don't have much time."

Sarah started across the embankment, and I followed grudgingly. "I'm a grown woman," I whispered. "Not a girl."

"Wait here," Sarah said then banged on the office door.

The man who came out of the back looked exactly as I thought he should, pot belly, balding pate, even the wifebeater tank top. I couldn't hear the conversation, but I figured it went a little like, 'I've got this hot little number outside, and I need a room for an hour.' And the guy would be like, 'Can I watch?' I shivered at the thought. Just gross.

Sarah came out with an honest-to-God door key in her hand and walked down to the far end of the motel, opening the room closest to the car. "Come on."

Once we entered, I finally snapped. "Okay, what the fuck are we doing in this bumblefuck, nasty-ass, bed-bug-ridden rat's nest?"

Sarah turned around and looked at me, genuinely stunned. Then she doubled over with laughter. "Wow! I have never heard you swear like that before. I mean, I've heard you say a curse word here and there, but a sailor's string like that? Oh, Lordy."

"I'm serious, Sarah," I started, but Sarah's laughter was infectious. And with all the stress, my emotions were a jumble. I laughed at the absurdity of it all, and it took several minutes to stop.

After we'd calmed down, Sarah spoke up, turning abruptly serious. "We are exactly fifty-three minutes from Davenport, give or take. I need you to put your phone on speaker and call your parents. Do *not* tell them you are with me and do not tell them where you are. They need to think you are alone. No one knows I'm with you, and we want to keep it that way as long as possible."

"What did you say to the guy?" I asked.

"I told him that if anyone came here looking for two women, to tell them that we just checked out. I also paid him two hundred bucks and had him give us the only room with a back door."

Sarah pointed through the little kitchenette. "This is actually his apartment. I also said we wouldn't be here for more than two hours. Now, call your parents."

I looked at her skeptically but made the call. My mother picked up on the first ring, and I put it on speaker so Sarah could hear.

"Miranda, are you okay? Where are you?"

Sarah shook her head.

"I'm safe, Mom," I said through trembling lips. "I'm, uh, fine. I just wanted to let you know." I had no practice talking to my parents. We didn't have much of a relationship, so I looked at Sarah, who was tapping her watch and motioning at me to continue.

"Do you want to talk to your father? He's right here."

"Mom, it's past four in the morning. I'm sorry I woke you. But if you want to put Dad on, that's fine."

Sarah shook her head in disbelief, but I waved her off.

My father's voice replaced Mom's alto. "Miranda, where are you?"

"I'm safe, Dad. I can't tell you where I am right now. I'm sorry. It's just not safe for me to do that."

"Miranda Anne Danbury," he ranted loudly. "You tell me where you are this instant."

Sarah scowled at the phone.

I shook my head and rolled my eyes. "Dad, I'm not twelve anymore. Raising your voice won't work. I've faced down scarier people than you—in just the last few hours even."

"You know what? I'm your father, and you will show me some respect, young lady."

"Don't you dare call me that," I snapped. "After all you've done to me over the years, you don't ever get to call me that ever again. Mitchell was just murdered right next to me, his brains splattered across my suit."

The line became very quiet. There was a bit of a shuffle, and then my mother returned. "I'm sorry, honey. Your father's just stressed. And we're both worried about you."

I laughed in incredulity, and my voice turned shrill. "Worried about me? You didn't even call me! It's not like you don't have my number. Mitchell was shot on live TV, and where the fuck were you?"

My face flushed, and I glared at the phone, willing it to melt in my hand. For thirty-four years, I'd been their good little girl, never embarrassing the family that was supposed to love and protect me. I'd be god damned if I played that game right now. I opened my mouth to give them what for, but Sarah reached over and pressed the end call button.

"What did you do that for?" I asked, my tone icy.

"Because they were getting you wound up, and that wasn't the point of the call. Has your mother ever taken the phone from your father that way?"

I blinked, looked at the phone, and then back at Sarah. "No. Never. She wouldn't dare—" I stopped short, catching on to the implications.

Sarah read it in my eyes and nodded. "Someone else was listening in. They were afraid you'd hang up before they got a trace. Is there anything in that phone you need?"

I thought for a moment about all of my political contacts, which were now useless. Then I thought about the banking apps, the calendar, everything. Nothing on the phone would help me now. "No," I finally said and held it out.

Sarah took the phone and reset it back to factory settings, then shut it down and pulled out the SIM card. "That's that then." She reached into her pocket, pulled out a small flip phone, and handed it to me. "Here, for emergencies only. My burner number is already programmed in. Just hold down the one button, and it will dial me directly."

"What about your phone? If they figure out you're with me—"

"It's in the car right now, but I'm about to get rid of it too." She wiped down my phone and left it on the nightstand, then wiped down all the surfaces we'd touched with a towel and the doorknob as well as the key, which she took back to the owner, and we went across the median to the Mustang and waited for forty-five minutes.

I sat impatiently, watching the motel and stroking Remington, who had been meowing up a storm when we'd returned to the car, clearly miffed at being left behind. "What are we waiting for?"

"Them," Sarah said and started the Mustang, leaving the lights off.

Two black SUVs rolled down the road past us and pulled into the Bug Inn parking lot. As quietly as the muscle car would allow, Sarah steered us out of the Hilton parking lot and headed west down the highway, further away from Davenport.

Forty minutes later, Sarah pulled off the side of the road, fiddled with her phone, smashed it with a tire iron, and chucked it off down the embankment into the darkness below. Then she made a loop at the next exit and headed back east.

"*Now* where are we going?" I asked.

When Sarah didn't answer, I quit asking. I couldn't think in my total exhaustion anyway, so I put my seat back and closed my eyes. Despite everything. Despite all that had happened, with everything being completely out of my control, I felt the safest I had perhaps ever. Minutes later, I was out cold.

About two hours later, Sarah gently woke me. "Come on. Let's get a good night's rest."

I looked up and realized we were in a parking garage. "Where are we?"

"The Palmer in Chicago, but don't get too comfortable. It's just for the night."

I stared at her, dumbfounded. "Sarah, The Palmer is a seven-hundred-dollar-a-night hotel."

"That's why we're only staying one night, and it's the only place I could get a room. I've already checked in and had them take our bags up. I figured I'd let you rest while I got us squared away. We're under the name Joan Lambert."

I looked at Sarah, puzzled. "Umm, wasn't she the whiney one that got eaten?"

Sarah grinned at me. "Wow, now I didn't expect that."

I chuckled softly. "I didn't grow up under a rock. It's only the best sci-fi horror film ever made."

Sarah went into the trunk and dug out a bag with a disposable litter box, a small bag of litter, and some cat food.

"Where'd you get that?" I asked, taken aback by Sarah's thoughtfulness.

"Walmart just outside Moline. You were out like a light, so I let you sleep. Can't have the cat pooping on the floor at The Palmer, now can we? And she has to be hungry by now."

"I—I—" I stuttered, then placed a hand on Sarah's arm. "Thank you."

"It's for the cat," Sarah deflected. "Don't get any ideas. I still don't like you."

Though I knew that Sarah was probably trying to be funny, the joke hurt, but I didn't say anything. Instead, I quietly followed Sarah into the high-rise hotel, desperate for a bed.

CHAPTER THIRTEEN
Sarah

I led Miranda up in the elevator. Only the panel's beeping punctuated the frosty silence as we passed each floor. Finally, on the twenty-fifth, we exited and found our room.

"It's not very large," Miranda said, gently placing Remington on the bed and turning to meet my eyes. "And there's only one bed."

Miranda's expression was inscrutable, reading only a tired sort of perfunctory acknowledgment, and it left me cold. It wasn't that I expected anything from her, but any sign of gratitude would have been nice.

"I can take the floor," I said and gestured to the bed as I dug into the closet and found a spare blanket. "You want the shower first?"

"Please," Miranda responded, her movements robotic, her speech bland and colorless.

"Miranda, it will be okay," I said gently, trying to show some encouragement and optimism, misplaced as it might be. But Miranda simply ignored the statement and disappeared into the bathroom, leaving me to my thoughts.

My heart twisted for her as I watched her close the door. I couldn't even imagine how she must be feeling. In a day, her entire life had simply unraveled like someone had yanked a key thread from a tapestry, and the entire thing just fell into a pile of so much string and embroidery. An entire life was destroyed with a single bullet, and I didn't mean Mitchell's. He was dead. His troubles were over. Miranda's were just starting.

Agents would start digging into Miranda's past, her finances, everything. When a husband dies, the wife is always the first suspect. What was worse, I knew I'd get caught up in that because of one careless afternoon, not that I regretted that afternoon, not really.

Remington stared at me from the bed, her feet curled up under her, making her look like nothing so much as a cat-shaped loaf of calico bread. Even her tail was tucked away. But her eyes seemed accusing as if to say, 'You loon, she's not into you. And even if she was, her husband just died.'

"You don't think I know that," I muttered to the feline before stretching the blanket onto the floor and lying on it. I couldn't hear the tears, but I knew Miranda shed them in the one place where she could do so with privacy, hiding her emotional breakdown in the noise of the falling water. And my heart started to break for her. I sniffed and wiped my nose. Of course, why I was pained over the emotional turmoil of Miranda Reichert, I couldn't say. She was the fucking enemy of everything I believed and stood for. Wasn't she?

" Shit," I murmured and rolled over to stare at the ceiling.

When Miranda emerged in a T-shirt and panties, her skin was bright red, and I sighed in sympathy. She'd been showering in scalding water, something people do when they feel they'd never get clean. Miranda looked down at Remington and then at me but said nothing.

The look was cold, a void of numbness. I'd seen it a hundred times on victims of various violent crimes, mostly in training videos. As a Secret Service Agent on protection details, I never saw it. Well, just once—in the mirror the day after the accident.

I knew the woman was in shock, but it still hurt that Miranda didn't even offer one side of the bed. I also knew I was being irrational, but it didn't matter. Feelings were feelings, and it was best to feel them than pretend they didn't exist. Despite Miranda's bitchiness, I had a soft spot for her. It was that simple, and I wasn't confused or in denial about that.

"You suck," I whispered to Remington and then scratched her

fur while she brushed her teeth. She rolled over and exposed her stomach, and I obliged, making sure the cat was purring loudly with a few belly scritches.

"Look," Miranda said after she set aside her toothbrush. "I don't mean to seem ungrateful, but tell me again why you're doing this?"

"Does it really matter? I'm on your side." I didn't want to get into the discussion. My feelings were about as clear as mud, anyway. *This is why you never fuck a client,* my inner voice chastised me. But I knew it was more than that. She needed me, and it felt good to be needed for a change.

If I was honest with myself, I knew I was enjoying playing the hero, even if only for a moment. Of course, that assumed Miranda hadn't set all this up from the start. But I couldn't believe that. Miranda Reichert was a lot of things, but a murderer? No. No way.

Miranda nodded but said nothing else. Instead, she climbed into the bed. Remington snuggled into her stomach, and Miranda picked up where I'd left off, stroking the cat's belly.

With a sigh, I ran a hand through my hair and blew out an exasperated breath. For a moment, I waited to see if Miranda would offer me the other side of the king-sized bed, but she didn't, so I dragged myself into the bathroom for a shower.

Finally getting clean under the spray, I stood and thought about my predicament. "What the absolute fuck am I doing?" I whispered to myself for about the fortieth time so far. *You're doing the right thing,* the voice in my head whispered back. *That's all that matters.*

Was it, though? I was now on the run with the wife of a murdered politician right after I'd slept with her. On the surface, this wouldn't just look 'not good.' It would look fucking bad, as if we'd arranged to have Mitchell killed. Of course, that wouldn't hold up under any kind of serious investigative scrutiny, but I knew that not every case got proper effort, and sometimes other pressures intervened, like the desire to close a case, personal bias, and, worst of all, politics. And in this instance, if this, whatever it was, ran as deep as I suspected, we would make pretty good patsies.

I tried not to think about it, but the image of awful headlines came to mind, like, "Did a disgraced lesbian former Secret Service agent and Senator's Widow plot murder?" or a short line Fox News ticker, perhaps, "Gay assassin kills senator and absconds with his wife."

We needed to get off the grid for a bit and soon. The longer the Bureau had to investigate this, the better the outcome for us would be. In the meantime, all I needed to do was keep my hands to myself and Miranda safe. Under no circumstances could I get intimate with her again. That was an absolute certainty. It would only make things more complicated.

It was a one-night stand, I reminded myself as I shut off the water. Of course, now, I was hip-deep in something huge, and I had no idea how deep the waters actually were.

Clean and teeth brushed, I opened the door to ask Miranda once more what exactly 'it' was we'd gotten into, but the woman was out cold, Remington, her heroic little defender, snoozing quietly next to her.

I shook my head and smirked at the sleeping pair, who, despite the circumstances, were absolutely adorable. I lay down on the floor. A moment later, Miranda's hand flopped over the edge of the bed, and she made a noise in her sleep like she was having a bad dream. I reached up to take it, and for a moment, she squeezed my fingers. I lifted up and looked at her, but she was still fast asleep. Finally, the hand went slack, and Miranda slid it back to her chest.

I snorted and shook my head again. Just before I passed out, I wondered who was the more ridiculous guardian here, me or the tiny little cat who had survived a hail of bullets.

CHAPTER FOURTEEN
Sarah

"Where are we going?" Miranda asked about two hours south of Chicago.

I looked at her, then glanced at the cat, relaxing in the back seat. "Some place where you and Remington will be safe. At least for a good long while. Just trust me. I know what I'm doing."

"I still don't understand why you won't tell me," Miranda griped and turned to look back out the window. The night before, she'd clearly been tired, but now her eyes had a haunted look. It was the look of someone staring at the end of everything they'd worked for, the face of someone lost. It pushed a deep swell of empathy into my chest, but it was something I didn't want to feel, not for her.

"I need a cup of coffee," I said finally, breaking the dark silence between us. "There's a Dunkin' up ahead."

Miranda continued staring out the window at the passing landscape. "It is really pretty."

I snorted a laugh. "This is flatland, honey. Wait until you see where we're goin'."

Miranda glanced over at me, clearly irritated at the teasing, but she didn't say anything, seemingly content at this point to go wherever I took her. Which, in my estimation, was a bit odd. Miranda had always seemed like the ice queen control freak, but there was something under that, a real person, and now that person was poking out, exposed, vulnerable. Miranda didn't like it, or so it appeared, but she didn't seem to know how to stop it.

For my part, I was more nervous than a ten-tailed cat in a room full of rocking chairs, cursing the flutter in my belly that wouldn't go away. Just being next to Miranda was distracting, and it made my heart thud in my chest—not because something actually could happen, but just because in my clearly damaged brain, somewhere, I must be holding out hope for something.

"I'd like some coffee, too," Miranda said, then quickly added, "and a donut for Remington, plain, no powder or anything."

I laughed. "A donut? Your cat eats donuts?"

"Yes, and she's sensitive about it, so don't tease."

I laughed even harder. "Yeah, real sensitive," I said sarcastically, looking back at the cat, who was curled up with his eyes closed.

A few minutes later, we were back on the road. I sipped my coffee, as did Miranda. Remington seemed content to sit in Miranda's lap and nibble at her donut.

"Make sure she doesn't get crumbs on the seats."

Miranda turned, and the frost had returned to her eyes. "Sarah Lou Rogers, tell me this instant where we're going. I deserve to know."

I finally relented. "I'm taking you home. It's the one place I know I can protect you from just about anything except the wrath of God."

"Where's home," Miranda asked, and I realized we'd never really discussed it.

"Letcher County, Kentucky. Coal country." When Miranda didn't react except to nod, I reached for the radio but then paused. "Are you ready to hear what's going on?"

Miranda suddenly looked terrified, as if the radio might jump out and bite her. "Is it bad?"

"It's not great. I've been catching bits here and there."

I hit the touch screen and touched the button for CNN.

CHAPTER FIFTEEN
Miranda

I killed the radio after only twenty minutes. My insides were squirming with terror, and it filtered into my voice. "They think *I* did it! They think *I* arranged to have Mitchell killed!"

"They didn't say that. They said you're wanted for questioning." Sarah's words and voice were calm, but her white knuckles on the steering wheel belied her tension.

"It doesn't matter. You don't understand. Mitchell's supporters are rabid people. They'll assume I did it. They'll try to find me. They'll try to kill me. I'd always received threats of one kind or another, but no one ever—Oh, my God. I'm going to be sick. Pull over, Sarah."

Sarah swerved across two lanes of traffic to the honking protests of other drivers as we traveled down I-65.

As soon as the car stopped, I opened the door and bent over, emptying the morning's breakfast of eggs and toast into the thin grass on the shoulder.

When I'd finished and closed the door, Sarah pulled a bottle of water from the back and handed it to me. "Here, you're white as a sheet."

I took a sip and broke down. Any control I'd managed to project since last night crumbled to dust as the weight of the circumstances landed on me. My voice came out high-pitched and tinny, choked with tears. "Twelve years. I suffered with that man for twelve years, and even with him dead, I'm still not free.

My life is over."

Sarah signaled and got back on the highway, driving fast. "I need you to hang on for just a bit. Can you do that for me? I'm taking you home. We'll keep you safe there."

I turned and looked at her in utter disbelief. "Kentucky? Are you insane? After what those nut jobs are saying? That's the core of his base, especially Appalachia. Pull off, I'll take my chances."

"No," Sarah said gently, placing her hand on mine. "Listen to me carefully. No one will even know who you are. And my family isn't like that. You'll be able to trust them. You'll see. We will get you clear of this."

I so wanted to believe her. She sounded so confident, so—sure of herself, but I knew better. *This isn't going to end*, I thought as I looked out the window again. I couldn't help the tears running down my face. I felt so alone.

"You know," I said with a sniff, abruptly switching subjects. "I never really traveled in the US. Isn't that strange? I've never seen any of this. It really is beautiful countryside." I turned to Sarah and dried my eyes. "I would really like to see your home."

"No, don't do that," Sarah snapped.

"What? Want to see your home?"

"Give up!" Her voice rose. "I can hear it in your voice. I am going to get you out of this. You're not going to prison, and I'm not going to let anyone hurt you."

I had had enough. I was tired of Sarah's incessant badgering about this. I just wanted to curl up in a corner, but I raised my voice, engaging this time instead of retreating again.

"What the fuck am I supposed to do, Sarah? I've been all by myself for the last twelve years with that abusive prick. I supported him, helped write his shitty legislation that was as close to evil as I could imagine, hosted his parties, and endured the bruises and the broken arm and the cracked skull. I'm tired. I'm fucking tired. Do you hear me? I'm fucking tired."

Sarah gripped the steering wheel hard. "I saw it in your eyes when you took the stage. You knew! You expected to die on that stage!"

"No, I didn't," I retorted, but my voice faltered. The truth was I didn't know exactly when or where it would happen, but I'd expected it. I'd known it was coming. 'Nothing better than a Senator in mourning to garner votes,' the email had said. 'Just like the ending of a tragic love story in the movies. It'll be Jack and Rose or Romeo and Juliet.'

"Yes, you did! You expected a public and bloody death, yours. Only I got in the way, and it ended up being Mitchell. You are free of him, you know. This is just the aftermath, and we'll fix it!"

"How, Sarah! How? The only thing keeping—" I stopped short.

Sarah glanced at me. "The only thing, what?" She prodded, her tone lower, obviously curious about what I had been about to say.

I looked back out the window. I couldn't do that. I'd already dragged Sarah in too far. I'd go with Sarah to her home, and when the time was right, I'd go back to D.C. and try to buy our way out of this trouble with what I had.

I could see Sarah's jaw working and the tightness in her eyes. Then, without warning, she pulled off at the next exit and into the parking lot of a CVS. "What color?"

"What?" I asked. "What are you talking about?"

"What color hair do you want? Pick something you'd never pick in a million years, but you've always wondered what it would look like?"

I suddenly understood. "A blue to purple ombre."

"You'd need my mom for that," Sarah said, pressing the point. "Something simple. Blue or purple?"

I thought about it and settled on a deep, unnatural ruby color. Sarah left the car and returned with the red hair dye I'd requested. Then she drove us to the nearest hotel and got a room.

"I don't want to stay long," she said grumpily as we stalked into the room. "I'd like to get to my folks before supper time."

In the bathroom, I fingered the bottle. It wasn't like me to do something this extreme, ever. I was supposed to be quietly confident and reserved, the good little girl I'd been raised to be, supporting my man, never the center of attention, even at thirty-four, the spat with my father notwithstanding.

But the more I fingered the bottle, the more I realized that this needed to be done, and, well, fuck it, my life was over anyway. I had never dyed my hair like this before. I'd once considered it, even researched how to do it, mostly as something outlandish in the hopes that Mitchell would freak and either leave me or beat me to death and end it. That had been a low point.

As I stood in the shower and rinsed the rest of the dye from my hair, I thought about what Sarah had said. Maybe she could help me. Maybe Sarah could get me out of this.

No, I told myself. This was more than Sarah needed to deal with, and I had more than enough information to trade for my life. At least, I hoped.

An hour and a half later, clean, showered, and with ruby-red hair, I sat in the passenger seat, and we got on the road again. I kept glancing at my reflection in the mirror and touching my hair. It was so different and, in a way, almost liberating. It was stupid, I knew, but for a second, I felt a bit of control, a kind of control I'd never had in my entire life. "I thought you said that bright colors attract attention."

Sarah glanced over, grinned for a moment, then grew a little more serious. "They do, but a drastic hair color change will throw off the eye, making the face seem wider or narrower. Also, it keeps some, especially the conservative types, from really paying much attention to your features. One advantage of where we're going, most of the folks are white, and identification is a major challenge across racial lines. Mama can do something about the length. You don't dare let me cut it. Here." Sarah handed me a pair of reading glasses. "When we're around people in public, you'll want to wear these."

I stared at the gray-framed glasses. At least they were stylish. "With these on, I won't be able to see very well."

"Just keep them perched on your nose. Trust me. You'll understand the value at some point. In the meantime, keep them in your pocket. I'll get you a pair of prescription-less when we get home."

Home. I thought about that word and realized I didn't really know what it meant. I certainly understood what most people thought it meant, but I'd never had a place like that where I could leave my heart and know it was safe. Home, for me, simply didn't exist. I'd never been comfortable in Silver Spring or Iowa—and Connecticut, well, I didn't want to think about that.

I tried on the glasses and looked in the mirror. I couldn't argue with Sarah's choice. I did look different. Very different. I looked about ten years younger. They weren't terribly strong, but my distance vision was for shit when I wore them. I perched them on my nose as Sarah suggested, then realized the wisdom of it. I could push them up if I felt uncomfortable about being recognized. They were as much for me as they were to throw people off.

"There it is," Sarah said, pointing at the sign as we crossed the bridge into Louisville and The Bluegrass State, pulling me from my musings.

A strange anxiety began to creep into my chest, pressing on my lungs. This place. This state. This was where it was all happening, and we were driving right through the heart of it.

"Do you need a break?" I asked as we pulled off the highway and into a gas station. "I can drive if you need me to."

"Nope, just gotta do something."

I set Remington on the back seat to a plethora of protesting meows. "It's okay, baby. I'll only be a moment," I told her as I exited the vehicle.

Sarah had started the pump and was now hunched at the back of the car, removing the D.C. license plate and replacing it with a Kentucky one.

"Isn't that illegal?"

"It was. These," she indicated the D.C. plates, "are from a different car."

"You stole someone's plates?"

Sarah smirked. "No. These are off the SUV."

I crossed my arms, frowning. "Why?"

"Why was I driving with the SUV plates?" Sarah asked as she screwed the Mustang's legal plate back into place.

I nodded.

"They're registered under Kincer Group LLC, which my mamaw's trust owns. Rogers Security is a subsidiary. It keeps the liability far away from me and keeps the ownership private. You can't just look up whose name a trust is in. It requires a warrant. Something Mamaw taught me. If we'd been spotted, it would have taken them more than a minute to figure out who they belonged to. As for why, it was just another precaution, like the hotel bookings." Sarah moved around to the front.

"What if we'd gotten pulled over?"

"Then we would have been fucked. The cops would have impounded the car, and I'd have had to answer a lot of questions."

I couldn't fathom why anyone would do something like that for me. I certainly didn't trust someone enough to do something illegal like that. Not that I'd never done anything less than legal. *I'm married to a Senator, after all,* I thought. *Was,* I reminded myself. *I was married to a Senator.* Mitchell was dead. He couldn't touch me anymore, though it still felt like he was reaching out from the grave to take me with him.

A few minutes later, fresh plates on the car, we pulled out and headed down the road. As soon as Louisville disappeared from sight in the rearview, Sarah opened her up to ninety and flipped on the radio to a local station. I groaned as the twangy sounds of 'Wheels' by Dan Tyminski floated through the car.

"Country music, really?"

Sarah laughed. "This is Bluegrass, Miranda. These are the songs of my people. But if it bothers you, I'll change it."

I shook my head. *When in Rome,* I thought. Even if it only brought thoughts of Ned Beatty and someone saying, 'Squeal like a pig boy.'

CHAPTER SIXTEEN
Sarah

As we passed through Lexington, Miranda asked me to change the station back to CNN. I had been enjoying an old Led Zeppelin tune, and I'd already heard quite enough of the news. But she was right. We probably did need to hear what was being said.

A steady stream of commuters filled the highway out of Lexington, headed into the suburbs for the evening, moving on as if nothing had changed. For most of them, not much had. Mitchell's death would be something awful to hear about, but they'd brush it off and move on. The news cycle was a different matter.

This time, the topic of conversation was the brutal attack on the Reichert residence in Bettendorf. It turned out that two civilians were killed, including the security guard who had been out front.

"Did you know that guy?" I asked, only too able to imagine how much worse that would be for her, but she shook her head.

"No. I never really spent much time in Iowa. I left that place to Mitchell and his paramours. I only left Remi there because the housekeeper kept her fed, and Gina hated cats. She'd have let her out of the house to be run over or worse."

"Mitchell was cheating on you?" I shouldn't have been surprised. All men cheat. Even my father had once. It was just a sad fact of life, or so it seemed.

Miranda gave a quick nod. "There was no real marriage anymore. Mitchell and I were basically separated for most of the last six years, except for political appearances and events. He stayed in the guest room at home or with one of his girlfriends during the Senate sessions, which I preferred. Occasionally, he would come back from an event drunk and try to—it never worked out well, and I carried more than a few bruises from those nights. I was able to keep those covered, though. He rarely hit me in the face."

My eyebrows shot up, and I shook my head. Miranda made it sound like it was the most natural thing in the world, just how marriages worked. "Were you?"

Miranda looked over, her face a mask. If she was offended by the question, she didn't show it. "No, not until—" She trailed off.

Not until us, I finished in my head. "I wonder why there was only one cop. After Mitchell was assassinated, I would have expected a gaggle of FBI, Secret Service, and others around you."

She shook her head again. "How should I know? Right after Mitchell died, Berringer came in with a guy named Branford and called everyone off. Then he told me I should go home. I ended up taking a cab from the rehab building. That was it."

"Branford who?" Distant alarm bells rang in the back of my head, a memory of someone from my Secret Service days tickling my brain.

"I don't know. I first saw him three days ago. I thought he worked on Mitchell's campaign, but—" She turned quiet again.

As the miles wore on, the quiet in the car became stifling again. Miranda sat, almost statue-like, but still stroking Remington's head. Remington seemed perfectly content and had been amazingly well-behaved if you didn't count the donut crumbs that I would have to vacuum out when I got to Mamaw's cabin—that and the fur.

"You know. You keep doing that, she'll go bald," I joked, trying to lighten the mood.

A wan smile tugged at Miranda's lips, then vanished. "She's all I have left."

I reached out and put my hand on Miranda's thigh, patting it. "You're one of the smartest people I know, Miranda. You're in shock. But you'll pull yourself back together soon enough, I'm sure."

Again, that wan smile that'd become so common in the last two days.

We sat quietly after that, listening to the news for a while. I glanced periodically at Miranda and finally settled myself that the young widow was handling herself better.

As expected, wild theories abounded as to where Miranda had disappeared. The gunman that I'd shot remained unidentified, but given that he'd been found with his balaclava, they were calling him an assailant. The exterior CCTV surveillance that Mitchell had set up apparently showed them approaching the house and unloading on the crowd. And though we couldn't see it over the airwaves, we could easily imagine based on the description and our own recollection.

After a bit, there was a great deal of speculation and discussion about who Miranda's defender had been. And it was nice to hear at least some of the talking heads describing her as the victim in all this. Someone had leaked the fact that she, not Mitchell, had been the target of the initial assassination attempt. However, the commentator made it a point to mention that it was unconfirmed. As what seemed an afterthought, someone mentioned a conspiracy-laden theory floating online that the attack on the house was a false-flag operation to throw everyone off the trail of Miranda being the ultimate mastermind behind the Senator's death.

I finally turned down the radio and spoke. "Miranda, why are you being targeted? I'm about to take you into my hometown, and I need to know what kind of trouble I'm bringing to the doorstep. Please, I'm beggin' you, just tell me what you know."

She blinked slowly and took a breath but continued staring forward. "I really don't want you in this any further than you are."

I sighed and told her the one thing I had been keeping to myself. "They know we were in the hotel together at CityCentre."

"What?" She shrieked, and Remington jumped up, scampering into the backseat. "How?"

"Someone leaked it. It's on your credit card, and we were on camera entering the hotel and on the elevator ride. So, it's too late. I'm in it up to my neck. They still haven't identified me, but that'll only be a day or two if the Bureau hasn't already. So I need to know."

Miranda hung her head, surely thinking this was all her fault. It wasn't, but that would take time for her to figure out.

"Friday night," she began. "Before Mitchell announced his candidacy, I found his computer unlocked. It was an accident, but there was a map of the major swing states. Behind that was an email window. It wasn't his Senate email. It was something else. It looked like a secret account on some group server, web-based. He was talking to a group of men about 'The Patriots of the Thirteen,' some kind of para-military group, I think. They had a plan to rig state elections."

I raised my eyebrows, glancing at her, then back to the road. "Pardon?"

Miranda looked out the window, her reflection merging with the darkening landscape as we passed into the mountains. "They were extremely organized," she said, her voice barely audible over the road noise. "They were planning to use a private security firm to alter the voting machines in key states."

"Which states?" I asked, my voice steady, but my mind swam with the implications.

"Wisconsin, North Carolina, Michigan, and Arizona. They had connections with at least one of the governors," she hesitated before adding, "blackmail, I think. They were going to tamper with voter registrations, too, through a firm that had been selected to audit state databases. The email said that with those states under control, everything else would fall into place. There were also jokes about how no one would suspect anything from a grieving Senator. It would be assumed the sympathy vote carried him." As Miranda's words painted a picture of deceit and a broad criminal conspiracy, Remington crawled back into her lap and nuzzled against her, purring in oblivion.

"Jesus," I swore under my breath. This was bigger than anything I had imagined. It was outright sedition.

"Why didn't you tell someone—the FBI, Secret Service, the FEC, even?" The question was reflexive. But as soon as I asked, I realized what a weight this must have been for Miranda to carry. And who would have believed her?

Miranda's eyes grew dark and pained. "I didn't know who to trust," she admitted, her voice breaking. "If I went to the Feds, Mitchell would find out. And I couldn't risk telling you, in case you did the same. Then you almost took a bullet for me."

She wasn't wrong in that. I knew for a fact that Mitchell had connections at the Bureau. Someone would have told him, and that would have been it. And it wasn't like Miranda had had much time to come up with a plan.

Miranda turned to me then, panic in her eyes and her voice dropping to a whisper. "They have names, Sarah. They have dates, times, and places. And they have a backup plan."

"How do you have a backup plan for a dead—" Then it struck me. "Mitch Jr."

Miranda nodded.

My heart pounded against my ribcage as I thought about it, and I felt a little colder, as if the outside air was seeping into the cabin despite the closed windows and blowing heater.

Miranda continued, her eyes fixed on me. "They have allies hiding in corners of government and informants everywhere. If they were willing to kill me just to get a few votes, what would they do if they found me now?"

I didn't argue. I had seen the SUVs that had shown up at the hotel. They'd had government plates.

"And now," Miranda said, returning to looking out the window, "they have me. I'm never getting out of this—not alive, anyway."

I was about to refute that last remark when a subtle vibration from the cup holder caught my attention. My burner. I glanced down. It was Mike. I glanced back at Miranda and held up a finger. I stuck my earbud in my ear for some privacy. "Mike, talk to me, brother."

"Sarah, I just got a call from Director Thatcher," his voice was a little quick but still relaxed. "He was wondering where you were."

"And?" I prompted.

"I told him I have no idea, of course. Last I heard from you, you were at home in D.C." Not a lie. "He also asked if I knew how to get in touch with you. I told him no." An obvious lie. "But

I told him that if I heard from you, I'd let you know he called. He said you should call him, and I said I'm not the postal service and hung up. So, how bad is it?"

I smiled. "It's fine, you know. I'm just seeing the country, enjoying the sights."

"Alone, I hope." I could hear the smile in Mike's voice.

"I met a lady friend," I replied, giving Miranda a wink when her head snapped around.

There was a long pause. "You do like to live dangerously, don't you?"

"No other way, Mike. Now, it's my turn to owe you. I need another favor."

Another pause. "As far as I'm concerned, I'm still working with that last favor you asked. Let's call the stuff I sent you a down payment. What is it?"

"The Patriots of the Thirteen."

Mike whistled. "Well, they used to be kind of a Proud Boys wannabe group, but they're popping up on the radar more and more. They've gotten funding from somewhere, and a lot of it. But I don't have Agency resources anymore, so I don't know where it's coming from."

Branford. The name finally caught the gears somewhere in my head, and they began to turn with it. "Check Branford Cash."

Mike paused for quite a long while, and I could hear a fair amount of clicking around on his keyboard and mouse.

"Mike?"

"Hold on, I was looking up his tail number." He came back a few minutes later. "Well, I'll be damned. Flight Tracker shows his jet landing in Louisville three times this year, and guess who also went to Louisville on those same dates, almost exactly?"

A crooked smile spread across my face. "Mitchell Reichert, I bet. This is all starting to make a terrifying sort of sense."

"Yup," Mike said. "Let me do some more digging and see if I can figure out who the Kentucky connection is."

"Thanks, Mike. Keep me posted."

"Sarah," Mike said, his voice somber. "Be careful. This is getting deep."

"Deeper than you know, brother," I answered. "You need to be careful yourself."

"I'll be fine. You just worry about yourself and your...uh... date." He hung up.

Miranda was watching me from the passenger seat. "What did he say?"

"Nothing good, but this entire mess is starting to piece together." I glanced over at her. Miranda's face was like a porcelain mask, beautiful but devoid of all but a single expression: worry. Remington, still oblivious to the tension, continued to purr softly, now back in Miranda's lap.

I reached over and stroked Remington's head. "Don't you worry, I'll keep your mama safe." She looked up then swabbed my finger with a sandpaper tongue, which she then proceeded to use to lick herself.

"Miranda," I said softly, putting my hand on hers. "They don't have you. Not yet. And I'm not going to let them get you."

Miranda didn't pull away, and my traitorous heart skipped a beat. But just one.

CHAPTER SEVENTEEN
Sarah

I pulled off into a Walmart Parking Lot, and Miranda scanned the place, watching the bustle of families heading into and out of the huge building.

"What on earth is this?"

I turned my head slowly and stared at Miranda. "You've never been to a Walmart before?"

Miranda shook her head. "I mean, I've heard of them. I've seen them from the road, but no, I've never set foot in one. I don't think I've ever even been in the parking lot of one."

I laughed loudly and then snorted.

"Nice," Miranda said with a giggle, and for the first time, a genuine smile lit up her face.

I felt heat burn my cheeks, but I kept giggling myself. "Don't laugh at me. I can't help it that I snort when I laugh."

"I think it's cute," Miranda said, and my flush turned crimson.

"Okay, stop. You seem to be feeling better."

Miranda turned toward me. "Safer," she said softly and placed a hand on mine. "I'm sorry you got wrapped up in this."

I scoffed. "I told you, this is what I do." I gave her my most dazzling and charming smile to hide the truth. I'd been running hot since Davenport, and my nerves were starting to fray. Hearing Miranda say something positive had helped my mood considerably, as did the flush creeping into Miranda's face at the moment. "See something you like?" I asked, trying to keep the mood.

She smirked, then turned a bit shy, looking away. "You do have a pretty smile. So what are we doing here in Hickville?" Then her hand flew to her mouth, and she looked away. "I'm sorry. I shouldn't have said that."

I just brushed it off. "You grew up in a rich home in Connecticut. I can see this might seem a bit like slumming it."

Miranda frowned and then gently squeezed my hand. "No, that's no excuse. It was wrong." She watched me intently after the admission, and I had the distinct feeling that she was waiting for absolution.

"It's okay," I said, finally. "I heard a lot worse at Brown."

"You went to Brown?" She asked. "Did you know Kara Thune?"

My stomach dropped, and I frowned as I opened the door, suddenly feeling a little pissed off, but not at Miranda. "Yeah, I knew her," I said as I got out. "Come on." I didn't feel like going down that particular lane of memories today.

"I'm sorry," Miranda said when she got out of the car. "Did I say something wrong?"

I shook my head, and my answer was probably more snippy than intended. "No. It's just a long story and not a pleasant one. Let's get moving. I want to get home before it gets too late."

Miranda nodded, slid the gray reading glasses onto her face, and followed me into the store. Outside, people had been moving in and out, rattling carts across the pavement, loading bags into cars, wrangling children. Inside, though, it was barely controlled chaos. They moved in every direction, taking advantage of the unseasonably warm temperatures to do some shopping for either Thanksgiving or Christmas. More than a few stares turned our way as we walked through the aisles toward the clothing section, and I kept an eye out, but as I expected, no one seemed to recognize Miranda in the slightest.

"We need to blend in," I said as we strode into the women's clothing section. "Here." I grabbed a small flannel off the rack.

"Flannel? Really? It's a little, um—" Miranda seemed at a loss for words, then raised an eyebrow at me as if waiting for me to finish the thought.

I leaned in and grinned, whispering, "Dykie? Lesbo? Butch?"

Miranda snorted. "I was going to say—well, yeah."

"Hey now, kids pay a mint for this stuff at the Mall in D.C., so don't be knocking the flannel," I said with mock indignance.

"Point Taken. But I have a question."

"Hmm?" I continued looking through the clothing, selecting a couple of pairs of jeans.

"How are you paying for all this?"

I smirked. "I'm putting it on your tab. Don't worry. When this is all done, we'll settle up. Besides—"

"Sarah," Miranda interrupted, suddenly turning sullen and quiet. "I told you, I don't have anything anymore. I can't use my credit cards. I have a few thousand in my own account, but everything will be Mitch Jr.'s now. Mitchell left it all to him."

I ignored the protest. "Here, go try those on."

Miranda frowned but looked at the jeans, put them back, and grabbed a size smaller. "Those are too big. You didn't answer my question. It's likely I won't be able to pay you back when this is over."

I took her by the shoulders and stooped slightly to meet her eyes. "Hey, it's okay. I'm not hurting for money, and this is Walmart, not Louis-Vuitton. Hell, it's not even The Gap. So, quit bitching about it and go try this stuff on."

Miranda took a few minutes to grab a few shirts, sweatshirts, and sweaters and disappeared into the changing rooms. She came out in a pair of jeans and a white t-shirt with the light brown flannel unbuttoned over it. On her feet were a pair of buckskin-colored work boots.

I was forced to pause when Miranda asked how she looked. She was a haircut away from some cute butch woman from D.C. or New York. She'd always worn her clothes like armor, using them to keep everyone at bay. Her high-end suits and skirts had said, 'Ice queen at hand, back the fuck up.' But now, she looked sweet, and I just stared.

She waved a hand in front of my face. "Yoohoo, Sarah. How does it look?" When I didn't immediately respond, she added, "What is it? Is the flannel too much?"

"No. You look perfect." My voice was lower and filled with the intensity of the heat rising inside me. I bit my bottom lip for a moment, then realized what I must look like. "Um, yeah, you look great."

"You think so?"

A slow smile curved my lips. "Absolutely, and fucking hot."

Her brows knitted in bemusement. "Hot? I'm wearing a ten-dollar shirt and twenty-dollar jeans."

"It's not the cost of the clothes," I said lightheartedly. "It's who's in 'em."

She blushed furiously, and the afternoon of passionate sex we'd had at the CityCenter Hotel flashed through my thoughts. *Where did that come from?* I thought and shivered slightly.

Miranda almost skipped back into the changing room and returned in her own clothes. Then we stopped for a winter jacket. I took a few minutes to go through them before waving one in camouflage.

"Oh, no," Miranda said with a laugh. "I'm not wearing that. I draw the line at camouflage." She grabbed a black puffy jacket from the rack and pulled it on. "This will be fine."

I chuckled. "That's okay. I don't wear it either. I don't hunt. I really just wanted to see what you'd say."

She grabbed it anyway, though she held it like a dead thing, stepping in front of the mirror before sticking out her tongue and making a gagging noise. "Definitely not." She put it back, grinning, and turned toward me. At her glance, I felt a spark of electricity. Bees started buzzing about my insides until Miranda turned away shyly and pushed her hair back behind one ear. "What?"

"Nothin'," I answered just as shyly. "I think that's all we need."

We checked out and headed to the car. Once we'd loaded the bags, Miranda pulled a leash out of her Louis-Vuitton bag, and I gave her a puzzled look. "What's that for?"

"I have to walk Remington. She's been in the car for hours. I'm sure she needs to go, and she needs exercise."

My eyebrows shot up, and I started to laugh. "You walk your cat?"

Miranda reached in and placed the leash on Remington, then pulled him out in her arms. "She's a high-class cat, Sarah," she said. "Just like her mother."

I watched in amazement as she sat Remington on the ground, and the two trotted off, side by side, toward the grass.

CHAPTER EIGHTEEN
Sarah

Late afternoon sunlight streamed through the rear window, casting a golden glow into the interior. I glanced at the temperature on the dash. It was sixty-five, so I opened my window. The earthy smell of freshly turned soil wafted in, mingling with the sharp scent of late-fallen leaves.

Finally, I felt the pressure of the last two days lift the further we moved into the mountains. I glanced at Miranda, sitting there, stunningly haloed in the fading light and engrossed in the news.

There was still no mention of me at all, and I was thrilled, if a bit miffed at the oversight. That couldn't last long, but for the moment, the only thing anyone wanted to talk about was Mitchell and Mitch Jr.

Rumors were circulating that he was going to take up his father's torch and make the run for the presidency himself despite his lack of experience. I shook my head at that. He'd end up being just another Donald Trump but even less competent. It would be like giving the White House to Gomer Pyle.

At this point, the senator's missing wife was almost an afterthought other than the 'Where is she now?' mentions, which was both good and bad. It gave the Bureau more time to figure out what actually happened, but it also gave the public more time to speculate, and given the vacuum of information, they'd come to their own conclusions.

I tuned out the radio and tried to take in the drive. It had been almost exactly five years since I'd been home, but it felt like a lifetime ago. The relief I felt only minutes earlier vanished then, and my heart beat a little quicker as if trying to keep pace with the weird feelings in my chest. I was excited for Miranda to meet my family, but there was a lingering doubt about how that would go, and I finally decided I was far more worried about it than I should be. For the life of me, I couldn't understand why I should care what this woman thought. She'd helped Mitchell with his reign of bigotry expressed in bill after bill. I should be mortified to be bringing her home, and yet.

I tried to stuff down the embarrassment that niggled at me as well, reminding myself that the world was wrong. We weren't a bunch of dumb hillbillies. Yes, we were—hillbillies, that is—but that didn't equate to stupid or ignorant. It just meant we were from the mountains, and our culture grew there, as did our dialect. City folk thought mountain folks were stupid because we shortened words, and sometimes the accent was so thick that they couldn't understand us. But that didn't mean the 'hillbillies' didn't understand city folks. We did—every word.

That sense of community shame was replaced by another emotion as we crept closer to home: anxiety. I had panic attacks occasionally, something I kept to myself. And the weird trepidation I felt now, I could cut with a knife.

Again, I wasn't sure why I cared. It wasn't like I was introducing a girlfriend to the family. I was bringing Miranda there to keep her safe, that was all. But still, the feeling remained. Would Miranda think they were idiots? Would she think they were just backwoods bumpkins without two brain cells to rub together? That idea really rankled me.

I knew I shouldn't feel this way about my home, but I did. It was hard not to when the whole world had told me most of my life that that's exactly how I should feel, like some weird cultural version of comp-het.

The hills rolled and tumbled into each other, eventually beginning to rise into the Appalachian Plateau. Beyond, high and beautiful, were the Blue Ridge Mountains—home.

I pulled out the burner and popped a quick text, telling my mother to expect two more for dinner.

"Nice of you to tell me," she replied. "The damn house is a mess."

I chuckled at that.

"What?" Miranda asked, raising an eyebrow at my laughter.

"Nothin', just Mama bein' Mama."

The house was never a mess. But if Mama hadn't scrubbed every surface within an inch of removing the lacquer, it wasn't clean in her book.

Miranda went back to staring at the radio, listening intently to the nonsense theories about who killed Mitchell. But I wanted Miranda to see the beauty of this place despite the rusty skeletons of the many once-thriving coal communities, and I grabbed her attention.

"Hey, get your head out of that radio and look!" I gestured to the road ahead, where the asphalt lined up perfectly with the setting sun behind us, casting the gorgeous hues of fall in sharp relief against the backdrop of the darkening sky beyond, with the cloud bottoms painted in hues of pink and gold and red.

Miranda paused and then stared, blinking in awe. "It's beautiful. It reminds me of Vermont in the Fall."

"Same mountain range," I said. "And you're right, it is beautiful. You know, we get a bad rap as a bunch of uneducated rednecks running around, doin' meth and poppin' oxy, and bein' gun nuts, but it's not really like that. I mean, it's depressed financially, and small towns here have the problems that go with it, but it's not the bastion of ignorance that most people think despite the fact that politicians seem to want us to be that way. And my family are good people with manners and respect. I think you'll like them."

Miranda looked away at the trees rising up a high ridge to her right and then back to me. "I was always taught that the people who live down here are, well—" she trailed off for a second, clearly searching for something non-offensive. "Less educated."

"You don't think that of me," I said. It wasn't a question.

Miranda shook her head, and her voice was low, regretful almost. "No."

"It's okay. Kids don't run around barefoot in Appalachia because they've got no shoes. It's because they like it. And shoes cost money. You use them for important things, like work and church."

Miranda raised an eyebrow.

I snickered. "No, I'm not going to drag you to church, and you can probably guess why. I don't go. And my folks kind of respect that. They understand."

After we passed Polly's Produce and rolled into town, I pointed out the Walmart parking lot where she and Delbert used to cruise, the old auto parts store where I worked as a kid, and the high school where I spent my teenage years, closed now due to falling enrollment.

Passing the road that led up to the coal mine where my father and brothers work, I pointed that out, too, and Miranda nodded, seeming to take it all in silently.

"Of course," I said when we'd passed the mine road. "Some Ukrainian coal baron owns the mine now. Sapphire runs it, but, you know, it ain't like they're workin' for the U.S. no more."

And by her closed expression, arms crossed, and the worry lines deepening Miranda's eyes, I could tell that Miranda was scared.

I didn't blame her. It was unfamiliar territory, and rural towns had a reputation for being less than popular places for strangers, especially gay ones, not that Miranda had given me any inkling that I'd been more than a quick experiment and was probably straight after all. There weren't a lot of Asians here, either, though.

I tried to ease Miranda's worries—and maybe test the waters a bit. "You know, you should see this place in June. There's a pride festival up in Pikeville. And there are always a few rainbows around. And there are people of Asian descent here too. A few."

Miranda's head snapped around at that. "Really? I didn't think —"

I laughed. "I know. But the same slices of life we have in big cities like D.C. and Davenport exist here, too. And it ain't so bad. Like I said, I think you'll like my family. You know, for a long time, I didn't tell anyone where I was from. I didn't want people thinking I was a dumb hick."

Miranda finally smiled at that. "You aren't a dumb hick, Sarah.

I've never thought that, nor has anyone I know."

"I know, but still."

"Though," Miranda said, her voice a little teasing. "Are you hearing yourself right now? It seems like the closer we get to your parent's house, the thicker your accent gets."

I pressed my lips together as red crept up my skin. "Sorry."

"No!" she exclaimed. "You don't have anything to be sorry for? It's just an accent. My mom was born in Korea. You should hear her when she has a few glasses of wine in her and gets going. Besides, I think it's cute."

I laughed nervously at that. "Thanks."

Time had painted new shades over the town, and I noted a couple of new buildings, but there seemed to be a few more cracks in the facade than I remembered. The town was dying. Eventually, the last of the mineable coal would be hauled out, and the last of the jobs would vanish. Then Walmart would close, just like in every other dead mining town. And that would pretty much be it if something didn't change. We needed better education and some investment in infrastructure. A heavy internet presence wouldn't hurt, either.

I steered the car uphill, just outside of town, past the Craft Cemetery where Mamaw and Papaw were buried. Then I made the final turn on old Pine Creek Road.

Technically, we were in Mayking, outside the Whitesburg city limits, but there wasn't much distinction. Here, the trees were thicker, and the houses more spread out, but it was all the same otherwise.

As we made the final turn onto the gravel driveway of the family house, my breath caught. The two-story split foyer home of my childhood loomed in the headlights, a relic of seventies architecture, with its faded orange siding and worn-out roof. Papaw and Dad had built it, and it had seen better days. But the towering oak tree still stood in the yard. The aging red door was the same, though it had a new coat of paint. And the lights in the windows were inviting. They all whispered a word I hadn't realized I'd longed to hear until just now.

Home.

And I was terrified.

CHAPTER NINETEEN
Sarah

Turning off the engine, I doused the lights. For a moment, I just sat there, taking in the place, wondering how much I had changed in just the last five years. I hadn't been home since before I left the Secret Service, and that alone worried me. It was irrational. Mama and Daddy loved me just the same, but still.

More than that, though, I just hoped they got along with Miranda. They didn't like Mitchell, I knew, and that kind of dislike could rub off on the people around them. It was human nature. And what if Miranda didn't like them? *Why do I care about that?* I wondered.

The longer I sat, the more my heart squeezed with anxiety. I gripped the wheel, more nervous than a fox in the dog pound.

Miranda gave me a quizzical look. "Um, are we going in?"

I blinked, then blinked again, shaking my head. "Yeah, yeah. Sorry, just lost in thought. It's been a while. Come on."

With a deep breath, I stepped out of the car, followed shortly by Miranda. Moments later, the front door burst open, and there stood Dad—older and wearier but with the same warm smile. His beard was a little more trim than when last I saw him and with a bit more salt than pepper in it. Behind him stood my two burly brothers, both still covered in coal dust. The three of them trotted out like a gaggle of geese, followed by my mother.

My dad broke the silence first. "Sarah, is that you?"

I gave a wan smile and dug my hands into my pockets. "Hi,

Daddy. I want you to meet Miranda." I nodded my head toward her.

My father's eyes went wide, and he shook his head. "Nice to meet you, Ms. Reichert." Then he turned to me. "I saw you on TV. Scared me half to death." He reached up and put a hand to my stitches. "You okay?"

"Nope, not even a little bit," I answered. "It's been a crazy three days. Let's get inside."

"I shoulda known you'd be mixed up in this," Delbert said as I popped the trunk so he could get at the bags. I waved a flat hand in front of my neck, telling him to can it.

Mom pulled me into a hug, and I squeaked. "Easy, mama; my ribs is broke."

She let go. "Sorry, sweetie. You'll have to tell me everything." She reached a hand out to Miranda. "Welcome to Whitesburg. Everyone, and I mean everyone, is looking for you."

Miranda nodded solemnly. "I know. But we'd like to keep them looking, if at all possible."

Dad looked Miranda up and down appraisingly, and Miranda returned his stony glare with one of her own. But then he did something she very likely had no idea was coming. He stepped up and hugged her. "I'm sorry for what happened. Sorry for your loss."

Miranda froze, clearly stunned for a second, unsure what to do. Then she wrapped her arms around him and hugged him back. I smirked. Dad gave the best hugs, they were hard to ignore.

Miranda tried to pull away, but Dad wouldn't let that happen yet; he gave her a heavy squeeze. "Welcome to the Rogers home," he whispered, and then it was brief, easy hugs and light tears all around.

Mom took Miranda's arm. "Let's get you inside and cleaned up, honey. You must be tired. Supper's gonna be on soon, and you look like you been rode hard and put up wet. I'm Roberta, by the way, but you can just call me Bobbie."

Miranda shot one last desperate look my way as my folks hustled her into the house, but I just nodded in return and shooed her on, mouthing, "It'll be fine."

"Miranda Reichert? Really?" Delbert said as he dragged the

Walmart bags, my duffle, and Miranda's bag from the back. "What are you thinkin'? She's wanted by every federal agency."

"I'm sure," I nodded. I hadn't heard that particular development; it must have been recent, but I wasn't surprised. I knew it was coming. Her husband got shot, and then she vanished into the ether. "She didn't have anything to do with it, Del."

Del screwed up his face. "Well, I knew that when you rolled up with her. But she's in trouble, isn't she?"

"Yeah," I answered. "Serious trouble. And so am I."

Jason just walked up and pulled me to him, taking care to avoid my ribs. "Hey, sis, welcome home. Nice car, new?"

"Yeah, Mach-1, four-hundred-seventy horses, and all the bells and whistles. Oh, and thanks, Jason. I needed some coal dust on me. I'd missed that smell. And your B.O. Good gawd, you stink."

"Oh, sorry," he said and backed up. "I haven't showered yet."

"No shit," I said with a pert grin.

"Um, Sarah?" Del inquired, staring down into the hatch.

"Yeah?"

"Why is there a cat staring at me?"

I reached down and picked up Remi. "This is Remington, she's Miranda's cat."

Del raised an eyebrow at that and screwed up his face. "Mama's allergic, you know that. You can't bring her inside."

"Well, she'll have to suffer. I'm not leaving her out here. We're going up to Meemaw's in the morning anyway. She'll make it through the night."

Del laughed. "Well, you get to tell her."

Inside, I scurried up to my old room and locked Remi inside with small bowls of food and water and the disposable cat box, fresh with litter. To Remi's credit, she didn't make a sound, and I decided that she knew this was a covert operation. Instead, the cat darted under my old bed. I winked at her. "Good girl."

As we gathered around the worn wooden dining table in the cozy kitchen, the smell of Mom's fried chicken enveloped the room, mingling with the rich aroma of string beans, turnip greens with bacon, and the buttery scent of cornbread. There was a kind of magic in the air—the sorcerous combination of home-cooked food and the warmth of my family. But I also felt the underlying current of tension.

Miranda looked anything but comfortable, probably because she knew they'd all been following the news. But it wasn't my folks' way to pry. Being nosy was a trait I had picked up in law enforcement, so everyone kept quiet about it. I knew some of it was just Miranda being scared in general, but Miranda was probably wondering what they thought of her. Did they think she had something to do with his death?

I placed a hand on her leg under the table, reassuring her the only way I could. She didn't move or push it away, but neither did she look at me. However, after a moment, she reached down, giving mine a gentle squeeze. 'I'm okay,' the gesture said. 'I feel safe.' And I smiled to myself and removed my hand, knowing that Miranda had understood.

Mom fluttered around like a petite whirlwind, making sure everything was perfect. My dad, Carl, sat, as always, at the head of the table. Delbert and Jason, both towering figures, squeezed into chairs that looked comically small under their bulk across the table from us. Per usual, Mom's seat stayed empty as she served everyone.

In the meantime, I just fiddled with my silverware, waiting for the damn to break and for them to pepper us with the inevitable questions.

Miranda glanced around, her gaze sweeping the family photos and memorabilia that adorned the walls. Her eyes seemed to pause on my graduation photo from FLETC. Then she passed on to the two photos beyond: one a shot of me at the range for Special Operations training holding a medal, and the other my graduation photo from Brown.

Seeming to sense my unease, she pulled her gaze away from the photos and glanced my way, unspoken sympathy painted on her expression before looking back at the photo of me in my cap and gown. I could tell that Miranda had spotted the incongruity, the obviously proud moment marred by the fake smile plastered to my face. *Damn*, I thought. *She really is fucking perceptive.*

Dad said grace, and we all tucked into the food. The conversation started as it always did, with Mom asking Dad how his day was.

Since I was a kid, Dad's voice had always seemed to carry a weight to it, heavy and resonant. It was probably just because he'd been such a huge figure in my life that, even now, older and seemingly smaller, his words seemed to fill the room. He talked about the mine, some new layoffs, and the fact that he was just happy that he and the boys were still working.

I waited for him to finish. He didn't take long. But then again, he never did. Once the pause had stretched and made it clear he was done talking, I spoke up, getting ahead of my brothers and their questions. "Dad, you ever heard of a group called 'The Patriots of the Thirteen?'"

He frowned and narrowed his eyes. "Yeah, we got some of them around. Why do you ask?"

Miranda gasped quietly.

I froze and screwed up my face, my fork paused mid-air. "Who the fuck are these guys, anyway? I've never heard of them before this week, and now I'm hearing they're everywhere."

"Language at the table, Sarah Lou," Mom called from the Kitchen, and Dad scowled at me.

I scowled right back. This wasn't the first time I'd sworn in front of him, nor would it be the last. I was a grown-ass woman, and he could get over it. Besides, the boys swore all the time, and he never gave it a second thought.

After a moment of making his displeasure known, he leaned back, his chair creaking slightly under his weight. "They came up to me a few months ago. Wanted me and the boys to join."

My brows knitted together. "What? Why?"

"Seems like they're convinced the government's gone bad. Runnin' their mouths 'bout how we need to get back to the roots of the thirteen original colonies or some nonsense." He let out a humorless snort. "As if they got any idea at all what that means. I'm pretty sure they're just more of those white nationalists like we had in the sixties."

"And they think what? They're going to overthrow the government?" I asked.

"They reckon they can, or at least give it a good shakin' up. They've been stashin' guns and doin' some militia trainin' out in them there woods," Dad said, his face stern, eyes narrow. "And you should see what they got, Sarah. There's some real dollars flowin' to them from somewhere. An' that right there was the kicker for me. I knew in my bones they're bein' played, patsies for some kinda power grab. Ain't nobody just throwin' money at a militia without some scheme in mind."

I glanced at Miranda, who was listening intently.

"You didn't join?" I asked, though I already knew the answer.

Dad snorted. "Hell no, don't be ridiculous."

"Carl, language," Mom interjected softly as she gathered up his plate.

"I told 'em they're outta their minds. But they've got a few folks riled up 'round here. Some of 'em good people, just kinda lost after the layoffs, and some others lookin' for any excuse to make trouble. I figure only a couple of 'em are honest believers, though. The rest are just pissed off 'cause the rich get richer, and we're getting the short end."

The room was silent for a moment, except for the ticking of the old clock on the wall. Mom refilled the glasses with sweet tea.

No one spoke for a while, and I could tell that everyone was suddenly on edge. The question had hit a nerve, and no one wanted to be the first to spill the rest. I could tell I wasn't going to like it.

"I don't understand how people can get so twisted," I said finally, my voice low, and shoveled a fork full of potatoes in my mouth.

Dad reached across the table and placed his rough, calloused hand over mine. "Sarah, there are folks around here that are legitimately scared. Some of 'em reckon white folks are losin' grip on America, and it sets 'em on edge. They're thinkin' that black and brown folks'll give us a dose of our own medicine from the past couple of hunnert years. Makes 'em jittery. They forget that folks is just folks, and we didn't have no problem pullin' together durin' the strikes back in the seventies.

"But the real problem is jobs. Everything's goin' electric, solar, wind, and gas. Coal's goin' away. We all know it. Besides, it's runnin' out. Letcher's all but dry. And when it goes, this town will dwindle to nothin'. Just druggies and subsistence farmers.

Just like Thurmond."

Dad referred to Thurmond, West Virginia, which died in the fifties. In forty-eight, it was thriving. Ten years later, it was dust. Now, it had a population of five.

"None of us think workin' in the coal mine is the best job on earth. And we're not stupid; most of us know that Climate Change is a thing, but it's what we got, and without it, t'ain't no town, Sarah, you know that. There ain't no jobs here but the mine and Walmart.

"Some folks have gone to meth and heroin to make 'em feel better, or booze." At that, Delbert shifted uncomfortably, and I shot him a sympathetic look.

'Sorry,' I mouthed, but he just shrugged.

"We feel used, Sarah," Dad continued. "All of us do, even me. They use us to take the coal out of the ground, then folks in New York or Washington get rich, and we stay poor. Then, 'cuz some scientist somewhere says the planet's gettin' hot, they stop and turn to somethin' else, and we get left behind—no pension, no savings, no nothin'. We were Democrats up here for a long time, fightin' for the union. Then they turned on us and started talking about shutting down coal altogether. We all heard Hillary. And before you say nothin', I know she was talkin' about bringin' in different jobs here, but who here would believe anything the government would say by now?

"So we turned Republican up here because Trump said he'd protect our coal jobs. He didn't. Now, they want to build a four-hundred-million-dollar prison between here and Pikeville. A prison! And who are they gonna put in it, I wonder? And, yeah, it's a job, but who wants to work at a prison? And they could do a lot better stuff here with that money than build a jail. What are we supposed to do? I love this place and don't wanna live nowhere else."

I nodded. He wasn't wrong, and I knew all this. But from the look on her face, it was the first time Miranda had heard it, which I thought odd, given all of Mitchell's fossil fuel pushes. But then again, he probably didn't know what the real situation was either. For him, it had just been politics, I was willing to bet.

Dad continued. "All that makes 'em scared. And when they're

scared, they latch onto any ol' thing that makes 'em feel big, don't matter if it's hogwash. You, outta all people, oughta know that one."

I looked down, a flush of heat coloring my cheeks as I remembered my own brush with extremism as a teenager. It was brief and stupid, but I did some things I wasn't proud of. I didn't want to think about the night I spent in jail for just being around when my cousin Dee set fire to one of the coal trucks. That had been it for me. Dad had let me sit there all night before he came to pick me up. I'd been lucky. I got off. Dee ended up in prison for three years at seventeen.

"So, who came at you?" I asked, noting that my accent had thickened up more, even since we'd walked in.

"Honeycutt."

I scoffed. "Leeland Honeycutt? He's not even from here. He's a fuckin' carpet bagger from Cincinnati."

"Language at the table, Sara Lou," Mom admonished with more vigor this time. "Mind your manners, girl. You're not too young for a switch!"

I looked down for a second. "Yeah, Mama. Sorry, Mama."

Dad didn't bother to chastise me, instead responding to my earlier point. "I know, right? You should see his house. He's never had a hard day's work in his life."

I looked at Miranda, who was paying shrewd attention with penetrating eyes as Dad talked.

"Do you know anything else about them?" I asked finally.

"No, and I don't want to. They're nothin' but trouble, Sarah Lou. Mark my words; it'll end bad for Leeland and those idiots."

Things grew quiet again, but as the evening wore on and the shadows grew long and dark outside, we changed the subject, lightening the conversation. Miranda, who was silent throughout dinner, finally spoke up as I got up to help clear the rest of the table.

"That was delicious, Mrs. Rogers," Miranda said, her voice carrying a genuine warmth I hadn't expected. "I don't think I've had a better meal."

Mom smiled, her face lighting up. "Thank you, dear. And, I told you, it's Bobbie, please."

Miranda smiled, and for only the second time since I'd pulled her out of her home in Davenport, it reached her eyes. There was even a bit of a sparkle as she continued. "Please don't take this as ingratitude, but I kind of expected a different welcome."

Jason was the first to jump on the comment. "Why? Because you're hot, and you're hanging out with our idiot sister? I won't lie. That's a surprise. I mean, look at her."

I threw a leftover green bean at him. "Asshole."

"Language at the table, Sarah Lou," Mom snapped from the kitchen automatically. "Don't make me tell you again!"

Miranda flushed slightly and grinned. "It's not like that."

Delbert screwed up his face. He didn't believe that for a minute.

"Seriously, Delbert," I affirmed. "It's not like that. Miranda's straight."

Miranda looked at me like I'd lost my mind. "No," she said softly. "I'm not. I thought you'd figured that out, Sarah."

My face burned, and my brothers both gave a long 'whoah,' followed by a whistle. "Wow, little sister, she must like you!"

Miranda turned six shades of red herself, but then she said, "You're sister's been really nice to me, and she saved my life, Delbert. The least I can do is defend her from her lunkheaded brother."

My eyes went wide, and I blinked rapidly, trying to believe my own ears. Jason laughed, as did my Dad. I had no idea who had just popped out of Miranda's mouth, but it hadn't been the same person I'd been dealing with for the last few months. I finally walked around and put my hands on Miranda's head and cheeks.

"Well, you don't feel feverish, but still," I said and then grabbed up Delbert and Jason's plates and silverware.

Everyone laughed again. And just like that, Miranda was one of the family.

As the laughter died down, Miranda turned to Mom with an earnest expression and a hesitant voice. "Bobbie, can I ask you something?"

"Of course, dear," Mom answered, wiping her hands on a dishcloth and settling into my chair right next to Miranda.

"Well," Miranda began, both hands a little tight on her iced tea glass, "I'm curious about when Sarah came out. How did the family react? I mean, being in a small town and all."

I grinned, and Mom's face softened as she leaned back in her chair. "Oh honey, we weren't surprised. Sarah was always more than a bit of a tomboy, working on cars with Carl and her brothers, always begging us to cut her hair short. She was never into things you might consider traditionally girls things, and she never once mentioned a boy at school." Mom chuckled, then looked up at me with loving eyes and said, "Besides, she's our daughter. There's nothing in this world that could make us love her any less."

Miranda looked visibly relieved, and I felt my heart swell. My family's acceptance had always been a source of strength, and it was good to hear Mom reaffirm it. Mom's gaze then turned toward Miranda, who was now fiddling with her napkin, folding and re-folding it.

"You know," Mom said gently, "it doesn't matter who or what you are. You're here with my daughter, and that makes you part of our family for as long as you need. You're welcome here."

Her eyes welling up, Miranda bit her lip to keep from crying. Then she nodded her head, and her voice was barely audible. "Thank you."

Miranda's smile returned, but this time, it was different, sadness and worry lingering at the edges. I realized she'd probably had just about enough when Jason had to say just one more thing.

"So, Miranda, wanna hear embarrassing stories about Sarah's childhood?"

The table erupted into laughter again as Miranda enthusiastically nodded, pawed a little at her eyes, then gave me a sly, sidelong look. "I would love to hear it."

I rolled my eyes, then looked down at the table and flushed. "This is my client, Jason," I warned, but he just shushed me.

This was not where I wanted this conversation to go, and I groaned, knowing exactly which story he was going to tell and that I'd probably never hear the end of it from Miranda later.

"Well," Jason said, leaning back in his chair and waving a chicken bone for emphasis. "When Sarah was about twelve, she decided she was going to be the world's greatest detective—like a female Sherlock Holmes."

"Nancy Drew," I interjected, shooting him the finger and going to the kitchen to get a beer from the refrigerator.

Jason nodded. "Sorry there, X-10, Nancy Drew."

Miranda interrupted. "Wait, X-10?"

I sighed as I walked back in and sat on the other side of her. "My uncle used to call me that. It's from an episode of The Little Rascals where Alfalfa decides he's going to open up his own detective firm. Anyway, it doesn't matter. Would you like to get yourself cleaned up?" My voice was a little pleading, hoping to distract her from the humiliating tale as I returned to the table.

Miranda put her hand on my arm. "No," she said in a firm but sweet voice. "I want to hear this."

Jason continued, and I sighed loudly once more. "One day, she heard old Sally Gibson talking about a missing family heirloom, and Sarah swore she would find it."

I buried my face in one hand, then took a long swig of my beer.

"So, she gets this notion that the heirloom's buried in Mrs. Gibson's garden," Jason continued. "But instead of asking or telling anyone, she sneaks into Mrs. Gibson's garden late one night with a shovel she took from the shed. Mind you, she's wearing a homemade cape made from a bedsheet and goggles 'cause she thinks that's what detectives wear."

"It was a disguise," I interjected, "not a detective's uniform."

Miranda burst into laughter, and I couldn't help but giggle, too, shaking my head and feeling that same flaming heat color my cheeks once again.

"So, she starts digging, right," Jason said, resuming the story, "and she's so focused that she doesn't notice Mrs. Gibson watching her from the window. She's dug up half the carrot patch before Mrs. Gibson finally loses it."

"And?" Miranda asked eagerly.

"And," Jason howled with laughter, "Mrs. Gibson storms out, waving a broom and chasing Sarah out of the garden! She's shouting about her ruined carrots and how Sarah's detective career better involve paying for the damage!"

Miranda fell into stitches, and the whole family laughed along.

I was now beet red and I looked across the old wooden table at my brother, giving him the finger.

"Sarah Lou Rogers!" Mom scolded. "You know better than that."

More laughter.

The rest of the evening was filled with shared stories and warmth. Miranda even talked a little about growing up in Connecticut. I listened intently, surprised at how comfortable Miranda had seemingly become. She didn't share much, just a few stories about friends at school, but at least she was relaxed and had let go of the elephant in the room for a bit.

I smiled. Miranda, who just a few hours ago seemed like a fish out of water, now looked like she belonged. Like she'd found a place, even if just for a little while, where she could relax, be herself without judgment, and feel a little safer.

And for that, I was infinitely grateful.

CHAPTER TWENTY
Miranda

I took a deep breath, feeling my shoulders drop, finally, as Bobbie ushered the two of us toward the stairway leading to the upper floor. I'd had enough—enough of running, hiding, being afraid. My whole body hurt with the constant tension of the last three days, and a headache was starting to sprout over my right eye. Despite how nice everyone was, I only wanted to go to sleep, to be unconscious and unaware of everything—not alone, but not 'switched on,' if that even made any sense.

"There's only one spare room, girls, so you'll have to share. Hope that's okay?" Bobbie casually offered.

I turned and answered quietly but confidently before Sarah could stumble out a response. "That's fine, Mrs. Rogers. I'm sure we don't mind sharing a room."

I smirked slightly as Sarah's cheeks flushed, and I decided it was probably one of the most adorable things I'd seen. Clearly, Sarah thought more of our afternoon together than she had let on. Of course, so had I, and, strangely, away from D.C. and the politics and being prim and proper, I didn't mind it so much. The thoughts of Sarah and that afternoon seemed to quell some of my misery rather than making me anxious. They felt less intrusive and more—fond, I decided the word was. However, my emotions were a little mixed. I hadn't felt bad about the encounter, just frustrated and angry that my interest in women was patently clear and there was nothing I could do about it. But now—

I dismissed the thought and took the towel that Bobbie offered from the linen closet. Then, I helped Sarah carry a couple of mothball-scented blankets so she could sleep on the floor. As nice as dinner had been and as sweet as her family, I didn't think for a minute we could be together or that she'd be interested. Her words echoed in my head, 'You're a hypocrite and a liar. . . I'm here because you hired me. . .' She wasn't wrong, and it filled me with self-loathing as the worm of guilt and regret dug painfully at my chest. I felt traitorous. Mitchell's speeches, his legislation, even the way he spoke in private conversations where I'd sat idly by, they all felt like little betrayals, each one tacit permission to treat queer people with disdain or outright hatred—to treat *me* that way. I was one of them, wasn't I?

Our footfalls raised muffled creaks from the carpeted floor as we made our way to the bedroom. Inside, I sat on the bed, numbly staring out the window. I offered a distracted nod as Sarah left to take a shower.

Lesbian, I thought, like I was trying the word on for size. *I'm a lesbian.* It was a weird revelation that sent a shock through me. I couldn't lie. The realization scared me, but I wasn't one to fool myself. I'd never pretended that my situation with Mitchell was pleasant. I'd never convinced myself that somehow I'd grow to love him. I'd just accepted that I was stuck with him. And so, I'd done nothing. I'd stayed celibate, at least until it had become too much—until Sarah. And I wouldn't fool myself now. That afternoon with Sarah had told me all I needed to know. And it wasn't that I couldn't let go of it. I could, but I didn't want to. Even though it had been quick and hot in a hotel room with no strings attached, it felt like something small and precious.

I glanced back out the window. Bedroom windows in split foyer homes were so weird, so high on the wall. It made them seem so far away when you were sitting in bed. That distance to the outside world, prison-like and dark, made me feel so alone, but the sound of the water moving through the pipes and the running shower lulled away the blooming melancholy. The noise was comforting. I lay back on the bed and just listened to it.

It didn't take long before my thoughts lingered on what she must look like in the shower. I imagined the water flowing down her well-muscled back, trailing glycerin rivulets across her shoulder blades and down to her gorgeous backside. The need was agonizing. I wanted to march in there and pin her to the shower wall. Given what she thought of me, it was a stupid idea, but the fantasy itself was maddeningly enticing. I snorted, thinking again about how I'd just wanted to get it out of my system. To prove it wouldn't be any better than sex with men. To prove that I didn't care, that I was broken. To prove I wasn't gay.

"Good job," I muttered and sighed, stroking Remington's fur. Then I laid back and thought about that afternoon anyway. *Fuck it*, I thought.

Sarah had been working for me for several months. I'd kept a professional distance. A Danbury didn't make friends with the help, but more and more, I'd been finding myself admiring the younger woman. I wasn't sure what it was at first, but just over two weeks ago, Sarah had looked me in the eye, and I felt something electric with her strikingly blue 'Paul Newman' eyes drilling into me. My breath had caught.

After that day, I found myself watching Sarah more and more often, catching surreptitious glances from the corner of my eye. I felt stuck, ideating on how she walked and stood like a block of marble, eyes always searching for danger. She exuded a quiet professional strength, her eyes hidden behind a pair of Aviators.

Finally, unable to deny the attraction—I mean, who could?—I decided it was time to get it over with, so I booked a hotel room. Then, as we were leaving the mall that afternoon, I made an excuse to take the hotel elevator to the fifth floor. I still couldn't remember what I'd actually told her, something about staying in town at the hotel so I didn't have to drive all the way into D.C. in the morning.

The butterflies in my chest and stomach had zoomed around all the way up in the elevator, and my heart had banged in my neck and ears. As soon as we'd stepped inside, I'd pressed my lips to hers. I'd intended the kiss to be chaste and unhurried, but when I'd felt her cool, moist mouth under mine, I'd lost all control, pinning Sarah to the door—

"Hey, you sleeping?"

I started almost violently from the reminiscence, and a hot

flush flew up my features. I cleared my throat, suddenly dry, "I—I —no. I was just thinking."

Sarah's face split into a wide grin.

"What?" I asked, my voice defensive and a little high-pitched.

The grin turned crooked, and Sarah shook her head gently, giving a little half-shrug. "Nothing. You just had this contented smile on your face. I'm glad you're feeling at home here."

I blinked. "Oh, yeah. It's nice here. Quiet. And I like your family. They seem really nice." *God, shut up, Miranda,* I thought as I pulled myself from the bed.

Sarah was dressed in a worn FLETC T-shirt and loose blue shorts, practically showing off her toned arms and thickly muscled thighs. After staring way too long, I tore my eyes away and grabbed a T-shirt and a pair of panties from my bag. When I turned back, she stood uncomfortably close.

"Do you have--um," I stumbled for a moment under her intense gaze, then looked down to find she was holding a pair of drawstring pants. I cleared my throat again. "I was going to ask if you had some pants or shorts I could sleep in." My hand brushed Sarah's as I took the offered bottoms. "Thank you," I whispered, and my voice sounded low, almost husky. Again, I tore my eyes away and practically scurried from the room.

Inside the bathroom with the door closed, I quickly stripped and turned on the water, mostly to hide the sound of my heaving breath, which I was sure the whole house could hear. Once in the shower, I let the warm water wash over me and felt a little more centered.

What is wrong with me? I chastised myself as the water sluiced down my body, more remnants of the red dye I'd used earlier flowing down the drain and turning the water a momentary soft pink. I didn't think I should wash it until tomorrow, so I just lathered up my body. A fresh razor, the plastic cover still on it, sat on the edge of the tub, and I stared at it for a minute. It was exactly my brand.

There was a soft knock at the door. "Um, I'm in here," I called from the shower, but the door opened a crack anyway. It was Sarah.

"Sorry, you forgot your towel. I'll leave it here on the toilet seat.

And I bought you a razor at the store. Did you find it?"

I almost burst into tears at the thoughtfulness of the gesture, simple as it was, and I tried as best I could to keep my voice from shaking. "I did. Thanks."

"That is your brand, right?"

"Um, yeah, it's great, thank you. Please close the door. You're letting in the cold." My voice came out a little bitchy—and more than a bit shaky.

"Yeah, sorry," she said, and I heard the door close. I slumped, propping myself up in the shower with one hand.

I slid a hand down between my legs, massaging myself. Imagining that I'd asked her to join me, my mind wandered to a place where there was none of this insanity, and it would be okay. It wasn't hard to imagine her soft, wet tongue making long, languid strokes across my wetness. I grabbed hold of the shower curtain, and my fingernails dug into the plastic, bunching it in my fist.

"Oh," I whispered as the water poured over my head and down my body. I breathed harder, imagining her hands around my hips and ass, pressing me to her as she sucked and licked at me. "Please," I said softly until finally, my legs shook, and I came, throwing my head back and my face into the spray. The orgasm was swift and passed quickly, leaving me panting slightly. Nothing like that day, but enough.

I leaned back forward and let the warm water cascade over me once more as deep fatigue settled into me. The water began to lose its heat, and I realized I'd been in too long. Taking a few minutes to drag the razor over my legs and armpits, I pulled myself together.

When I finally emerged from the bathroom, my thoughts turned from heated and pleasant to morose. I needed sleep, but there was something else I needed to deal with, and Sarah was clearly too much of a lady to broach the subject.

Clad in the drawstring pants and T-shirt, I sat down on the bed and looked down at Sarah. Pursing my lips, I gave the mattress a pat. "Sarah, come up here. Let's talk."

Sarah frowned and seemed to hesitate for a moment, but then she rolled up and sat down by my side, looking at me intently.

"What's up?"

The air in the room felt a little heavy as the scent of coconut shampoo wafted from Sarah's hair, almost soothing in its gentle sweetness. I took a breath and blew it out. "First, I want to say thank you. I wouldn't be here without you, and I appreciate it."

Sarah nodded, listening quietly.

"Secondly, you don't have to sleep on the floor. I should have said so at the hotel. In truth, I would rather not sleep alone, but please, I hope you're not expecting anything."

Sarah shook her head, and her voice sounded a bit defensive. "Of course not, Miranda. Mitchell just died. I'm here to protect you, that's all."

I blinked slowly, then let out a relieved sigh. "Okay."

After a moment's silence, just staring at each other, Sarah asked, "Is there anything else?"

I shook my head. "No. I just—no, not really."

The corner of Sarah's mouth crooked up slightly, and she chuckled. "I'm happy to be your teddy bear if that's what you need. I don't mind."

I snorted at the unexpected joke and then looked away, tucking a strand of hair behind my ear, my voice a whisper. "Thanks." Then I slid under the covers and turned on my side, staring up and out the high window.

Sarah joined me under the covers, and we lay there in silence. Once again, I felt like the entire world pressed down on me. Sarah shifted slightly and then again, clearly trying to get comfortable. For a long time, I lay there, the sheet bunched in my fists, unsure of what to do.

Finally, I turned, my movements causing the old mattress to creak softly as I moved closer and put an arm over her midsection. Then I buried my face in the warmth of her back. Soft tears flowed in quiet sobs as I cried. It was just too much, all of it. The shock had finally worn off, and I couldn't keep it in anymore.

Sarah rolled over and put her arms around me.

I was grateful for the gesture. In the dim glow of the moonlight streaming through the narrow windows, I was finally able to calm myself. I listened to the wind rustle the leaves outside until my tears ceased. I closed my eyes and drifted off to a fitful sleep filled with frightening dreams of masked, faceless men, guns, and fruitless running.

CHAPTER TWENTY-ONE
Sarah

The grogginess of sleep still clung to my eyes as I stumbled from my room, chasing the smell of sausage and bacon. That and the chatter of familiar voices had lured me out of the warm bed toward the kitchen.

"Morning, sunshine," Mom said as I trundled in.

"Coffee!" My words came out as a zombie-like groan, making her laugh.

So did Miranda, gesturing to the coffee pot. "Ready and waiting," she said as she finished rolling and cutting biscuits like an expert.

I blinked at the clock, willing my eyes to focus. "It's eleven a.m. Why the heck didn't ya'll wake me up?"

Miranda slid the biscuits into the oven and then turned, her hands covered in flour. "You were out cold. I thought you needed the rest after two full days of driving."

I scooted awkwardly, both Miranda and I moving first left and then right as I went for the coffee. Finally, I just chuckled and said, "Shall we dance?" Then, I waited for Miranda to pick a direction before reaching for the pot.

Miranda moved out of the way and looked down shyly. "Sorry." My brows knitted at the sheepish response, but I said nothing, instead pouring myself a cup of coffee and dropping into a seat at the table.

I watched Miranda as she moved expertly around the kitchen,

dressed in a pair of my old high-school gym shorts that drew my eyes the length of her legs down to her perfectly manicured and polished toenails. "I didn't know you could cook," I said finally, a light grin playing on my lips, carefully hidden behind my coffee cup.

She glanced back at me and rolled her eyes while her hands flawlessly placed a second bunch of biscuits on a baking sheet. "I'm not useless, despite what people may say or think. When you're a politician's wife, you find things to do to keep yourself sane. Cooking classes was one of them." There was a twinkle in her eye, a glimpse of playful mischief that made my stomach flip a little.

I realized then that I was seeing something different—no, someone different. Gone was the starched politician's wife, and in its place stood a woman, much more self-possessed and friendly. She definitely looked more comfortable than the night before. Then I realized that there was something else. Miranda's hair was cut to shoulder length in a bob. "That's quite the change of hairstyle."

"Bobbie's doing this morning while you slept," She said, again showing that uncharacteristic shyness. "I wanted one of the sides shaved, but your mom refused."

I raised an eyebrow at that. "Really?"

Bobbie turned around to check the grits, speaking over her shoulder. "I told her absolutely not. I'm sure she'd look stunning in anything, but there's looking different, and then there's drawing way too much attention."

"She's not wrong," I said, still gazing at Miranda, watching her every move and mannerism. "You would look fabulous, but it's a bit extreme, don't you think?"

She pouted for a moment, then checked the biscuits. "I figured you'd like it."

I thought she was just playing around with the side shaving thing, but I realized suddenly that Miranda actually wanted the haircut, and I was taken aback. "Wait, you're not joking?"

"No," She said seriously as she loaded the biscuits in the oven, her butt sticking out behind her.

I wondered if Miranda realized what she was doing to me as

my heart sped up and a shiver ran down my neck. Then I had another thought that tightened my chest, wondering how constricted Miranda's life must have been if she wanted to cut loose like that at thirty-four. Just as the weight of it started to settle, Miranda's pout morphed into a burst of laughter, and Mom joined in. The tightness eased, and my lips turned upward.

"Ha ha, you two," I chided as she took another sip of her coffee. "Well, I think you'd be beautiful with any haircut, even bald."

A flush crept up the back of her neck like a blooming rose, and she put her hands flat on the counter as if steadying herself.

"Sorry," I whispered. "I wasn't trying to embarrass you."

Miranda shook her head. "It's not that. I'm just—it's hard to explain. Don't worry about it." Then she turned playful again. "Scoot! Go sit down. Food's almost ready."

With a bit of a twinge of unpleasant tension, I did as I was asked. For a moment, watching them, I could easily forget the last couple of days, but I knew that Miranda was just trying to get comfortable in a new place as a coping mechanism. I couldn't imagine the swirl of emotions that Miranda must be feeling: anger, fear, heartbreak, even, maybe.

Finally, I knocked back the rest of my coffee and stood. "Well, since it'll be a bit before breakfast is ready, I'm going to head into town and pick up a few things at Walmart."

Miranda turned around, looking uneasy.

"I won't be long," I said. "I promise. No one knows you're here."

She snatched up my coffee cup and grabbed one of the travel mugs from the cabinet, filling it. "Take this for the road," she said softly. "And don't be too long, or the biscuits and gravy will get cold."

I took the cup, and our hands brushed. I pressed my lips together, and Mom looked at me over Miranda's shoulder with a sly smirk.

I gave her a questioning look. "What?"

"Nothing. Just be careful out there, Sarah, and be quick. The less people that know you're here, the better."

"I will, Mom; no lollygaggin'," I replied and kissed Mom on

the cheek. I turned toward Miranda and awkwardly looked away, but Miranda touched my upper arm.

"See you soon," she said, then gave me a peck on the cheek.

One corner of my mouth turned up as I nodded and fled the kitchen, my heart pounding in my chest.

At Walmart, just over ten minutes later, I stopped by the optometrist section and grabbed a pair of frames with plain window glass in a style not that different from the readers Miranda already had. Then, I made my way to the clothing section, passing by the cheap lingerie to pick up a few practical pairs of underwear for myself. Finally, I passed down the feminine products aisle by the pharmacy, grabbing some light flow pads. I knew I'd need them soon. I expected Miranda would, too. As I rounded the corner to head towards the checkout, I nearly bumped into someone.

Fuck, I thought as I looked up. It was Leeland Honeycutt. His wiry frame, gray hair, and rat-like face hadn't changed much. He was just older and more creepy-looking. Next to him, in civilian clothes but still with his badge on his hip, stood Sheriff Wiley Fields, his corpulent frame reminiscent of a belted jelly donut.

"Sarah Rogers, as I live and breathe," Leeland oozed with his oily smile, his beady eyes flicking up and down my body in a sort of disgusting appraisal. His voice was slick, his smile sly, and his predatory gaze made my skin crawl. I hated this man. Had since the day I met him years ago.

I schooled my features and reminded myself that I'd sat across the table with everything from terrorists to South American drug lords to the former President. Leeland was nothing but a puny old twig by comparison. "Leeland. How's business?"

"Oh, you know, always somethin' buzzin' in Louisville or Lexington. Sometimes even Washington, D.C.," he drawled with a cocksure smirk. "But this here lil' town of Whitesburg, bless its heart, reckon it's been draggin' its boots through the mud lately, ain't it?"

"That slow drag has been going on for more than forty years," I replied. "It's nothing new." Then I narrowed my eyes at him and turned a little snide. "You know, though, it's funny how you got interests all over Kentucky but seem content to let Whitesburg drop plumb into the shithouse."

Leeland's eyes squinted back at me, but then he changed the subject. "You been watchin' the news lately?"

"Haven't been keepin' up," I lied casually. Then I turned and walked down the T-shirt aisle, flipping through some of the eighties throwback T-shirts.

Leeland and Wiley followed. "Someone murdered Mitchell Reichert. There'll be hell to pay for that."

I snorted. "Good riddance," I said. "He was a liar and a cheat and probably dirtier than the North Fork." I was being flip, but my blood ran cold, and I stepped slightly to my right, further down the aisle, to put a little distance between us.

Leeland placed his hand on my shoulder with a serpentine smile and leaned back in. "You might be interested in coming out to see what I've got going on, Rogers. There might be something in it for you, seeing as how you got a raw deal from the Secret Service. You know, your brother's on the reserve detective squad at the department. It'd be good to have you workin' with him if nothin' else more prestigious could be arranged."

I dropped a warning gaze pointedly to his hand, and Leeland removed it. After a moment's thought, I finally decided I needed to know what Leeland was up to and what he knew, so I agreed to come by.

"Say, is that your blue Mach-1 I spotted outside?" He asked, tipping his head toward the storefront's glass doors.

"Might be," I answered with a smirk and a raised eyebrow. "Why? Lookin' to race?"

"Maybe," he said but shook his head in the negative. "How many horses you got in that thing?"

I grinned. "Almost five hundred. How 'bout you, Wiley? I bet I could turn one of those nice interceptors out pretty good."

Wiley gave me a dark look of disgust. "Street racing's illegal, you know that."

"Never stopped you in high school," I retorted and finally selected a cropped t-shirt that read NASA on it in 80's style retro coloring and smiled to myself. Miranda would never wear it, but I got it anyway.

Wiley smiled at me, but it didn't reach his eyes. "Keep yer head on a swivel, Rogers."

"Will do," I answered before making my way to the checkout. The whole time, I could feel their eyes on me. It gave me the willies and made the hair on my neck stand up. I started to worry that someone might have seen us pull away from Miranda's after all.

I checked out as casually as I could, doing my best not to look at Leeland and Wiley, but it was difficult. I felt only slightly better as I left the store to head home, but as I pulled out, I spotted them standing outside the store, talking and watching me drive away.

"Shit," I swore under my breath, that wasn't good. Of course, what did I expect? The whole world had seen me dive across the stage to save Miranda, and someone here had been bound to recognize me.

As I walked back into the house, I couldn't help the nagging feeling about the entire encounter. In the kitchen, I found Miranda and Mom sitting with plates ready. The smell of sausage and fresh biscuits was heavenly, and it lifted my mood. I put the bag of stuff from Walmart on the counter and joined them. "I ran into Leeland Honeycutt and Wiley at Walmart."

Mom's face darkened. "You heard your father, Leeland's bad news."

I nodded and started fixing myself a plate.

Miranda looked between them. "Who is this guy, anyway?"

"A businessman who acts like he owns half of Kentucky," I explained as I tore my biscuits into small pieces and poured gravy on them. "But something was off about him. The way he looked at me was just…weird. Like he knew somethin' he shouldn't."

"You think he knows I'm here?" Miranda asked, the edge of panic rising in her voice.

I shook my head. "I don't think so, but he asked about my Mustang. When we peeled out of your neighborhood, you didn't see anyone behind us, did you?"

"Not that I remember, but I wasn't exactly at my best."

Mom sighed. "We better keep an eye out. No telling what that man's up to." Then she sneezed. "By the way, which one of you brought a damn cat into my house."

"Language at the table, Mom," I chided with a grin.

"Do as I say and not as I do, young lady," she shot back automatically as she slathered gravy across her biscuits. "Now, who owns the cat?"

I chuckled. "Sorry, Mom. It's Miranda's. I'm gonna take her up to Mamaw's this afternoon anyway, so it's just for a little bit."

Mom gave us both an irritated look before she started eating, every so often coughing or sneezing. Finally, she got up, opened the cabinet over the refrigerator, and found an allergy pill.

We all dug into the meal, and Mom regaled us with the local gossip, but despite the warm food and the safety of the family home, I couldn't help feeling like things were about to get a lot worse.

CHAPTER TWENTY-TWO
Sarah

I winced and briefly stroked the dashboard as the Mustang banged over every rut, divot, and deep hole in the old dirt road. "Just a bit further, baby. I'll level the road this year, I promise."

Remington was curled up in a tight ball in Miranda's lap, jerking slightly with every big bump that scraped the undercarriage. And though Miranda seemed unfazed by the bumpy drive, I thought that was more shock from the last few days than anything.

Earlier that morning, she'd come out of her shell, but as the day wore on, I could see she was looking a bit more haggard and a lot more tired. We spent most of the day cleaning house and had a nice lunch. Miranda and Mom talked about nothing while I just sat around and listened. Now, in the early evening, she was obviously cooked. I was sure that she'd been trying to put on a good show for my mother, ever the polite woman Miranda was. But that's still a lot of mental effort for someone who'd just survived an assassination attempt, and it had to be exhausting.

"You ever been out anywheres like this?" I asked, keeping both hands on the wheel and moving slowly. I was happy the dirt was dry, and there weren't too many leaves for the low-profile tires to slip on. Again, this was *so* not what my baby liked in the way of street quality.

"Well, my family had a place in the Berkshires, but I doubt you could call it a cabin."

I glanced over to find Miranda giving me a mildly amused grin. "What?"

Miranda shook her head and chuckled. "Just your accent. It's like soup. The longer you're here, the thicker it gets."

I noted that she didn't say whether that was a good thing or a bad thing.

"I'd love to see it in the Summer," Miranda said, changing the subject as she watched the trees bounce slowly by.

"Once this is over, maybe you could."

Miranda didn't say anything, but it wasn't a no, and I found myself wondering what it would be like to have her here for longer than just a few days. *She'd probably lose her mind.*

The cabin finally came into view, standing among a group of fat oaks. The log walls were crafted from sturdy timbers, and they were well-maintained.

"Wow," Miranda said, looking at the place. "It's so—you."

I looked over at her, mouth agape. "What is that supposed to mean?"

Miranda laughed. "Just that it suits you. It's beautiful. Did you build it?"

It was my turn to laugh. "No. Mamaw and Papaw built it in the fifties. Papaw passed away from lung cancer when I was little, but Mamaw stayed here until she died about fifteen years ago. She left it to me."

"Why didn't she leave it to one of your brothers?"

"Jason was too young, and Delbert was struggling with alcoholism. Besides, I was always Mamaw's favorite," I giggled and gave Miranda a wink.

"He seems fine now," Miranda commented as I pulled to a stop in front of the large garage that flanked the left side of the home.

"Yeah, he's recovering—eight years sober," I said, then gestured through the windshield at the house. "Delbert oversaw some updates for me about four years ago. And he comes out here from time to time with his friends to hang out and, of course, to steal my Jeep. He made sure the contractor did his best to maintain the overall aesthetic."

Once we'd reached the paved driveway and stopped, Miranda got out and walked around a bit. "I think the moss and lichen in the cracks add a touch of rustic character, don't you?"

"What?" I exclaimed and marched around to the side, looking where Miranda pointed. "Damnit, I told Delbert and Jason to look out for growth." I blew out a breath. "Nevermind. Yes, I guess it does add a bit of somethin', but that somethin's gotta go. The wood will start to rot underneath it if it hasn't already."

I leaned against the hood of the car as Miranda meandered around the place, looking at the porch adorned with two hand-made Adirondack chairs that needed refinishing and an old, weathered wooden bench. Then, she disappeared from view as she went around the rear of the building.

"A hot tub? Nice!" Miranda called, and I gave a wide grin.

"Wondered how long it would take her to find that," I mused as Miranda made her way around the other side and back out front.

Miranda stopped and crossed her arms. "I couldn't see much inside. Are we going to go in or just stand out here?"

I couldn't get rid of my shit-eating grin, so I popped the trunk and threw Miranda the keys. "It's the angular brass one." Then I watched as Miranda unlocked the door, and a light beeping reached my ears. "Shit," I cursed and darted to the door. Inside, I entered the code and shut it down. "So, what do you think?"

Miranda gawked. The cabin's interior was a mix of rustic and modern. Directly ahead and to the left of the door sat a long dining table with eight chairs. Beyond lay a modern kitchen with beautiful stainless steel appliances plated in black enamel to maintain a kind of cast iron appearance. The gorgeous oak countertops sat on cabinets of midnight blue. It all looked almost brand new. "The cooking I would do in here," she murmured.

"What might you cook?" I asked.

"Private thoughts, *Sarah*."

I scoffed. "Then don't say them out loud, *Miranda*."

Miranda turned and looked back at me, donning an impassive, icy glare. But I saw right through that. The ice queen was all facade, and now I knew it. I'd seen Miranda's face in Mom's kitchen, the flush to her cheeks when she caught me staring, but I kept my thoughts to myself. Miranda was in a brittle place, I knew, and I would oblige whatever constructs she needed to stay in one piece.

"What's this?" Miranda asked, looking at an inscription carved into one of the supports. She traced the line as she ran a finger over the letters. "JD and MK"

I snickered, knowing what was coming next. "Those are Mamaw and Papaw's initials. Jessica Danbury and Michael Kincer."

Miranda turned around slowly and narrowed her eyes. "Is Danbury a common name around here?"

I laughed. "No."

"You do realize that's my maiden name."

I chuckled again. "Yes."

Miranda's face began to flush, and a look of concern flashed through her eyes. "Is there a possibility that we are related?"

Finally, I couldn't hold it in anymore, and I busted out laughing at the irony of the situation. "That is indeed a possibility, though Connecticut has a lot of Danburys, as I understand it."

Miranda looked non-plussed at the teasing as I kept laughing. "What could you possibly be laughing at? This isn't funny. We slept together, Sarah."

I finally stopped laughing and walked over to place a hand on Miranda's forearm. "We're not related. We probably have a common ancestor back about four or five generations. Mamaw was born in Boston, and your dad was born in New Haven from a long line of Connecticut Danbury's."

Miranda raised an eyebrow. "I'm not amused."

"Oh, come on. I'm sure you can appreciate the irony of the joke. Appalachian folks are always accused of sleepin' with their cousins, and after going all the way to Washington, D.C., I slept with someone who could have been my cousin from New England." I started to laugh again. "It's priceless, especially the look on your face."

Miranda still had her eyebrow raised. "Are you quite finished?"

"I am," I said with a last snort and walked outside, scooping up Miranda's bag and Remington from the car, who seemed perfectly happy to just sit tucked on one arm. Inside, I dropped the bag and stroked her head, and she purred loudly. "You're just a little slut."

Miranda was looking at the bookshelves now, running a finger across the titles. Shock registered on her face when she turned around to see Remington in my arms. "She let you pick her up?"

I shrugged, a little bemused. "Yeah, how do you think I got her into Mom's? Was I not supposed to?"

Miranda turned back to the books. "Huh. She hated Mitchell and Gina. Even some of the security guys got a good scratch from her."

"Sounds like she's a good judge of character." I closed the door and let the cat down onto the floor. She immediately began investigating her surroundings, sniffing here and there. I moved Miranda's bag to the sofa and went to the fireplace. "There's not much wood in here. I'll get a fire going, but I'll need to chop more shortly. There's no central heat, just an electric heater in the guest room, the fireplace, and that old wood-burning stove over there." I pointed to the far corner of the living room at a classic wood-burning stove that looked like it had been in the place since it was built.

Miranda continued her exploration of the small cabin, noting the upstairs loft and its large king-sized bed in a beautiful box frame. "Did your grandfather make this?" She said, and I looked up to see her running a hand across the beautiful knot-work carvings on the headboard.

I trotted up the stairs. "Yeah. He had a gift. I tried once to get him into working in other mediums before he died, but he wouldn't have none of it. I never knew why, and he never said."

She sat down for a moment and examined the headboard. The knotwork was interspersed with beautiful fairies flitting from flower to flower. "I'm assuming he made it for your grandmother?"

"Oh, the wee folk?" I said with a snicker. "Nope, Papaw was always talkin' about fairies. That was his thing, I guess. Never saw one myself, but he swore they were out there. But I won't lie. Midsummer up here is something to see. It's about as magical as you'll find anywhere."

Miranda stood and flattened out the quilt where she'd been

sitting. "And the bedspread?"

"That's Mamaw's handiwork. She took to needlework until her eyes went bad."

She ran a hand over the blanket. It was made from a hundred different squares of cloth, each featuring a different wildflower in bloom, no two alike. The stitching was exquisite, not a thread out of place. I loved that quilt.

"When did her sight go?" Miranda asked.

"Oh, that was years ago. This quilt is probably fifty years old."

Miranda gawked at it. "Fifty? It looks like someone finished it yesterday."

"We make things to last here. It's probably been hemmed a few times, but Mamaw had a touch for it, that was for sure." I took Miranda by the shoulders. "Listen. No one knows we're up here. The house isn't in my name, not directly. A few of the locals know about it, but no one comes up here. You're safe here."

Miranda nodded, but her brows were still knitted together. "You said there was a guest room?"

I drew Miranda back down the stairs and back down the hall past the kitchen. "That's the bathroom," I pointed to the first door on the right. "Opposite is the guest room. It's actually pretty roomy. There's a queen in there. And over there," I pointed at some accordion doors by the back exit, "is the laundry room."

Miranda entered the cozy guest room. Like most of the house, the furniture looked handmade and sturdy, done in natural wood tones. A queen-sized bed sat against the back wall under a wide double window. Another quilt, similar to the one on the bed upstairs, covered it, though not as ornate. A painting hung on one wall showed an eagle swooping down and snatching up a fish from a lake.

She snorted. "That's a little rustic and stereotypical, isn't it?" She asked, pointing at the painting.

I laughed. "Mamaw hated that damn thing. Papaw got it at a flea market and absolutely refused to get rid of it. This was the only place Mamaw would let him hang it."

Miranda chuckled. "I don't blame her. It's kind of cheesy."

I grinned. She wasn't wrong. "I can take it down if—"

"No," Miranda said quickly. "It's fine. I just thought it was a little funny. I'm just glad there's no hunting trophies."

I laughed. "No, no hunting trophies. It's not a lodge. And Papaw stopped hunting in his thirties. Something happened, but I never heard what. I always meant to ask Mom about that." I stuffed my hands in my pockets and started to back up. "Well, look. I'll let you get settled. The wardrobe is empty, you can use it. Make yourself at home, okay."

Gazing at the wardrobe, Miranda ran a hand over one of the doors. The decorations were positively scandalous, given where we were and when Papaw had carved them. Two beautiful fairies were carved into the doors; they could be dancing or gazing at each other lovingly. It was hard to say. They were both female and quite naked, with their fingers intertwined. Miranda turned back to me and walked over, giving me a quick peck on the cheek. "Thank you."

I flushed, suddenly feeling bashful, but I nodded. "You're welcome, Miranda. Try to relax here for a bit and recover. It's been a long few days for both of us. I'm going upstairs to take a short nap. We have enough firewood for the night. I'll cut some more tomorrow."

Miranda nodded, and I trotted upstairs to put away my clothes in the loft closet and get some shut-eye.

CHAPTER TWENTY-THREE
Miranda

Three days went by, and Sarah was quiet. We didn't really talk much. She made a few phone calls, getting the lay of the situation back in D.C. through her contacts. We watched the news for a few minutes each night, but there wasn't much to see, just a lot of speculation. Eventually, thankfully, other stories started to filter into the news cycle. Mitchell was laid in state at the capital, and a small part of me felt strangely bad for missing the funeral. Mitchell's parents had died years ago, but even so, the crowd for his memorial was large, mostly other politicians and a few of his donors. I snorted at that. The man didn't really have any real friends, people who just liked him for him. Of course, neither did I.

Rather than sit inside all the time, I spent most of my afternoons and evenings sitting on the porch and reading a book or taking in the view. I looked out across the valley beyond into what I now knew to be Virginia. We were right at the line. It was an odd feeling, knowing how much closer to D.C. we were than I'd first thought. From somewhere in the distance, I heard the soft laughter of children playing and a splash of water that conjured up images of young kids swinging on a rope and dropping into a lake or deep stream.

Cupping my tea with both hands, I blew the steam away into the frosty air. The rolling mountains and trees below the cabin already lay in deep shadow, and I hugged the warm lambskin jacket Sarah loaned me closer around my body, taking a moment to tuck the wool blanket up underneath the hem to keep out the cold air. I was cold, but I didn't want to go inside. Besides, it was nothing compared to Connecticut this time of year.

I didn't know much about birds, but the one that now sang above me in bright tones seemed to signal the coming of night as the last rays of the sun slunk down behind the cabin and a sliver of moon, no wider to my eyes than the edge of a curved embroidery needle slipped itself free of the far horizon.

"It's beautiful, isn't it?" Sarah asked from the doorway.

I just nodded. I couldn't see Sarah, but I could feel her presence. She seemed to fill up the space around her, not in a looming way, but with confident control and not a small amount of bravado. I found it comforting. It gave me a sense of safety and security I'd scarcely known all my life, even as a child—especially as a child. And despite the warnings going off in my head, I leaned into that feeling of security for as long as it might last.

Sarah's solid footfalls heralded her approach as she moved to me and leaned over. I looked up, and our lips met in a soft, chaste kiss.

Sarah's eyes went wide, and she backed away. "I'm sorry. I was just going to give you a peck on the forehead."

I took a sip of my tea to hide the curl at the corners of my mouth then giggled. "It's okay."

I played it off, but I'd done it on purpose. I didn't know why. It was just a sudden urge, a whim. And truthfully, I wanted to feel her lips again. And when Sarah had pulled away, I'd felt like I lost something. No. I felt unsatisfied. I'd wanted her to deepen the kiss, but she didn't. I wanted Sarah to hold me like she had the other night at her parents' home, but more. I sighed. I needed to stop. I was going to confuse her—and myself, even more than I already was.

I turned my gaze back out to the night sky and the field of stars, rapidly being covered by a thick layer of dark clouds riding in from the west. On the gentle winds, I could smell the aroma of threatening snow.

As if in sync with my thoughts, Sarah looked out across the valley from one of the support posts and murmured, "I expect snow tonight. They say there won't be any, but I beg to differ."

I stood quietly, setting down my cup of tea, and walked over to Sarah, putting my arms around her waist. I couldn't help leaning against her back and resting my head against her shoulder blade. "Can we just stay here?" I asked softly as a second bird somewhere in the darkness returned the call of the first, perched above us.

"For a while," Sarah answered, placing a hand over mine.

Just the way Sarah said it made my heart flutter, that Kentucky drawl, the way it drew out the word 'while,' almost languorous in its delivery.

Sarah turned around and stared into my eyes, and I froze. I wondered what she saw in mine. Did she see the yearning gulf I felt in my chest right now? Did she sense the desperation and need, my heart screaming for someone to care for it? I hoped so—and not.

Her hot breath slid solicitously into my mouth and filled my lungs. Eventually, I drew away, feeling a trembling in my lips and hands. But was it the cold? Her proximity? Or the edge of panic?

Returning to the table, I snatched up the discarded blanket, dropping back down into the chair. My heart was racing, and I grabbed at my tea, almost spilling the quickly cooling liquid. But despite the cold tea and the night turning rapidly frigid, a flush of heat rushed up my breast and throat. This wasn't supposed to happen. I wasn't supposed to be indulging in feelings for Sarah. This wasn't some romantic getaway. People were after us. And after it was over, assuming we both came out okay, what then? There was no way this would work. But then, a thought intruded. This really was nice.

"You've never had any real friends, have you?" Sarah asked.

I looked up at Sarah, completely off guard by the question. I probably looked like a frightened deer, caught in those amazingly blue eyes, so I turned away. Gazing out into the deepening darkness, I watched a few snowflakes make their way to the ground as the rear porch light came on automatically.

"No," I said finally, my voice a little choked, and I swallowed behind my words. "I had one friend in primary school and for a bit of high school, but we're not friends anymore. It's why I asked if you knew Kara."

Sarah closed her eyes and crossed her arms defensively.

I knew I shouldn't, but I pressed anyway. "What is it between you two?" I tried to keep my voice gentle, but it came out accusatory anyway. I didn't know why.

Sarah stayed silent. She just looked at me, pinning me again with that intense stare.

Then my eyes went wide as it struck me. Then I laughed, though I didn't really mean to, "You and Kara Thune? Oh my God, what is that even like? If I'm some kind of spider, then she's a block of arctic ice. God Sarah—"

"Hey, you didn't know her then."

As if, I thought, as irrational, hot anger boiled up in my chest. "Oh yes, I did. Now, it all makes sense. Every time she came home to New Haven, she talked about this *man* she was seeing, how great *he* was, how *he* loved to go to the beach, and they'd just sit and eat ice cream together, but how she didn't think *he* was long-term material. She didn't want to be married to a cop."

Sarah's face grew pale, and her eyes glistened in the pale lamplight.

I'd overstepped. I'd let that damnable control freak out of its box. Instead of stepping back when Sarah got upset, I'd picked a fight. *Shit,* I thought. *Nice going, Miranda.*

Sarah started toward the cabin door, but I caught her arm, grabbing it tight as she tried to pull free.

"Look, no," I said, suddenly feeling desperate. "I'm sorry. I shouldn't have said anything. I didn't know it was serious. I didn't mean—"

When she turned back to me, I saw her tears hot and fierce. "I'm so sorry," I whispered. "That was wrong. I keep saying the wrong things."

I heard Sarah swallow and sniff, and an ache began to build in my chest for her. I didn't know what to say, so I let go of her arm.

Sarah stalked inside, returning moments later with a photo album and a handkerchief. She wiped her eyes and dropped the album in front of me.

The book was small, maybe only about thirty little pages, each with one or two instant photos. Every photo was poorly composed and faded, and each one showed either both women together or Kara alone doing mundane things: posing by a boat, sitting and reading, eating ice cream. It wasn't just a book of memories, it was almost a shrine to Kara. And they seemed to be having the time of their lives. In one, clearly taken by someone else, Sarah and Kara were locked in a passionate kiss on a beach. Behind them stood a large gray cedar-sided Cape Cod style home that I recognized.

"I know this place," I whispered. "I've been to that beach."

Sarah nodded somberly. "Kara's parents' place near Chatham. That was the last time we were together. Two weeks later, she left me. We'd been a couple for four years, and that's the only evidence that it ever happened."

Buried in the back, folded and worn, lay a small piece of paper. It read, in Kara's handwriting, "I'm sorry. I can't." It was signed with just a 'K,' nothing else. "You could have ruined her at any time," I said, again my voice just a whisper amid the now thick snowflakes.

Sarah just shrugged. "And that would have done what, exactly, besides make me an awful person?"

"I'm not like that," I said, my voice sounding small, almost childlike. I didn't know where the words came from. Somewhere deep inside, I just didn't want Sarah to hurt so much, and I certainly didn't want her to think I was like Kara Thune.

Sarah turned back and crossed her arms, still leaning against the support. "That's why I don't do relationships. It's just too damn easy to get your heart ripped out."

"I wouldn't know," I murmured, my gaze turning back out to the darkness.

"You've never been in love?"

I jerked. The question stung, and part of me wanted to run away from this place right then and escape from Sarah Rogers. But it was the other feeling, the one I couldn't deny, that held me in place. I wanted nothing more than to go and wrap this woman around me, curl up in a dark place with her, and never come out. Because Sarah made me feel safe. She made me feel like I wasn't alone. I'd never felt safe, ever, and it angered me that—well, I didn't know what I was angry about, but I was suddenly enraged.

"No," I snapped, unable to control myself. "I've never been in love. My parents practically auctioned me off to Mitchell, who, as you now know, was a bastard. So was my father. My mother was useless." The words just poured out of me, and now that I'd started, I couldn't stop. "My father abused me for years. When I failed at something, he ridiculed me. When I made mistakes, he said things like 'your brains are in your ass.' And then, when I turned thirteen—" I jerked my words to a halt, stopping just before— I stopped and took a deep, sniffling breath through my nose and blinked back the burning in my eyes.

"Anyway, my mother's solution was to ship me off to boarding school, where I was ridiculed and made fun of because of my braces, my academics, my lack of athletic talent, you name it. And I had to fight every god-damned day to make something, anything of my life that I could call my own. And now, here I am —with nothing."

I stood, letting the blanket fall, and stomped back into the cabin, returning to the tiny, claustrophobic room that had become my only refuge over the last few days. I tried to take a deep breath, but I couldn't, and my hands shook. My entire body was filled with a horrid anxiety I couldn't understand. Hyperventilating as my chest seemed to squeeze tighter and tighter around my lungs. My head began to buzz, and I started to panic. *Jesus*, I thought. *I'm dying right here and now.* The longer it went on, the worse it got. "Sarah," I tried to call, but it just came out as a wheeze. "Sarah!"

Sarah appeared in the doorway to the Cabin. "What is it? What's wrong?"

I gasped for air, scrambling with my lungs at each sobbing breath. "I can't—I can't breathe. I—" I waved my hands frantically as if I could use them to scoop the air into me.

Sarah stepped in, closed the back door, and grabbed me. She carried me into the living room as my eyesight became spotty and lights danced at the edge of my vision.

"Tilt your head back and breathe, Miranda," Sarah said, her voice gentle and level. "You're having a panic attack."

"I'm—I'm trying."

"Let me ask you something. When was your first kiss? With a woman, I mean?"

I looked at her, terror still clouding my thoughts. "Wh—What?"

"When was the first time you ever kissed a woman?"

"Wh—Why?" I croaked, my throat parched.

"Just answer the question."

I tried to get the words out. Just the mention of it brought back that first moment when Sarah's lips seemed to burn mine and set my body on fire with need. It seemed so long ago, that afternoon. Slowly, my breathing hitched, and the hyperventilating slowed. "The—" I paused to swallow and take in another shallow breath. "The first time…was with you." I just managed to get it out, and I suddenly became aware that I was sitting upright on the sofa.

Sarah knelt before me, holding my hand, eyes full of concern. "Let me get you some water."

I clutched at her arm, digging my fingers into the fabric of her sweater. "No! Don't go! Just stay here for a minute."

"Okay," Sarah nodded, taking a seat next to me.

I leaned in, placing my head on Sarah's shoulder and putting my arms around her waist. Her muscular frame was an anchor, keeping me from fading away, and I stayed there for a long while until Sarah finally picked me up and carried me up to the loft, laying me on the bed.

"I'll get you that water," Sarah said and disappeared downstairs.

I lay there, unmoving, my mind a swirling mass of nothing. Not a single thought could I hold in my head. I tried to stay in the moment; thoughts of the past or the future seemed to spike my anxiety, so I kept my eyes fixed upward as I tried to find and count the knots in the wooden ceiling.

A moment later, Sarah returned with a glass of water and a small yellow pill.

I took the water and stared at the pill. "What is that?" I whispered.

Sarah smiled. "Just clonazepam. If you don't want it, I'll put it back."

I looked at it for a moment longer, but the anxiety I felt wasn't really going anywhere. So I took the pill from Sarah, stuffed it in my mouth, and sent it down with a swallow of water.

"Have you ever had a panic attack before?" Sarah asked as she began changing into a pair of sleep pants and a t-shirt.

I shook my head. "No. And I don't ever want to have one again." The sight of Sarah's body, the way the light moved and shifted over her back muscles as she peeled off her clothes, seemed to take away a bit of my shakiness. For a moment, I wondered if I could draw Sarah, assuming she'd let me. She really did have an impressive physique, and I had once been a fairly decent artist. I looked away for a moment, nibbling at my bottom lip, not wanting to think about why I'd given up drawing and painting.

Sarah pulled a set of pajamas from her dresser and gave them to me. "You want me to turn around?"

"No, please don't," I said softly as I stripped and put on the PJs. I didn't want to be out of her sight, naked or not. Somehow, just knowing she saw me helped. Then I lay back down and slid under the covers.

Sarah crawled in with me and lay on her back, her arms spread. I lay on her shoulder, throwing one leg over her. My arms were tight about her as I hung on for dear life.

"D—Do you get them?" I asked, my lips still trembling.

"That's why I have the medication," Sarah replied, her voice low as if I might break apart if she spoke too loudly. "I don't get them on the job; I'm too focused. But in the wee hours, when I'm alone. It—well, things come back to me. Most times, it's nothing at all, just a horrible fear squeezing at my chest. It's a trauma response. Or so my therapist tells me."

I thought about that for a moment. "So, I'll likely have another one."

Sarah shrugged lightly. "Probably. It's the way of trauma. Humans are much more fragile than we like to think. Our defense mechanisms can keep us alive over the short term, but at some point, you have to process things, or it stays with you. We're not designed to live in flight or fight mode for long periods. Like you've probably been doing for years."

I fingered the locket I'd given to Sarah. "Safe," I whispered.

"Hmm? What did you say?"

I glanced upward, but from where I lay, I couldn't see Sarah's eyes, just the curve of her jaw and her pretty mouth. "I was just thinking. I don't understand why I suddenly had a panic attack. I feel safe here. Safer than I've ever felt in my life."

Sarah's breath came out in a light huff. "I don't know. I'm not a therapist. But sometimes, when we feel safest, I think our brains decide that's the moment that we need to feel whatever it is we've suppressed. I wish I had a better answer."

"It's okay," I said through a long yawn. "Just thanks for being here."

Sarah wrapped her arms around me then. "Is this okay?"

"Mmhmm." I felt the medication kick in, and my thoughts became sluggish. The anxiety dissipated, and I just felt tired. It wasn't too long after that I drifted off to sleep, Sarah's arms wrapped around me.

CHAPTER TWENTY-FOUR
Miranda

I woke the next morning to strange sounds. First, I heard a grunt, Sarah's, for sure. Then there came a whack and what sounded like wood knocking around. The sounds repeated. Then again. This went on for several minutes before my brain kicked into gear, and I remembered that Sarah had said something about cutting firewood the day we'd gotten here. But she hadn't. Given how cold the cabin was, we probably should have done it before now, but, well. I took a deep breath, remembering the panic attack I'd had.

"Well, that was—awful," I muttered to myself as I slid out of the bed, pulled the quilt around my shoulders, and hunkered my way to the front of the cabin—where my breath caught.

Outside, in nothing but a sports bra, brown cargo pants, and work boots, Sarah stood, placing a short log on a tree stump. It was mesmerizing. I could see each etched muscle of her shoulders contract and bulge as she hefted the axe. Sweat fell across her shoulders and rolled down her back. The axe came down and split the log in two directions, sending each piece to a separate pile. Then she picked up one of the halves and split it again.

Pressing my lips together, I opened the door, shocked to find the outside temperature was much warmer than I'd expected, so I sat down in one of the chairs with a loud creak, the quilt folded into my lap.

Sarah turned toward me, the axe still in her hands. And when she smiled at me, it was as if the world fell away. I'd have liked to point to some feature of Sarah's that had caught my attention, but it was everything: the stunning cobalt of her eyes, the slightly boyish cut of her black hair, and God, that smile, flashing bright and warm, not to mention her fit and toned body.

I flushed into a blotchy mess from head to toe. Embarrassed, I tried to hide my flustered state by crossing my legs and resting my chin in my hand, but my elbow slipped off the arm of the chair, only making my mortification worse.

Sarah laughed a bright tenor sound that sent a barely suppressed shiver straight down my spine.

"Well, shit," I cursed to myself and then grinned at my own misfortune, finally bursting into heartfelt laughter of my own.

"You might want to see to that," Sarah said as she set down the axe and started toward me, gesturing at my arm.

I furrowed my brow. "What?"

"Your arm, you scraped it on the edge of the chair arm. It's bleeding."

I looked down. "Oh!" A long scrape ran the length of my forearm, tinged with lightly flowing blood. "Oops."

Sarah held out her hand. "Come on. I've got a first aid kit in the house. We don't want it getting infected."

"It's a scrape, Sarah, not a war wound," I griped but took the other woman's hand and let her lead me back into the cabin.

"Don't worry about the quilt. I'll wash it."

I looked down at the quilt, noting the blood, and before I could respond, a tightness formed in my shoulders, and anxiety flooded me. Then I felt dizzy again, just like last night. "Oh, God, Sarah, I'm sorry," I said, my voice a little shaky.

Sarah looked back at me with amusement. "For what?"

"It's your grandmother's quilt—"

"So—so what? It'll wash."

"But I got blood on your grandmother's quilt. It's—" I began again. My hands shook slightly.

Sarah snatched the quilt out of my hands and tossed it aside with a chuckle. "It's not the AIDS quilt, Miranda. It's just a blanket. If Mamaw were here, she'd probably say something like, 'and that's why we cain't have nothin' nice.'"

I wrung my hands and looked down.

"Come over here," Sarah said, leading me to the couch. "Why don't you sit here? You're white as a sheet."

I did as Sarah asked, unable to think straight as fear gripped my chest again. *What is going on with me?* I thought, feeling my jaw tighten and my shoulders bunch. It was something, something about a blanket—a blanket and a fine china teacup. I just couldn't remember.

Fingers snapped in front of my face, and I jerked. I looked up into Sarah's eyes, now filled with concern.

"Miranda, what is it? The quilt? I was only joking."

"Nothing. Just—Nothing." I said and moved to rise.

Sarah reached out and touched my arm.

I stared down at Sarah's fingers and then back to her eyes. And then, just like that, I sat back down. It wasn't that I wanted to share the memory—quite the opposite. I wanted to run, but I just couldn't make myself get up.

Sarah dropped to one knee in front of me and waited patiently.

The moment dragged on, with neither of us speaking. I could hear my breath, loud as it rushed in and out through my nose. My chest felt as if it were sinking away from me. Finally, I spoke in a voice so small and tiny I could barely hear myself. "Good girls are more careful."

Sarah's eyes widened just a bit, then she put her hand out, letting it hover just millimeters over mine. "Is it okay if I hold your hand?"

I nodded, and Sarah's hand wrapped around mine. The first thing I noticed was how warm it was—and calloused. I squeezed it tightly.

"Did your father tell you that?" Sarah asked, finally looking back up into my eyes.

I nodded.

"You want to talk about it?"

I shook my head, then swallowed. When I next spoke, my voice was subdued. "He's a malignant narcissist and abusive. There's not much else to say."

"He didn't—" Sarah didn't finish the thought, leaving it

hanging, but I knew what she was asking. Had he molested me?

"No," I replied quietly, shaking my head once more. "Nothing like that."

Sarah nodded. "Can I get you anything?"

I finally found my voice again, speaking with more confidence. "When you finish with my arm, could you make me some hot chocolate? I saw some on the counter when I was looking around."

Sarah gave me a soft smile, nodded, and stood slowly.

I put my hand on Sarah's and added, "Please." It was a small thing, but somehow, somewhere along the way in all the politics and backstabbing of D.C., I'd forgotten that manners weren't just a front. Politeness was something people appreciated.

While Sarah pillaged the kitchen for the chocolate and whatever else, I stared at the floor. The assassination broke me. I knew it. Something inside me had come undone; the knot around the box where I kept all of the awful things that I'd done or that had happened to me had sprung loose. What I needed was therapy—I knew that, had for a long time. My parents had always been dead set against it, and Mitchell forbade it. *I should have been stronger,* I thought. *I should have just done it and not told him.*

A few minutes later, the microwave dinged, and Sarah returned with a steaming mug of hot chocolate with a bobbing fat marshmallow.

"It's the shitty powdered kind," Sarah said. "But I did find a bag of marshmallows."

I took the mug slowly and blew on it, letting the smell calm me like it had when I'd been a kid. Meanwhile, Sarah slowly tended to the scrape on my arm with the first aid kit. When she'd finished, I gingerly drank the chocolate as she stepped back outside and brought in some wood to get a fire going.

"I'm sorry," I blurted as Sarah lit the kindling.

Sarah sat upright, head tilted and brow creased. "For what? I already said the quilt is no big deal. It's okay."

"No." I swallowed, the sound seeming loud to my ears. "This is the second time in as many days that you've had to deal with— well, with whatever this is."

Sarah finished getting the fire going, then finally turned back to me with a smile. "Miranda," she paused and scooted back over to the sofa, placing a hand on mine. "You don't have to apologize for anything. You feel how you feel. We don't control that. I reckon you're just full up. You've had to deal with a lot." Then Sarah just stood and, with a squeeze of my hand and with her jaw tight, she just walked out the door, leaving me completely befuddled. Had I said or done something wrong?

A few minutes later, I heard the Mustang rumble briefly and then watched Sarah pick up the chair where I'd scratched my arm and carry it off the porch. Confused but unwilling to move just yet, I drank my hot chocolate until I heard the sound of a saw. I blinked. *Is Sarah destroying that beautiful Adirondack chair? She couldn't be, but it certainly sounds like it.*

Frowning, I set aside the chocolate and got dressed, marching out to the garage. "Sarah Lou Rogers, what are you—" I stopped just at the edge of the garage door. Sarah stood at the back of the garage, in gloves and goggles, as sawdust flew around. The view wasn't quite as jarring as it had been watching her chop the wood, but still, the woman was just as amazing to look at as she worked.

I stayed quiet, secretly watching as she used a router saw to round off the edges of the chair and sanded down the rough wood with a small power sander.

She was meticulous and completely engrossed in the work, clearly not noticing the audience at all. Her hands moved the sander around the chair with careful but practiced ease. After re-contouring the edges of the arms, Sarah started on the rest of it, sanding down the older wood. Her hands roved over the wood, checking for splintered spots or loose knots, anything that might catch on a shirt, a pant leg—or an arm.

Heat crept into my cheeks. The more I watched the sweat bead on Sarah's torso and the muscles flex in her arms and back, the warmer I felt until I finally backed up, slowly and quietly. I made sure to turn away only when I was sure she couldn't see me.

It was over an hour later when Sarah finally rejoined me in the living room. I sat quietly on the sofa, having sprayed the comforter with some stain remover I'd found in a cabinet above the dryer and thrown it in the wash. My eyes followed her as she trundled into the kitchen and dug into the refrigerator, drawing out the water pitcher and upending it. Tiny rivulets of water rolled down her neck, joining with the beads of sweat hovering there before sliding down the exposed top of her breasts.

"What were you doing?" I asked innocently, keeping my face carefully neutral.

Sarah set down the pitcher and wiped her brow with a dirty forearm that just pushed the sawdust and sweat around on her head, then she shrugged. "Nothin'. Just refinishing that chair. I should have done it a long time ago. I'm going to go get a shower."

I said nothing but turned back to the now roaring fire to hide my completely out-of-control smile.

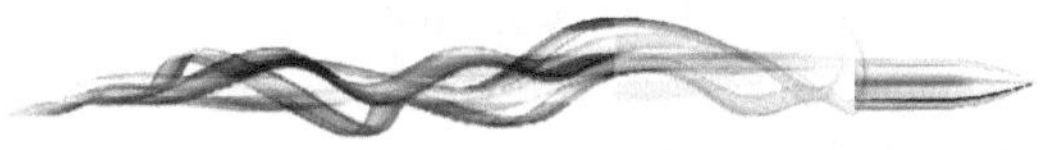

Sarah came back downstairs a half hour later dressed in a pair of jeans and a t-shirt. Without a word, she headed into the kitchen and started digging out ingredients, ground beef, brown sugar, chili powder and a few other things.

I drew myself up off the couch and grabbed a seat at the kitchen table to watch her. "Are you making chili?"

Sarah looked back and nodded with a smile. "Yeah, I have this recipe I got from a chili cookoff in Texas. It's real good, and I've always wanted someone to share it with."

"Can I ask you something?"

"Sure." Sarah pulled some pork sausage from the refrigerator. "By the way, this won't be quite the recipe that I would normally make. I just have ground beef, not steak."

"Why did you leave the Secret Service?" I asked quietly.

Sarah stiffened, but only for a second. "I fucked up. Do you know former congresswoman Luisa Sanchez?" Despite her best efforts, I could hear the tremor in Sarah's voice.

"Not personally. We never really crossed paths except for social functions. Remember, she was a kick-ass Democrat congresswoman from New York, and I was the evil bitch who ruined everything she tried to do."

"We were involved briefly," Sarah almost whispered. "And then one day, I was assigned as a protection detail for her kid. There'd been a credible threat, and as a personal favor for someone in the White House, my boss put her daughter under my protection."

"Oh, no," I said, raising my hand to my mouth. "You were driving the car."

Sarah paused as she cut the onions, washed her hands, and grabbed a towel to wipe her eyes. She didn't look at me though, not at all. "Yeah, I was drivin'. You know the rest. Little Maria was killed instantly when we got t-boned by the truck. It wasn't my fault. It was dark and raining, and the guy driving the truck ran the red light. But it came to light pretty quickly that Luisa and I were having an affair."

I furrowed my brow. "But—you just said it wasn't your fault. And Sanchez wasn't married. You were two consenting adults."

Sarah did turn then, a frown full of guilt and misery on her face. "You know better than that, Miranda. The Bureau did the investigation, and the SAC had it in for me, a guy named Phillip Cameron. Even though it was ruled an accident, Cameron just wouldn't quit, and eventually, he uncovered the affair. I won't lie. He's an ace investigator, but he's also a bigot. When he figured it out, mostly from credit card receipts where Luisa and I had split tabs to avoid suspicion, he reported it up to our Deputy Director."

I shook my head. "I know Phil Cameron. He's an obnoxious racist shit. He was pretty cozy with Mitchell, too."

Nodding, Sarah wiped her eyes and nose one last time, then went back to cooking. "Anyway, I was asked to resign. They were afraid someone would leak the affair and cause a scandal. I'm sure you know that Luisa resigned from Congress after that. Then the story just died away, and everyone forgot about it."

"That must have been awful," I said, trying to imagine what she had gone through.

Sarah didn't say anything as she finished putting the ingredients into the pot.

When I couldn't stand the silence anymore, I got up and walked over to Sarah. "I'm sorry," I whispered as I wrapped my arms around her. "I didn't realize."

Sarah returned the hug. "It's okay. It's ancient history now. I don't like to think about it. But honestly, you probably deserved to know."

"Thank you," I said, watching her put the lid on the chili pot.

We didn't talk much after that. The chili was good—she served it Cincinnati-style over pasta. But before we retired to our respective beds that night, I caught her arm and turned her toward me. "You're a good person, Sarah," I whispered. "And thank you for keeping me safe."

She just nodded and pulled away, heading up to her room.

CHAPTER TWENTY-FIVE
Sarah

By the end of the next week, Miranda's episodes were an all-but-forgotten memory, though since then, I'd woken every morning to find fresh coffee in the pot and Miranda sitting out on the refinished Adirondack.

The chair looked good. A few of the carvings were further worn down, but that was the price of my poor upkeep of the cabin. If I'd been paying attention, Miranda wouldn't have been hurt, and more importantly, she wouldn't have had to relive whatever memory had upset her so much. I'd already figured that there had been abuse, and it certainly explained a lot, most notably, her choice of husband, assuming it had been her choice at all, really.

That following Saturday morning, I stepped outside to find Mom sitting in the other chair, talking to Miranda. She had her cosmetology kit with her. They were both in relaxed clothing. The snow had long gone, and an unseasonably warm spell had blown in, taking the temperature up to springtime levels.

"Hey, Mom, what brings you here?" I asked as I sipped my coffee and leaned on one of the supports, fiddling with a loose thread on my sweater.

"I thought maybe Miranda could use a new look. She's been stuck up here with just you."

I sneered at the way she said 'just you,' like it was a bad thing.

Miranda raised an eyebrow, and a slow smile spread across her face. "Maybe a pixie cut like yours, Sarah."

I blinked. "Okay." I drew out the word and narrowed my eyes, wondering if I was being punked again.

Miranda burst into laughter, as did Mom.

"God, you're so easy," Miranda said through her giggles, but there was a twinkle in her eye. "I asked her to fix the coloring. This red looks ridiculous."

"I think it looks just fine," I said with a chuckle. "Takes ten years off you."

Miranda rolled her eyes. "What are you doing today?"

"Leeland's," I sighed and took another sip of coffee. "If I don't see what he actually wants, he'll come lookin', and we don't want that. The man's as stubborn as a mule in the mud. Besides, I want to get the lay of the land. There's somethin' going on over there; I just know it in my gut."

"Well, be careful," Mom warned. "That man's slicker than snot, as your father would say."

"I know. But I'm not worried. At heart, Leeland's a coward. He won't want anything tied to him. If he comes at me, it'll be sideways."

Miranda gave me a nervous look. "Please be careful."

"What about Fields?" Mom mentioned just as I was about to go back inside.

I snorted and gave her an incredulous look. "Wiley? He's just as cowardly, if not more so. How he ever got elected Sheriff, I'll never know. Besides, he's just Leeland's gopher. I don't expect him to even be there."

Mom and Miranda stood, following me indoors. The small TV in the corner, tuned to the news, caught Miranda's attention as her name was mentioned, and she blanched.

I put a supportive hand on Miranda's shoulder. She covered mine with hers and patted it gently, giving a soft chuckle. "That doesn't even look like me."

I stared hard at the picture, a stark contrast to Miranda's current appearance with the ruby red bob haircut and glasses. "No, not anymore."

"Hush, you two," Mom hissed. "I'm trying to listen."

The commentator continued her coverage. "And we keep up

hope that Miranda Reichert will be found soon."

"Jesus," Miranda said, placing a hand over her mouth. "My sister must be worried sick. Can't I get a message to her?"

I shook my head. "Text or social media can be traced. Letters pick up things like oils and dirt from the local environment, and given that this is a high-profile assassination case, the lab at Quantico would be all over it. She'll survive for a few weeks."

She nodded.

As we watched, the analysts and talking heads started babbling about Miranda's possible involvement in her husband's death, and Miranda quailed.

"Some people still think I had something to do with Mitchell's death."

"No," I said with more confidence than I felt. "They're just speculating, milking as much from the news cycle as they can. As soon as I figure out what's going on and who we can trust, we'll go to the feds, but we need to understand how deep this goes. It's not like they can pin it on you anyway. Unless there's something you're not telling me."

Miranda shook her head. "No, not really."

I raised an inquisitive eyebrow at that but let it be for the moment as Mom headed me off, flipping off the television. "You're safe here, sweetheart. No one will find you. And if they do figure out where you are, well, let's just say there's a history here of protecting our own. And we're damn good at it."

"It'll be fine," I said, giving Miranda's shoulder a gentle squeeze. "I promise. I'll be back in a couple of hours. Hopefully, with more information."

CHAPTER TWENTY-SIX
Sarah

A half-hour later, I found myself navigating the winding road that leads to Leeland Honeycutt's sprawling estate. Leeland blew into town twenty years ago from Cincinnati, a distant relative to some of the local Honeycutt clan, not that he ever spent any time with them.

It wasn't clear how he had made his money, but he started buying up old stores, which had been bankrupted by the arrival of Walmart, and leasing them out. There had been an insidiousness to his arrival. He slowly infiltrated the town's politics, adding in a flavor of corruption that wasn't obvious at first but had all the nuances of someone creating their own personal little kingdom.

The grand entrance to Honeycutt's was beyond ostentatious and suited his seedy reputation. Ridiculously expensive wrought-iron gates adorned with ornate filigree and intricate patterns flanked the driveway. I rolled up in my old Jeep and pushed the call button on the box outside the gates.

"What can I do for you?" A soft feminine voice called over the speaker.

"It's Sarah Rogers for Boss—" I stopped abruptly. I'd been about to say Boss Hogg, something I'd taken to calling Leeland when I was younger. "Mr. Honeycutt is expecting me."

There was a click and a buzz, and the gates swung wide. A long, winding driveway lined with trees rolled out beyond, taking me further into the heart of the property. I rolled past manicured lawns, now brown with the fall weather. Barren flower beds, cleared of their usual blooms, waited patiently for next spring when the tulips would come up.

A quarter mile in, I pulled up onto the half-moon driveway in front of the main house, a magnificent mansion completely incongruous when compared to the average house in town. Truthfully, though, it was absolutely breathtaking, and I'd have thought it beautiful if I didn't know the owner so well. Leeland was a smooth talker who knew how to bend people to his will. He'd always been a taker, never giving back to the community. Or any community he exploited, for that matter. He'd squeaked out from under four indictments for public corruption over the last decade. Just like Mitchell, he used his influence to push people around and exploit their vulnerabilities for his own gain. For a minute, I thought maybe he'd end up just as dead, but probably not, and at that moment, I wanted to be anywhere else. Just the thought of Leeland anywhere near me made my skin crawl.

Leeland stood on the stairs of the portico as I exited the car, a self-assured smile etched on his face. "Well, I wasn't sure you were coming," he said, his voice dripping with charm. "Welcome to my humble abode. Please, come inside."

I had to fight to keep from rolling my eyes at the false modesty in his voice. What an asshole, I thought.

"I said I'd be here, and I am. I do what I say I'm going to do, Leeland."

If the dig at his tendency to go back on his word bothered him, he kept it carefully hidden. Instead, he just smiled and opened the double doors with a slight creak. A beautiful chandelier hung from the ceiling, casting a dazzling display of light across the hardwoods in the late afternoon gloom. Intricate paintings and sculptures adorned the walls, though I didn't recognize any of the styles or artists. None of them were masterpieces, I was sure. And a few were obviously reproductions unless the Louvre had been robbed recently, and I didn't know about it.

"Nice place," I said as we walked down a long hall toward a large room with a wraparound couch and a massive television.

"Well, thank you, Sarah," Leeland said as if he was surprised by the comment. "I like it. It's quiet out here. None of the noise of the city."

It finally hit me what I hated so much about this man and his home. It reminded me of D.C. People in D.C. lived their lives in a mad scramble to 'get ahead,' making laws and decisions or working in an uncaring bureaucracy that steamrolled communities like mine. No one really cared how it affected people here. What was worse, I'd bought into it, leaving home with no intentions of returning, at least not permanently. It was an ugly feeling. My family was made up of good people who worked hard to make an honest living, and people like Mitchell and Leeland soiled that.

I followed Leland through the main sitting room and was assaulted by the scent of something sickly sweet and probably expensive—it smelled like perfume. Then I saw her, a woman sitting in the kitchen with bleach-blond hair, relaxing in a bathrobe and slippers, showing quite a bit of leg. It wasn't Leeland's wife. I did my best not to react.

"Oh, that's just Barbara," Leeland said as he followed my gaze. "She's from Baltimore. She's only here for a few days, but she's certainly pretty."

I just nodded and kept my breathing steady.

Leeland gestured for me to follow him, leading me into a lavish study adorned with leather furnishings and rich mahogany bookshelves.

"Scotch, right?" He offered, pouring himself a glass.

I narrowed my eyes but accepted the glass, taking a sip of amber liquid wrapped around a fat sphere of ice. I spied the bottle as he poured his own, a MacAllan Twenty-Five, and almost snorted. Not that I was complaining. It was smooth and delicious, the burn sliding precipitous and welcome down my chest.

"So, what is it you've got going, Leeland?" I asked, not wasting time with chit-chat.

"To the point," Leeland oozed and sat down across a large mahogany table holding a stack of files and large envelopes. "I like that."

I just raised my eyebrow, waiting for him to get to the point.

He pushed the files across to me, the weight of their contents palpable. "Sarah, my dear, I believe it's time for you to see what lies beneath the surface of this country," Leeland said, a predatory gleam in his eye. "This is why we're doing this."

"You still haven't told me what it is exactly that you're doing," I commented as I opened the file, revealing a trove of information —evidence of corruption, deceit, and manipulation within the ranks of politicians all over Kentucky, including our illustrious and, in my opinion, asinine Senior Senator. Each page told a story of compromised principles and broken promises. Leeland's voice resonated with conviction as he shared his plans to expose and dismantle the corrupt system, bringing justice to those who have long evaded it.

Leaning back in my chair, I listened intently. For a minute, I felt a surprising sense of conflict brewing within me, torn between my disdain for Leeland and my longing to see my hometown thrive again.

He laid out his vision of revitalizing the coal industry in Appalachia, promising to bring back lost jobs and restore hope to a struggling region. I couldn't argue much; his words had an allure. But you can't bring back coal mining jobs when there's no coal to mine, and in Letcher County, just like Harlan, there isn't any. And, I reminded myself, he was long on words and short on specifics. Not to mention the other visions that accompany what he says. Even if there were more coal to be mined here, it came with a cost—exploited workers, devastated landscapes, and dead miners. It wasn't Hillary Clinton who drove Appalachia to Donald Trump; it was the slow emptying of the coal fields. No mines meant no jobs, and no jobs meant no union, and no union meant no fight. Humans thrive on a certain level of conflict. Without some conflict, we lose our purpose. We get lost.

Leeland leaned forward, his gaze locked with mine. "Sarah, I know you don't like me, but I believe that deep down, you want the same thing we want: a better America. Join us, and help us reshape the future."

"Great speech," I replied, dropping into a thick drawl. "But I reckon your designated representative, 'fore someone shot him that is, sounded a might preachy, ya know? And you know where I stand on that."

Leeland laughs and stands, grabbing a cigar from a cigar box on his desk. "Cigar?" He offers.

I shook my head, watching him cut his cigar and light up.

"Nobody's perfect. But we're not looking to be some religious organization that decides how people should live."

I raised my eyebrow at that. I knew better. The sleazy salesman was in full form now. And I met his gaze, putting some steel in my voice. "Leeland, I've seen firsthand around here what happens. Yeah, a lot of people would like the return of coal, and I don't blame them. People without jobs feel useless and lost, but it isn't just the US where this is an issue. Besides, that's bullshit anyway. There's almost no mineable coal in Letcher County. That's why Sapphire sold most of their holdings last year."

Leeland turned a slightly surprised expression toward me but then schooled it back to impassivity. But I caught it, and I felt pretty thoroughly insulted. He honestly thought I had no idea what was happening here. I wasn't stupid. I hit the website for the Mountain Eagle, the local newspaper, almost every day. I paid attention to the geology reports, trying to figure out when Dad was going to end up out of work, wondering how long before I'd have to supplement my parents' income and help them with the taxes on the house.

"Leeland, look. I get your point. Everyone's upset. Hell, I'm upset. There's hardly any coal left. The mines are closing up, and there's no jobs. But promising to magically make it go away don't make it happen, and besides, there's no momentum in Washington to actually do what you're talking about anyway."

A flicker of disappointment flashed across Leeland's face. "Sarah, I respect your point, but remember that change requires sacrifice. The world is not always black and white."

I narrowed my eyes, waiting for his next words very carefully when the door opened.

"Dad, your business associates are here," Leeland's son Garrison said. I looked up and caught sight of two figures. The first one gave me a moment of pause, to say the least.

Standing behind Garrison was Branford Cash. He didn't know me, but I knew him. He was a well-known money launderer for both South American drug cartels and the Russian Mob, which means the Russian Government, too, given that Russia is still under hella sanctions over the ongoing conflict in Eastern Europe. Branford was a slippery character, and we had never been able to nail him with any strong evidence when we investigated him for counterfeiting at the Secret Service.

It was the second man, however, that stole the heat from my blood, Aleksandr Petrovich, a wanted hitman for the Russians and anyone else who could afford him. And he knew me. I had sat across the table from him for six hours and grilled him over an assassination plot against the Vice President just a year before I was drummed out. Ironically, his nickname was "the Ghost," and I was willing to bet my life that he took the shot that killed Mitchell Reichert.

"Have them wait on the veranda," Leeland snapped, his voice full of irritation. Clearly, he hadn't wanted me to see his associates.

I kept my expression neutral as I turned back to him, and Garrison closed the door.

"Look, Leeland. You've got your own business to attend to. But I tell you what, I'll think about it."

He nodded and smiled. "What if I told you that I could get you back into the Secret Service? Would that sweeten the pot?"

I raised my eyebrows at that and gave him a slightly eager expression. "You could do that?"

"It's possible."

I nodded. "Well, that does make things more interesting. I'll let you know."

He nodded back. "Well, don't take too long. Oh, that reminds me, Garrison said he saw you drive into town with a woman. You got a new girlfriend?"

I looked back at him. "Who, Molly? We're just friends. I'm hoping it'll be more, but you know how these things go. Courtin' and all."

"Sure do," he said with a wink, smiling that serpentine, oily grin and bidding me goodbye. "I'm sure you can see yourself out."

"Sure can," I answered. "Thanks for the Scotch. It's delicious." I downed the rest and slid my glass across the table, causing the fat ice ball in it to jingle around, then walked casually from the room and out the front door to my waiting car.

"Holy Jesus, and fuck me sideways," I breathed in relief as I climbed into the Jeep and fired her up. My hands were literally shaking. *Oh, Leeland,* I thought. *You are in so far over your sleazy little head. And so am I.*

CHAPTER TWENTY-SEVEN
Sarah

On my way back to the cabin, I peeled off at Walmart to check the undercarriage of the Jeep. Underneath, attached to the frame, dug way up under the hood, I found a GPS tracker attached.

"You little shit," I muttered to myself and took a good half hour to see if there were more: opening the hood, checking underneath, lifting the seats, you name it. But that had been it. I looked around the parking lot, spotted a state trooper's patrol car, and had a fun idea. "Track this for a while," I muttered.

The weight of my discussion with Leeland was sludge-like and heavy, and I wondered how much to tell Miranda. She deserved the truth, but God, the Russian Mob? This was so far beyond me. She had been worried about dragging me into this mess, and now I understood why. But I'd jumped in with both feet, now, hadn't I? *Well,* I thought as I pulled into the driveway. *I best get to hoeing my own corn.*

I took a deep breath as I got out of the car and stopped for a moment, taking in the loam scent of the woods and the fragrance of the big pine just across the road from the cabin. It was soothing and calmed me a little. The air had turned even more unseasonably warm, too, which was nice once I got past the thought that it was because Mother Nature was being run ragged.

The door opened with a mild creak, and I looked up. Miranda stood in the doorway.

I gasped. "Holy shit!"

"Language, Sarah Lou," my mother called from inside the house.

Mom had cut and dyed Miranda's hair, alright. It was short. Way short. The sides were shaved above the ears, and the rest sat stylishly on her head, curving over to the left side in a short cascade of purple and black ombré. She was wearing the pair of gray glasses I'd bought her. She looked nothing like the woman I'd risked my neck for in Davenport. Hell, I barely recognized her. And she looked damn hot in a pair of tight jeans and one of my flannels, partially unbuttoned. I wouldn't say it showed off *every* curve, but still.

She gave me a shy look. "Well?"

I blinked, then a slow smile turned up at the corners of my mouth. "Uh…uh…" I stammered, trying to get my tongue to work right. "It…It's amazing. You look—just—wow. You look hot. You're gonna have to beat 'em off with a stick."

She laughed, and her smile was wide and pretty. "Seriously. Do you think it looks good on me?"

I nodded vigorously and grinned like a fox in the hen house. "Yeah, it suits you, but hell, I thought you were jokin'."

Miranda still had a shy look about her, as if she wasn't sure what to make of it herself. "I was," she said, her fingers rubbing against the shaved back of her neck. "But when you said you thought I'd look beautiful even if I were bald, I decided to go for it."

"Well, you look like a movie star, or maybe—"

"Don't say K-Pop," she said quickly and gave me a lighthearted look of mock irritation.

I snapped my lips shut and pressed them together, then I said, "Hey, what's wrong with K-Pop?"

"It's vapid crap," Miranda said, crossing her arms. "And do you know how they put those bands together? I mean, really? It's disgusting exploitation."

"We'll just have to agree to disagree on that one," I responded and walked toward the door, following her into the house. "I like K-Pop."

"Well, there's no accounting for taste," Miranda shot back.

"I like you too," I murmured under my breath. "So I must have some taste."

"What did you say?" Miranda asked, looking back over her shoulder at me.

"Nothin'," I replied, stuffing my hands in my pockets and looking anywhere but at her.

Mom sat on the couch, snickering at our bickering as she read a book. From the looks of the table, they'd been going through Mamaw's collection, mostly her old romances from the eighties. I hadn't pegged Miranda as a romance reader, but then again, I could see it. Lonely women read romances. I certainly did.

"Well?" Mom asked, looking up as I sat heavily in one of the chairs. "What did the king snake have to say?"

I scowled scornfully at the thought of Leeland and glanced at Miranda, who was getting a Coke from the fridge. "Come over here; you might want to hear this."

"What?" Miranda asked as she sat down. I'm sure she could tell from my expression that nothing I had to say would she like.

I recounted my meeting with Leeland in as much detail as I could recall. I didn't sugarcoat it, and I didn't leave anything out, the files, Petrovich, or Branford.

"We're fucked," Miranda said flatly.

I nodded. "It don't look good."

"Doesn't," Mom corrected. "I taught you to speak like a human, not like some bumpkin'."

I snorted. "Yeah, and I grew up here, Mom. You weren't the only influence in my life, ya know."

Miranda was ignoring us as she gripped the edge of the table, her knuckles white and her face drained of color. "You don't think they're here for me, do you?"

I shook my head. "I doubt it. No one knows you're here. There's something else going on."

She took a deep breath, swallowed hard, and looked at me as if I had all the answers. "So what do we do?"

I shrugged. "Nothing we can do just yet. I'm waiting for the Bureau to go through Mitchell's machine. If we give them a chance to investigate further, they'll figure out that we had nothing to do with his murder. No one's going to recognize you looking like that, anyway." I shot her a wide grin, forcing it to my eyes, even though I didn't really feel it. "We have time, still. But by next week at the latest, I expect Mom and Dad will get a call from the Bureau asking about me."

"What do you want us to tell them?" Mom asked as she joined us at the table.

"Tell them that I've asked you to keep my whereabouts quiet until I'm ready to turn myself in for questioning," I said. "That's all. You don't have to say anything else. I just need to buy as much time for the Bureau to do their job as possible."

I tried to keep my face neutral, but in truth, I was having an internal conniption. This was the Russian Mob we were talking about and, quite likely, the Russian president himself. The FSB had a long memory and a history full of Novachuk and Polonium and dead turncoats.

Just as I was about to say something inane to try and lighten the mood, there was a knock at the door, 'Shave and a haircut'— Delbert.

His face was smudged with coal dust, and he smelled like sweat and hard work. He greeted us with a wide smile. "I'm gonna grab a shower, then I'm headed to Jester's place. They're having a small get-together, just family and close friends. Thought it might be good to be around some familiar faces and maybe for Miranda to get out of this place for a night."

I pursed my lips and shook my head. "I don't know. I mean, who'll be there?"

"It's just family," Delbert answered. "They're expecting a pretty big crowd, and the band's playin'," Delbert said that last with an arch grin.

Maybe surrounding ourselves with friends would be a good distraction. It would be all family. I just worried about what might happen if any of Leeland's cronies showed up. But Miranda stepped in before I could object further, placing a hand on my shoulder. "You know what? I'm tired of being cooped up in this cabin. A party sounds like fun."

I sighed. This was just like Miranda, no caution at all. "Miranda—" I started, but she gave me a hopeful smile and a bit of a pout. It struck me how different she was out here. Despite the panic attacks she'd had, she was slowly transforming into someone else. My dad always said that people change, sometimes right in front of you, and a little bit more of a taste of home did sound nice.

"Fine," I said to Delbert. "We'll meet you at Jester's, but if you get there before I do, you tell Jester I ain't playin', not tonight."

Delbert gave me a smile and left, my mother in tow.

"I mean it!" I called after him.

CHAPTER TWENTY-EIGHT
Sarah

Miranda and I both decided it was too warm for jeans. I put on a pair of my old cargo shorts and a T-shirt. I donned my shoulder holster and slipped a flannel over that, cuffing the sleeves around my elbows. I looked alright, I thought. Casual and comfortable. But when Miranda exited her bedroom, I almost fainted dead away. She was wearing that cropped NASA shirt I'd bought on a lark, a pair of skin-tight, ripped jeans that she found God only knows where, probably a pair of mine from years ago, but damn, did they fit. A pair of my mom's flip-flops adorned her feet.

"This okay?" She asked, then waved a hand in front of my face when I didn't answer. "Yoo-hoo, Sarah Lou Rogers, this is Houston Control. Is this okay?"

I blinked. "Fucking perfect," I answered with a goofy grin.

"Language, Sarah Lou," she shot back with a wink, and then we just stood there, staring at each other. And strangely, we were smiling.

I walked over and reached up slowly, running my hand across the stubble on the side of her head. "Wow, it's short."

She didn't pull away. Instead, she grinned up at me with those gorgeous brown eyes, and my gaze flicked to her lips, full and ripe for a stolen kiss. Gods, it didn't matter what she wore, how her hair was, or even her expression. She was stunning in every sense of the word. Underneath the veneer of the starched, ultraconservative politician's wife was a total flirt. I could see it in her gaze and feel it in the flush of heat running through my entire body. It was like the moment when Cinderella looked down at herself and realized how beautiful she really was in her ball gown, except from the outside. Obviously, I had always thought Miranda was pretty, but this was something else. My heart raced, and my breath deepened as the rush of warm feelings filled me.

She stepped forward and brushed an imaginary bit of something off my shoulder. Butterflies danced in my belly and made my breathing come a bit short. We were inches apart, and her lips parted slightly as if she were going to kiss me, but then she backed away. "Umm. . . We should probably get moving."

"Yeah," I answered, my voice low and husky. "We probably should." For a moment, neither of us moved as we still stared at each other. Finally, I took her hand and grabbed the keys to the Jeep. I knew two things right then. I was going to get her out of this in one piece, and I was so fucked.

We took the Jeep and followed Delbert from Mom's through the winding roads. The entire drive, I couldn't help but look in the rearview mirror. There was nothing there, but I could feel the size of the target on our backs now. The shadows of the trees that enveloped the road seemed darker and a little ominous. It was a strange feeling, not something I was used to, not here, anyway.

When we reached Jester's place up the road, between Mayking and Jenkins, the sky was drenched in shades of orange and pink as the sun set behind the mountains. A long line of cars and trucks lined the road on either side, most of them parked well into the grass and low ground cover, twenty at least. We were forced to park some ways away.

As we walked down the dirt road toward the sounds of music, laughter, and the smell of the cookout, Miranda stopped me. "Okay, so let me get this straight. Molly, right?"

I nodded. "Molly Min-Ji Davis."

She laughed. "That's almost as bad as Miranda Soo. That's not my birth name, you know."

I tilted my head. "Huh, really?"

"Nope," she said with a cheeky grin. "My birth name is Seo-Ran Soo—Danbury, of course."

"That's a beautiful name. Why did you change it?"

"Dad insisted. He said I needed something more American to blend into the political space."

We were just making idle conversation, but I was getting, I suspected, a rare glimpse here. "And did you want to?"

"No," she answered, and I detected a hint of resentment in it. "But my mother went along with it, too, so I did it. I think after this is all over, I'll change it back."

"Well, that's up to you, but it really is a beautiful name."

She smiled briefly and took my hand. "Come on."

The laughter and the clinking of bottles grew louder as we approached the house. The air was thick with the smell of barbecue, burgers, and the earthy scent of the forest. The sky glowed in amazing shades, giving the entire evening a truly magical feel. The only thing missing was fireflies. It was too late in the year.

We rounded the edge of the gravel driveway and strolled up to the huge yard out front. The sprawling farmhouse had ten rooms and a wraparound porch that hugged almost the entire ground floor. The whitewashed wood exterior reflected some of the evening sun from a dozen windows in hues of red, orange, and pink. Normally decorated with seats and a hanging porch swing, it had been cleared to make room for the musicians, who were still setting up.

Relatives from the Kincers, Adams, Gibsons, Rogers, Pace, and Hall families milled around. Most of them I recognized, but a fair few of the people there I didn't. A couple of old friends nodded or came up and gave me a quick hug, greeting us with smiles. They mostly spoke to me, but I could feel their eyes on Miranda. She was like a shiny new toy to everyone I introduced.

As we made our way through the crowd, I saw it was well set up for the party. There were long tables on the lawn covered in checkered tablecloths, barrels of ice-cold beer, and a smoking barbecue pit.

Jester's house, with its mix of rustic charm and grandeur, felt like the perfect backdrop for the gathering—a testament to the long family traditions that I thought I'd left far behind. Clearly, not so far as I'd believed. It felt comfortable and friendly.

Miranda pulled off her story flawlessly as she talked about our fictional meeting in D.C. at a coffee shop, and I couldn't help but admire how effortlessly she morphed into character. But then again, I shouldn't have been surprised. By her own admission, she'd been playing a part for twelve years, just a different one. Minutes after we'd entered the yard, Jenny Kincer, one of my cousins, and her gaggle of friends, turned into a bunch of squirrels arguin' over a nut, drawing her away from me in a flash.

I let her go, heading off to find a beer, before I spotted a familiar face from high school—Shelly Adams. The memory of our sloppy tryst during a late night under the stars crept into my thoughts. I imagined I could still feel the ghost of her lips on mine. There'd been nothing to it, but it was still a fond memory—my first time, hell, my first kiss.

Shelly's eyes flickered toward Miranda as I approached, and she leaned in, her voice teasing, "Where'd you find her? She's smokin' in that outfit. Good Gawd, Sarah."

I just smiled, a conspiratorial glint in my eye.

"Seriously, Sarah Lou. Wow."

I finally quit gawking at Miranda myself and answered her. "We're just friends, Shelly."

Shelly looked at me skeptically and laughed. "Then why does she keep looking at you like that?"

I looked up and caught Miranda's eye. A bit of a flush ran up my neck and covered my cheeks. "Uh, yeah, that," I muttered distractedly.

Shelly just laughed. "Yeah, that."

I couldn't look away from Miranda, and she kept stealing little glances at me, laughing and smiling with my cousins. "She and I met in D.C. when I was grabbing a coffee. She lives up towards Hagerstown, you know. The middle of nowhere."

"Kinda like this place," Shelly chuckled.

I laughed at that. "Almost."

Shelly leaned in close and whispered in my ear. "Well, I can see you two are in love."

I sputtered. "What?"

She just shook her head and chuckled. "Whatever. I'm gonna go find Boomer. Let's catch up tomorrow if you have time. I'm on shift at the Subway until four."

I nodded.

As the night unfolded, I kept a close watch on Miranda, making sure everyone was treating her with the respect she deserved. But I needn't have bothered. She was engrossed, soaking in stories about my childhood, laughing and drinking like she belonged here. She'd even kicked off the flip-flops and walked barefoot in the grass.

From what I heard from the various cousins who stopped by to say hello, she was pretty shy about herself but seemed to be taking in every story about me that she could get; apparently, the more embarrassing, the better. *Great,* I thought. *There are enough of them. Mostly stupid kid stuff.*

I was leaning against the porch post, looking up at the night sky, when a banjo was thrust into my hands. I looked down, then over to Uncle Lester, who jerked his head toward an empty seat on the porch. Apparently, Noah, the banjo player, was taking a break.

I threw the strap over my shoulder. The weight felt so familiar. Taking a few swipes at the strings, I plucked a couple of patterns to make sure they were in tune. Glancing quickly at Miranda, I noticed her wide-eyed stare, followed by a raised and daring eyebrow.

She didn't know this part of me—the mountain girl who'd played banjo and guitar since she was six. Uncle Lester, clearly tired of waiting, grabbed a microphone and hollered for me. "Sarah Lou, get up here!"

"Aw, shit," I cursed loud enough for everyone to hear.

Half the clan hollered, "Language at the table, Sarah Lou!"

I shook my head with a chuckle and launched myself up onto the porch, taking the offered chair.

Everything got a little quieter than I would have liked, all eyes on the band, and specifically me.

"I need to warm up," I said quietly to the rest of the band. "It's been a while. Unionhouse Branch, okay?"

"We can start with that," Uncle Lester said with pursed lips, "but after, we get cookin'. You got that?"

I snorted, amused, and turned back. "Lester, you ain't no Dan Tyminski."

He gave me a sour look. "And you ain't no Earl Scruggs, girl. Now we gonna play or what?"

"You just better keep up, old man," I shot back and nodded to my cousin Jimmy on the fiddle. "Hit it."

Jimmy and I counted off and fired the opening riffs of the song. Before I knew it, my fingers were dancing across the strings, and people were clapping along. Miranda just leaned against one of the tables with a beer and watched us intently.

As the music rose, my fingers rolled across the banjo strings. I stole glances at Miranda. Her eyes were wide and sparkling, her mouth slightly open as if trying to capture the music in the air, then she bit her bottom lip.

She looked like a painting, every stroke of her features full of emotion. I hadn't planned to play. I'd told Delbert to tell them I wouldn't. Maybe I'd been afraid of her seeing this. But if she was put out or turned off by it, she sure as hell didn't look it.

As I played, I could feel something steal over me that had nothing to do with Miranda. It was the music, like me, as much a part of these mountains and the people who settled here, and I wondered why I'd stayed away so long. I hadn't missed much about the town itself. Things like this, however, family get-togethers and playing the banjo, I'd missed them plenty. I just hadn't realized until now.

The banjo sang under my fingers, but Miranda's face kept grabbing my attention, as did the sparkle in her brown eyes. My heart thundered in my chest. The crowd stomped and clapped. At least once, a little smitten at Miranda's delighted attention, I fell off the beat, but I recovered quickly.

Awe twinkled in her eyes like she'd been walking through a desert and just happened on cool water, and I felt a pull I couldn't deny. It was as if, at this moment, the relentless current of the music had torn down all the walls between us.

The band and I played about a half dozen songs before I finally decided to stop. I'd kept up with playing some, but not enough. My fingertips weren't as calloused as they should be, but I barely felt them, and the final notes lingered in the air as the last song wound down. The applause was thunderous, but all I heard was the echo of the strings and the silent conversation in Miranda's gaze.

As I finally passed the banjo to Noah, I stepped down from the makeshift stage, eyes still on Miranda, and the electricity between us danced like a physical thing, an understanding, a wordless agreement that we'd crossed a threshold neither of us could or would step back from.

She walked toward me, her movements as light and graceful as the last melody hanging in the air. On a whim, I turned back, stepped up to the stage again, and leaned down, whispering to Lester, who handed me his guitar.

I stepped up to the mic. "Everyone, please meet my date for the evening, Miss Molly. Molly, this one's for you." I scratched the opening riffs of 'If It Hadn't Been for Love' by the Steel Drivers, and the band followed along as I sang a song about obsession, love, and the road to prison. It might have been a bit close to home, but she didn't seem to mind.

When I was done, my fingertips were aching, but it was worth every second to see her face as, for the first time, I was sure, someone sang a song just for her.

Shyly, she stepped onto the stage. "Umm...Ya'll know 'Daylight' by Allison Krauss and Union Station? It's the only bluegrass song I know."

I nodded. "I'm sure some of us do."

One of the Kincer boys handed the resonator to Lester, and we started up again. Miranda sang into the microphone. Her voice was angelic and sweet, stopping everything as the family all stared in amazement. Of course, I should have known she could sing; she could do damn near everything else.

A ridiculous grin slid across my face as I played the lead guitar, but it was Miranda they were watching. She had them all enthralled.

Afterward, we stepped off the stage and meandered a little ways away. "That was amazing, Sarah," she whispered breathlessly, the air from her lungs caressing my face and bringing gooseflesh to my arms. "I didn't know that side of you. It's like you're someone else, here, someone I really want to—" She trailed off, and I gave her a shy smile, looking away. My body was flushed from head to toe with a mix of embarrassment and desire.

We didn't share much in the way of words. She commented on a few of the more spectacular failures of my childhood she'd heard about. Then we split up again as I caught up with people I hadn't seen since high school, and she finally got herself a burger surrounded by half the guys at the party. One leaned in, reaching for one of her pickles, and she slammed her knife down into the wooden table.

"You do that again, boy, and you'll pull back a nub," she said with a glare, and I had to pinch my lips to keep from laughing.

I decided to rescue Will before she actually stabbed him. "Alright, Molly," I say, "go easy on my kinfolk. Willy, she's with me, honey." I gave Willy a jerk of my head, telling him to back up a bit. And like that, the guys all dispersed.

Miranda looked up at me. "They all know?"

I nodded. "They're family. A few of 'em don't like it, but they know I don't care and that it is what it is. It's the closest to acceptance I'll get from some of 'em. Besides, they're all afraid of me, so that helps."

She grinned and offered me the pickle that Willy had reached for, stuffing it in my waiting mouth. "Thanks," I whispered, leaning in close and kissing her on the cheek. "I'm gonna go get somethin' to eat myself."

She gave me an odd look and a weird grin, then shooed me off. "Well, go on, then, Sarah Lou."

Later, as the night finally wound down, Miranda and I shared a few glances, heavy with unspoken words. I wanted to talk about it, to reach out to her, but not here. Besides, now that all the women knew she was with me, they were all around her gossiping and chatting instead of giving her sour, jealous looks. I decided we could talk later. We had all night.

CHAPTER TWENTY-NINE
Sarah

Jason, Delbert, Miranda, and I chatted as I ate, and Miranda was in the middle of sharing an embarrassing story of her own out of nowhere. It was just a beer-drinking story about Miranda having had one too many. In the middle of her story, the band stopped playing, and a deep pall fell over the party; I shushed her gently and stood up.

There, walking through the crowd with two of his thugs, was Leeland Honeycutt.

"What the fuck is he doin' here," Jason whispered on my left as we got up and stood in front of the picnic table in a line, trying to keep Miranda out of sight.

Honeycutt spotted us and sauntered over, and I thought Miranda might run, but she sidled right up next to Jason and took his arm. *Good girl,* I thought. *Play it cool.*

Honeycutt oozed toward us with his oily smile and bright serpentine eyes, glimmering maliciously in the dark. "Don't let me stop the party," Honeycutt said, loud enough for folks to hear him but not really shouting.

I slapped my beer bottle to the table with one hand, spilling a little and wiping my hand on my jeans. "What do you want, Leeland?"

"Well," he said, lowering his voice. I was just passing by. I saw the lights, and I figured there was a party going on." Behind Leland stood two men I recognized: Jimmy Fields, the younger brother of the Sheriff, and Jacob Kincer, a distant relative. Both were about Delbert's size, broad-shouldered and hard-eyed, their arms crossed. They were wearing black polos and black slacks, clearly doing well on Leeland's payroll.

"Yeah, it's a family get-together, Leeland. The emphasis is on family. Which you ain't." I stepped forward, getting into his space, almost nose to nose. The scent of his cologne overpowered everything around it, and I wrinkled my nose. "You bathe in that Parisian crap?" I asked, an edge to my voice. "It's stinking up the place."

Leeland frowned, then his smile returned. "It's from London."

I rolled my eyes. "Whatever. So, I'll ask again." My voice was low and threatening now. "What are you doing here?"

I didn't bother to close my flannel, so my Sig was in full view.

"I hope you have a CCDW for that," Leeland commented, a friendly smile full of ooze and menace splitting his face. "Wouldn't want you to get arrested for a gun violation."

"Who's gonna arrest me here, Leeland? You?"

"My brother," Fields grunted, putting his hands on his hips. "Or maybe we make a citizen's arrest."

I slowly withdrew my pistol from its holster and handed it, grip first, to Jason before stepping up on Fields. "I'd love to see you try," I said with a smirk. "Nothing would make me happier than to knock your dick in the dirt."

A shuffle and a few appreciative "Ohs" passed through the crowd as Fields took a half step forward, looking down at me. Then he reached out and put his hand on my shoulder. I could tell by the gasps that everyone thought it was a bad move, which it was.

I snatched his hand and put him in an armbar, spinning him to the ground before putting my knee on his neck as I pulled my cuffs from my back pocket and slapped them on.

"That, brother, is called assault, and I think I'll make a citizen's arrest. Oh, wait. I'm a licensed PI in Kentucky. I can just detain you here and call your mama to come git you, boy. Tell her what you been up to."

Everyone laughed and several of our group stepped over to the ruckus, scowling at the interlopers. He was outmanned and outgunned, and he knew it.

Leeland frowned. "Let him go, Sarah. He didn't mean nothin' by it."

I raised an eyebrow at the order but unlocked the cuffs anyway, letting Fields off the ground, watching him cradle his right wrist, likely sprained. The point was made. I wasn't going to be intimidated, and I was anything but alone here. "Now, what do you want?"

Leeland started to answer, but Bill Jester walked out of the house, his shotgun resting over his arms. "Leeland, you try anything here, and I think you might find yourself less Rambo and more Butch and Sundance, you know? Now, this is a private gathering, and I want you off my property. We don't need no more trouble."

By this time, the family had closed in, completely encircling the group, and I knew for a fact that at least a couple of them were packin', too.

"And who might you be?" Leeland says, walking straight up to Miranda.

Shit, I thought, just waiting for him to say something.

"Molly," Miranda said, looking him up and down. "Molly Davis. Who the fuck are you?"

Leeland raised an eyebrow. "You kiss your mama with that mouth?"

She smirked, "I wash it out first." She didn't stare daggers at Leeland as I expected. She just acted nonchalant, going so far as to look at her nails and buff them on her cropped top.

"You get those done at Shelly's?" Leeland asked.

"Nope, got 'em done in D.C. before I came down here. That's where Sarah Lou and I met. She thought maybe I should come down and meet her brother while I'm on vacation. And I kinda like him." She leaned up and kissed Jason on the cheek. "Ain't that right, baby."

Jason flushed a bit and smiled.

"Leeland," I said, stepping between him and Miranda. "I think you've overstayed your welcome. Please don't make this any worse. Someone's libel to get hurt, and I just know you don't want that."

Leeland focused his gaze on me. "You thought about my offer?"

I nodded. "Yeah, and I'm still thinkin' about it. But coming here, disturbin' our fun with vague threats about permits and arrests, ain't helpin' your case."

Leeland turned away. "Come on, boys." Then he looked back at me. "Don't take too long on that, Sarah Lou. There may not be much time left before we decide that you can't be much help after all. Maybe you should come by with your friend. I like her spirit."

I narrowed my eyes at him but didn't react to the thinly veiled threat, instead standing in front of Jason and Miranda, watching as he and his goons sauntered their way back to his Suburban and drove away, peeling out and sending gravel flying.

"Asshole," I swore under my breath.

"I could have taken all three of 'em," Delbert said as we turned away.

I nodded. "Yeah, I know, but we didn't want 'em dead or horribly mutilated, Delbert. And that's what would have happened if you'd jumped in."

After he was well out of sight, Miranda leaned into me and started breathing heavily, as if she'd been holding her breath for the entire encounter. "Jesus, Sarah, that was close."

"Naw. This was par for the course. It's not the first time Leeland has intruded on a family event when he wanted something. But, I wish you'd stayed out of sight."

"He'd have picked up on that for sure, Sarah," Miranda whispered. "He may be a fool, but he's not completely stupid. If he'd looked past you three and seen me, he would have wondered why you were hiding the Korean girl, and that would have been that. We were screwed either way. At least now, he'll have to think about it more. And what was that about Delbert killing them?"

"He was a scout sniper in the Marine Corps," I said. "Despite his mild manner, he's an absolute badass."

"That's Gunny Badass, thank you very much," Delbert joked.

"Impressive," Miranda commented, her eyebrows raised. "Got any good stories?"

"Nope." Delbert abruptly left the table.

"Did I say something wrong?" Miranda asked, watching him walk away.

"No, he just doesn't talk about the war. He's still pretty angry about it, especially after the way we pulled out from Afghanistan."

The band fired up a couple of tunes to get things back in gear, but the pall was still there, at least for me. Just one more thing to worry about.

I looked at Delbert. "Hey, I said. Come over here. I need to talk to you in private." Delbert raised an eyebrow but followed me to the far side of the house, where we had a short conversation.

A half-hour later, Miranda and I said our goodbyes. As we left, absolutely everyone glommed onto Miranda, drowning her in hugs and 'come back soons.' She really did have a way with people.

CHAPTER THIRTY
Miranda

We stopped in front of the cabin door and looked at each other. As Sarah fiddled in her pocket for the key, I reached out and caught her arm. I wasn't exactly sure what I was doing, but my chest heaved with the emotions that turned over within. My lungs filled with deep breaths, drinking in the scent of her. Sarah looked at me almost shyly, her blue eyes always reminding me of the deep afternoon sky, unclouded and beautiful.

The connection between us was undeniable, and I wasn't a fool. I knew what I wanted as the breeze wrapped us in a quilt of chill air that raised the hair on my arms, or maybe it was just how close she was.

My hand slid up and across Sarah's cheek, my voice a low and husky whisper. "You're so beautiful, and that song together—It was—"

"So that's the way to your heart, is it?" Sarah joked nervously. The confident woman who'd been my balm and guide for the last few weeks vanished, replaced by someone uncertain.

I wouldn't let her get away. I squeezed her forearm a little more firmly, a warm and genuine smile that felt real and unforced spread across my face as I answered the silly question in a whisper. "It's the way to any woman's heart."

It was as if my world had fallen down to just this: Sarah's eyes and my hand on her cheek. My heart was thundering in my chest, and I didn't try to slow it. I stepped forward slowly. A vague image of that afternoon in the hotel room intruded on my thoughts, but I mentally batted it aside. That had been nothing. And this—this was something or at least the beginning of something—maybe. But the moment was stretching too long, and I heard the jingling of the keys as Sarah fidgeted.

Quickly, I closed the distance and pressed my lips to hers, feeling the need and longing that had been burning within me for weeks swell and glow until my thoughts and body were all on fire.

Sarah let out a soft, muffled sigh, and I gave a slow whimper as our breath mingled. She parted her lips to deepen the kiss into something much less hurried and yet much more powerful than we'd felt that day in the hotel. That had been burning lust, this—this was the inkling of love. And while terror scrabbled at my chest, I refused to let it sink its claws into this. I wouldn't run.

Now, the keys jingled earnestly as Sarah tried to find the right one blindly because I refused to release her. I slid my other hand into her hair, pressing her lips harder to me as I pressed my own body to hers.

Somehow, Sarah managed to slide the key into the lock and pull us into the cabin. She kicked the door shut behind us as we almost fell inside. I could hardly breathe, and the anticipation in my chest was almost a tangible weight. I couldn't get enough of her lips on mine, her hands roaming my back and bunching up the silly mid-riff t-shirt. My whole body was alight in a way I had never felt. I felt—desperate.

"Please," I breathed between kisses, almost gasping and tilting my head back as she nibbled at my throat.

"Miranda," Sarah whispered. Her voice was a mixture of vulnerability and uncertainty. "I know I shouldn't—we shouldn't —" She broke off as I placed a finger on her lips.

"Stop," I gasped, still a little out of breath. "It doesn't matter anymore. Let me take you to bed. I want it all." I peeled away her jacket, throwing it to the floor. Then I slid off her shoulder holster, tossing it to the sofa, where it landed with a soft bounce.

Sarah's eyes searched mine, probably for any hint of uncertainty. There was none. I grabbed her hand and led her up to the loft in the darkness. And then we were on each other again, my hands sightlessly tugging at her shirt, one sliding up underneath to cup a breast.

Sarah let out a breathy sigh and a soft moan of pleasure as I slid my hand around and into her hair, jerking her head back so I could get at her throat.

Slowing down, I ran my tongue slowly up her neck. I wanted to savor this. It was the first time I'd ever felt affection like this, and I wanted to explore every inch of her, feel every tumbling emotion. I wanted this to last. I've never had love before—not ever. And I knew it because I could feel it rising in my chest, painfully squeezing at my gut. I couldn't get close enough to her.

As I lifted her shirt over her head, I stopped playfully with it half off, covering her face and pinning her arms inside, leaving her abdomen exposed. With a gentle push, I shoved her backward onto the bed. Making love to a woman might have been new to me, but there were some things where it didn't matter. And Sarah was so in control all the time, trying to keep everything in order and safe for me. I knew implicitly that she needed this. She needed to surrender, and I wanted to give that to her.

I reached down and snatched the cuffs from their pouch on her belt and, with a bit of coaxing, tempted her to roll face down, where I finished removing her shirt and cuffed her hands behind her back. Then I tugged at her hair, lifting her face from the bed gently. I wasn't into pain, giving it or receiving it, but I was firm, holding her head steady.

"Just do as I say," I demanded in a whisper.

She closed her eyes and nodded her assent.

I pushed her back over onto her back. In my suitcase was a scarf I'd accidentally grabbed from my underwear drawer. I tied it around her head, covering her eyes, not that it wasn't already dark. But now, she could see nothing, and my eyes had adjusted. I could see the perspiration glistening across her chest in the dim and failing moonlight from outside. Her nipples sat rock hard, capping small breasts, a sacrifice to the amount of work she'd put into her sculpted physique.

As I ran my hand across her body, I watched her shoulder muscles bulge, her wrists tugging lightly at the cuffs in random spasms. A flush of warmth and lust filled me when I thought of how quickly she'd taken down Fields as if he'd been nothing more than a rag doll, how she and her brothers had immediately stepped in front of me when Leeland had arrived, protective, like a wall. She'd made that happen, and just the thought of it made me a little wet.

"So, big bad security lady," I smiled playfully, my voice hoarse and low. "Tell me. Do you like this?" I leaned in and took one of her nipples into my mouth, gently sucking and licking at it.

"Yes," she breathed.

"And this?" I slid my hand across the crotch of her jeans, pressing hard against her.

"Oh, yes," she gasped as a tremor passed across her lips.

"Do you want more?" I asked, a bit of a smirk starting to split my lips as I realized how much control I really had. I found myself wishing that we had something a little more elaborate here than just the handcuffs, but they'd have to do.

"Yes," she answered, her voice now just a whimper full of need.

The feel of her was electric, igniting a fire that coursed through my veins as I ran my hands across her muscular frame. "Beg for it."

"Please," she groaned and tilted her head back.

With gentle fingers, I slowly undid the buckle of her belt, sliding it loose. She tried to rise, maybe to make it easier, but I pushed her hips into the bed.

"No," I said firmly. "You just relax. You're mine for the night."

With a groan, she settled back to the bed, but whether it was a groan of frustration or desire, I couldn't tell. Probably both, and I let out a tinkle of laughter. "Oh, poor baby. Do you have needs?"

Sarah nodded vigorously, pressing her lips together as I undid the button of her pants and slowly lowered the zipper, lifting the waistband of her panties and licking along the exposed flesh. Her breath was heaving and deep.

CHAPTER THIRTY-ONE
Sarah

My entire body quivered with anticipation and a strange giddiness. No one had ever taken control of me in bed—ever. I lay there unable to see, my hands bound underneath me with no means of escape, not that I wanted to.

Miranda pushed my legs apart, gently probing places with her tongue: the back of my knee, my ankles, the crease at the top of my thigh, so close to my folds. Slowly, gently, she spread those folds of flesh, exposing my clit fully. She licked around them with long, slow strokes, leaving me heaving and a breathy "Oh" lilting from my mouth.

She slid a hand down my bare stomach, letting her fingers splay across my one thigh while she ground against the other, the slick of her wetness leaving a cooling trail. "God, I want you," She moaned and dug the fingers of her hand into my belly. She bit her way upward, stopping periodically to lay kisses and small, gentle nibbles that tickled slightly. But when she reached my breast, she bit down hard on the nipple, bringing a gasp of pain to my mouth.

"Ow," I protested, but she bit the other one just as hard. "Ow, Jesus."

"Too bad," she hissed at me and raked her nails down my chest. Her right hand slid into the hair at the top of my head and yanked my head back once more. "Now, tell me, do you want me?"

"God, yes," I moaned, unable to contain myself.

"Then give in to me," she breathed as she slid a hand down and massaged my clit.

I nodded.

"Is that a yes?"

"Yes." It came out as a deep moan. "God, yes. Please."

After that, she was gentle, though. Running her hands and mouth and tongue across every part of me until she lowered herself to my face, pushing her clit and folds to my lips. I nipped and sucked at her sweetness, running my tongue back and forth, listening to her moan as her dripping wetness coated my chin and lips.

"Oh, Sarah," Miranda gasped as she grabbed my hair again, this time pressing my face into her. I could hear the welling orgasm building within her. At first, there was a quiver in her legs, and I sucked and licked with more vigor. I wanted her to come on me, in my mouth. I wanted to take her to climax.

She pressed into my mouth so hard I could scarcely breathe, arching her back and riding me to a loud orgasm.

"Oh! God! Yes," she called to the night as her body shook.

Finally, she released me, moving back. I sucked in a great gulp of air, feeling a touch of light-headedness.

"Sarah, that was incredible," she gasped. But she wasn't done. She slid her hand back down between my legs, pressing her fingers into my clit, sliding it back and forth between two fingers. The gentle pressure was true torture.

"Please, Miranda," I begged, desperate for her to make me come or release my hands, something, anything.

Abruptly, her hands vanished, and her mouth rested on me, her tongue tantalizingly brushing against my opening. The feeling was beyond intimate. All of my reservations and worries dropped away as she finally moved her tongue across me and pressed against my pulsing bud. So thrown was I in the arms of lust, my rise to climax was blissfully short and my orgasm powerful, shaking my knees and forcing my head back in a loud moaning cry, deep and husky.

She continued licking and biting at me until I begged her to stop, my skin sweat-soaked and sticking to the sheets.

She fished the cuff key from my pants pocket and removed the restraints.

I pulled off the makeshift blindfold and grabbed her with both arms, pulling her close and kissing her deeply, tasting our mingled sweat and breath and sex. It was exquisite. And I held her like that, kissing her and running my hands down her back, through her hair, cupping her ass. Anything to bring her closer, as if she might slip away into the night, a specter of memory or a product of my own needful imaginings. But no harsh gust of wind came to blow her away into the darkness. No words dragged away the moment. And when I looked into her eyes, I saw not burning lust but need and desire and vulnerability. *She is here*, I thought. *And she wants me, and not just for a one-night stand.*

At that moment, I realized that I didn't want a one-night stand either. I wanted more. Maybe I always had, but I just hadn't found the right woman. Or maybe, before now, I just hadn't thought I deserved it.

We weren't done, though. After a brief respite and some water, we spent the rest of the night remapping each other's bodies, exploring every inch, exploiting those sensitive spots and places that drew harsh whispers and occasional giggles. We showered together, and I saw the water flow down her body, pouring over her back as she forced me to the back wall and dropped to her knees.

And there were tears. Not for the life she abandoned or the love I lost so long ago, but for the intervening years: for the years she spent subservient to the will of an uncaring man who both cheated on her and took her for granted—tried to have her killed. They spilled for the years I had stayed unattached and unable to find that certain someone who could make it all seem worth it again, for the years we'd run in parallel lanes from my time at Brown with her best friend to D.C., where we finally met, to Davenport where we were forced to run for our lives, until here, high in the mountains where we found each other.

And for a moment, just one, we were happy and carefree, forgetting the rest of the world existed. And no one could take it from us.

CHAPTER THIRTY-TWO
Miranda

I woke up at about noon the next day. It was quiet outside. In the distance, though, I could hear the sound of power tools coming from the garage. A fresh pot of coffee sat in the coffee pot with a post-it attached to the maker. "Breakfast in the microwave. Give it twenty seconds."

I poured myself a fresh cup of coffee and peeked into the microwave. A plate sat there with a helping of grits, some cheesy eggs, and two sausage links. I touched the eggs gingerly. They were cold, so I did as the note bid and heated them up. Another note sat on the table. "In the garage, refinishing the other chair. Come see me when you're done eating."

I snorted. "Okay. That's mysterious."

I finished eating and found something to wear. Again, the weather was way too warm for November, so it was a T-shirt and jeans. Outside in the garage, Sarah was finishing up sanding the second chair. She shut down the sander and pulled off her protective gear when I came in.

"Hi," she said with a crooked smile. "You sleep well?"

"Nope. This crazy hillbilly kept waking me up asking for sex."

Sarah laughed and smiled wryly. "I'm pretty sure you asked a few times yourself."

I blushed and changed the subject, but I couldn't wipe the grin off my face. "I suppose I did. How's the chair coming?"

"Just perfect," Sarah said, appraising her work. "I should have been back here a long time ago to refinish these. The carvings on the chairs are damaged now. I'm doing my best to restore them, but this one's going to take someone good with woodworking tools."

"It looks good to me. How long to refinish it?"

"A few coats should do it," Sarah said. Then she set down the sander and put aside the chair. "Can we talk for a few minutes?"

My lips pressed into a thin line as I tried to read Sarah's face, but all I could see in the other woman's eyes was joy. It twinkled in them like stardust. "Is something wrong?"

"No. Just the opposite. I was wondering what your plans were for when we get out of this."

"Oh," I said as my anxiety rose a little. "That sounds like a longer conversation than I want to have standing here in the garage. Let's go inside." I'd been avoiding thinking about that, trying to stay neutral on the subject. There was no question that Sarah liked me or that I liked Sarah, but the idea of something beyond this was too far away—and too complicated. So, we retired to the kitchen and I poured us each a fresh cup of coffee.

Once we'd sat down, I looked at her, a crease in my brow. I tried not to frown, but I couldn't help it. I understood what she wanted, and in a perfect world, I might want that, too. But we didn't live in a perfect world.

"Sarah," I said after a moment's thought. "You've been really generous and nice, and I don't want to burst your bubble, but I can't stay here."

Sarah blinked. "I don't understand; you asked just the other day if we could. I know we have to go back to get clear of this, but—"

I held up my hand. "Sarah, why did you move away from here?"

"I wanted more than Whitesburg could offer. It's why I went to college so far away."

"Exactly. There's nothing here. You said it yourself: The entire town is dying along with coal." I could feel the cold sinking into my chest, the lies tasting bitter in my mouth. And it hurt far more than I had expected it to. *Christ*, I thought. *When did I become such a wimp? I used to do this without a second thought.*

Sarah frowned, and I could see a touch of glistening liquid in her eyes. "Yes, but it doesn't have to stay that way. You're a national figure we could bring some attention to—"

"I don't want to live here," I said, my voice rising. "I don't want to live in some small town where I'm the only Asian woman, a novelty at best. A target at worst if we have another administration like the last one. I want to go home."

"But what about last night? I mean, I thought we both felt it was more than physical."

I twisted my coffee cup and pawed at the table briefly. "I'm sorry, Sarah. I just can't. There's so much you don't understand."

Sarah's eyes went wide, and I realized what I'd just said, but it was too late now. Sarah's voice turned quiet and subdued. "Oh, I understand, alright. The lesbian redneck girl is good enough to screw but not good enough to be a real partner."

That stung, but I barreled ahead. Sarah wasn't understanding, and I wasn't really explaining very well, probably because of what I wasn't saying, that Sarah's life would be in danger if this continued, that I didn't want her hurt. I just couldn't bear it. "Sarah, my life is in D.C. Everyone I know is there. I can't just pick up and move to rural Kentucky. Yes, it's pretty out here, but this is your place. I don't know anyone. It's not you—"

"Don't you dare finish that sentence with 'it's me.' That's bullshit. Obviously, I get it. I'm not good enough for 'daddy's good girl.'"

My eyes went wide, and a cold slice of deep rage burned in my chest. I gave her a hard stare, and my voice grew angry and brittle. "I told you that in confidence. How could you use that in an argument against me?"

"It's true, isn't it?" Sarah half-shouted. "Don't lie to me. It's that living with a woman who doesn't make seven figures doesn't fit in with your parents, especially when I can't take you on seventeen-thousand dollar shopping sprees, drive you around in Bentleys, or own a Lear jet."

I lost my temper then and said something fiercely cruel given all that Sarah had done, but I had to get Sarah off this idea that we could have some life together. "Yes! That's exactly it. You've protected me, and I appreciate it. But I need to be honest. I like a better lifestyle than—than this!" I gestured around the cabin. "It's quaint, but it's not what I'm used to. And it's not what I want. I still have a future back in D.C. Mitchell's dead, but with the notoriety this will bring, I have a shot at Congress. I could do some real good for people. Maybe make up for—" I stopped, realizing that I'd gone too far from the horrific look on Sarah's face.

Sarah stood, fingering the locket around her neck. "You bitch," Sarah said finally. "You're so full of shit right now. You're just afraid. And that sucks because we could have something good! You want to do some good, get the fuck out of the closet and stand tall."

"That something else your daddy taught you?" I yelled back.

"Yes! And I'm damn proud of it!"

I scowled at her. "Oh really? Look around, Sarah. This whole area fell right in line behind one of the biggest bigots on the planet, not for principle, but for jobs that were just as likely to poison them or kill them as pay them. That man they helped into office would have happily roasted you on a spit if it got him a hint of applause. They don't care about you. And standing tall isn't what coal country is known for anymore. They're known for doing anything they can to keep a mine open even though the mining companies don't give a shit about you, them, or one inch of this land that doesn't have a block of black rocks in it. I don't call that standing up for principle. They were delighted to vote for a man that happily said he likes to grab women by the pussy. So don't talk to me with this working-class hero shit because it's just that—bullshit."

"You know what? I almost took a bullet for you. I have protected you. And let me tell you what I learned from my father. When you start a job, you finish it. So no matter what vile crap you spew at me, I'm going to get through this with you, then I'll send you the fucking bill!" Sarah stormed, then charged out of the cabin and slammed the door shut behind her, rattling half the windows.

As soon as Sarah was gone, I put my head on the table, tears pressuring the backs of my eyes. "Shit." That wasn't how I wanted that to go at all. On the other hand, if Sarah hated me, she'd at least let me go when we got back to D.C., and she'd be safe.

CHAPTER THIRTY-THREE
Sarah

I hadn't put one foot outside the door before I was confronted by three men with automatic rifles, including Wiley's brother and two local boys, Jerry Hall and Jack Hilyard. It was a shame, really; both Jerry and Jack had been good friends in High School. They'd never seemed like the bigoted militia types, but then again, people change. They were led by a fourth, Leeland Honeycutt.

My hands went up.

"Inside," Leeland said, his voice laced with menace.

I reached back and opened the door, backing into the cabin. I was unarmed, and there wasn't much I could do. I prayed Miranda had gone back to her room or something and could make a run for it. But she was still at the table, her head down.

"Look, Sarah," she said, then she saw the three men and snapped her jaws shut.

"Well, lookie here," Leeland said, his voice full of venom. "If it isn't Miranda Soo Reichert, just the woman everyone's looking for. I'm glad I found you first. I have some people who want to talk to you. Take her."

Miranda stood quietly. "I'll come quietly, just don't hurt her."

I raised a hand. "Miranda—don't—"

A gunshot sounded in the cabin, and I glanced around frantically to see who'd been shot.

Miranda stared at me, eyes wide, just as the burning in my chest started. I looked down. Blood poured from the right side of my rib cage. Leeland held a nine-millimeter Glock in his hand, a puff of smoke still whipping from the barrel.

"No!" Miranda screamed and rushed over as I hit the floor. But one of Leeland's men, a hulking figure in a dark jacket, grabbed her and yanked her away, the ferocity in his movements making my blood run cold.

It took two of the men to carry her out. She thrashed wildly, raking her hand down Jerry's face, and he dropped her, but only to punch her, knocking her senseless.

Leeland stood over me, the gun pointed loosely in my direction. "You should have just joined us, Sarah. It would have been much simpler."

The taste of blood filled my mouth, and my eyes rolled up as the world went black for a moment. When I opened them again, Leeland was gone.

I crawled across the floor and dragged myself upstairs. My body was just shades of pain and despair as I fumbled for the burner phone on the nightstand. I dialed my brother's number, praying he'd pick up.

"Jason! They took her! They took Miranda! I've been shot," I gasped into the phone when he answered.

The truck bounced and jolted over the rutted dirt road, every bump sending shockwaves of agony through my battered body. Jason kept a tight grip on me, trying to keep me from moving too much as Delbert drove at insane speeds down the back roads to the highway. The wind rushed through the open windows, smelling of pine and the damp earth. *Shit,* I thought. *I fucked up. I should never have taken her to Jester's.*

Delbert's knuckles were white on the steering wheel as he navigated the winding road with a grim face. I could hear him muttering curses under his breath.

"Hold on, sis," Jason whispered close to my ear. "Not much further."

The pain was so intense I barely heard him. My thoughts

flickered between Miranda, the violence, and the overwhelming need to get her back.

The road smoothed out as we reached the highway leading to Pikeville. The truck's roar was deafening, and the morning slipped by in a blur.

The sounds of passing cars became more frequent as we entered the city. I tried to count them to take my mind off the steadily rising pressure in my chest. Then it happened. I couldn't breathe. I sucked and sucked, but no air came in.

"Shit," Jason swore, leaning down to listen to my chest. "Pneumothorax, Del, fucking floor it, man, or she won't make it. She's turnin' blue."

Jason was feeling around my side, then he dug into the glove box, pulling something out with a triumphant. "Yes." His face vanished for a moment in a haze. I heard the crinkling of something being torn open. Then Jason was back with a sympathetic expression. "Sis, this is gonna hurt like a motherfucker."

I nodded vigorously as spots danced in my vision. I still couldn't breathe, and the panic was literally suffocating. Then Jason jammed something into my chest between my ribs, and there was a hissing sound, almost like a deflating tire. My chest expanded into a balloon of inbound air, and my vision cleared.

"Fuck," I growled as he pushed the plunger back into the syringe sticking out of my chest. I coughed, feeling something hot and warm run down my cheek.

"Del, that won't hold for long. We need to book, man."

"We're almost there," Delbert shouted from the front. "Just hang on, Sarah. We're here."

As if on queue, the syringe broke, and I started to lose air again. My lungs wouldn't inflate, and everything went black.

I came to with a mask on my face. Nurses and doctors swarmed around me. I couldn't understand what was happening. My thoughts were sluggish, like trying to swim through peanut butter. I felt a pinch in my arm, then a burning running into my veins.

As the anesthesia took hold, my last thought was of Miranda's terror-filled eyes looking down at me as Jerry dragged her away.

I felt nothing at first as I slowly opened my eyes. Harsh fluorescent lights glared down at me, and I winced. My body felt like it had been through hell, which, judging by my scattered memories, wasn't far from the truth. The pain in my right side was so intense it took my breath away. I struggled for a moment to assess what I remembered and what I felt: a gunshot wound on my right side, a bump on my head where I hit the floor. The light didn't bother me, and my head wasn't spinning, so probably no concussion.

Whispering and the shuffling of feet told me I was not alone. "Miranda," my voice was barely audible, a scratchy whisper.

Delbert moved into my field of vision. I glanced around. Mom was sleeping in the chair next to me, and Dad was leaning against the window sill with a haunted look in his eyes. Delbert looked down. His eyes were likewise red and tired. "Hey, there, X10. Take it easy," he murmured.

"Miranda— where—" My voice broke.

"We don't know," Delbert's voice was strained. "Jason's talkin' to the state police. We'll find her."

"No, I've got to get—" I tried to sit up, but pain shot through me, and I gasped.

A nurse came in with a syringe and injected something into my IV. "You need to stay still."

As soon as she was done, Jason came in with one of the State Troopers, who took a statement. Interestingly enough, I came up clean with no warrants. No one was looking for me. I had to tell them about Miranda, though, which changed everything. The trooper left but said someone from Lexington would be by to talk to me. Bureau agents, I was sure. I had to get out before they showed up.

"The doc said you got a gunshot wound. It pierced the lung but stopped. He wasn't using hollow points, so it didn't fragment. You're lucky," Jason told me when he strode back into the room, his voice choked.

Lucky? Nothing about this felt lucky. Images of Miranda being dragged away, my fingers grasping for her, and the burning in my chest all flashed through my mind.

"What did they say?" Delbert asked.

"What the fuck do you think," Jason shot back. "They'll look for her. But they won't tell me anything else."

Delbert shook his head. "Well, these motherfuckers are in for a fuckin' surprise. I'm gonna find Leeland myself and carve his fuckin' head open like a pumpkin' on Halloween."

"I need to find her," I said, my voice firmer now. "But right now, I need to get out of here."

"You need to heal. We'll find her," Jason reassured me, but his eyes were grim.

"Go get the rest of the boys, and let's start diggin' out the long guns," I heard Jason say as my eyes closed for a moment. "You still got that Barrett Uncle Charlie left for you? I think it's time we turn the fuckin' tables. The Patriots of the Thirteen, my ass, more like the dead fuckin' patriots."

Their words became indistinct and unfocused, and I fought the sedative, but my arms were too heavy to lift. My thoughts became leaden, and I couldn't focus. The sedative the nurse gave me started to pull me under; I fought against it with a mixture of terror for Miranda and rage at the men who took her. *Delbert's right about one thing, these sorry sons of bitches are in for the worst fucking surprise of their short ass lives. They have no idea the can of whup-ass they opened.*

Then darkness claimed me again.

CHAPTER THIRTY-FOUR
Sarah

I wasn't out long. My body was one big bruise, and every breath seemed to pull shards of glass into my lungs. My right side hurt like hell, but I needed to get to get back to the cabin. Delbert was resting in the chair next to me.

"Help me up, Del." My voice was weak and almost tiny sounding.

"You need to stay here," Delbert said, but he started helping me out of the bed anyway.

"If the feds show before we leave, I'm fucked. I gotta get out of here now," I bitched. Delbert supported me as I wobbled out of the room and started limping down the hallway.

"What do you think you're doing, Ms. Rogers," one of the nurses said, a young Filipino man. He blocked our way.

"Sir, I don't mean no disrespect," I gritted out through my teeth. "But if you don't get out of my way, I'm gonna tear these butterflies open flattening your ass."

"Just a second, let me at least get the AMA paperwork," he said and stalked off.

The nurse came back with papers and a plastic bag. I desperately searched the bag, digging for Miranda's locket. I wasn't sure why I was so desperate for it all of a sudden, but it felt like a promise—like as long as it was around my neck, she was still alive. It was stupid, I knew, but still, I felt a sense of purpose as I finally found it and dropped it over my head.

"You need to stay," the nurse said as I signed the paperwork in all the places he indicated.

"I can't," I grunted in pain. "You don't understand. It's safer for everyone if I leave here."

"Quit arguin', Sarah. Let's go," Del said as he and Jason helped me out of a side exit and into the truck, which was parked not far away.

The ride back was quiet and relatively smooth now that we weren't flying over the dirt road to the cabin. My chest felt like it was on fire as Del drove back to Mom's.

"I need to get my stuff from the cabin," I grunted as they hoisted me out of the truck.

"No," Jason said firmly. "You need to lay down and lay low. The cabin will be crawling with cops and feds soon."

Jason handed me a pill. "Take this."

"What is it?" I asked, pretty sure I knew the answer.

"Percoset," He replied, and I scowled, but now wasn't the time to argue with him about his side gig. I took the pill to quell the pain.

"If they don't find me in the cabin, they'll just come back," I said. "There's really no safe place." Safe. Something about that tickled at the back of my head. 'Safe,' Miranda had said when she'd fingered the locket. "Fuck me," I whispered as Del set me on the bed in my room.

"Sorry, sis," Del said as he tried to make me comfortable.

"No, it's not that," I whispered, trying to breathe gently and keep quiet. I sat up carefully on the bed and took the locket from around my neck, opening it up. I dug a fingernail under the gold filigree around Miranda's picture, and it popped open. The photo slipped out, but there, behind it, sat a small SD card, like you might use for a camera.

"Son of a bitch," I said softly. "I'd had it all the time. Miranda, I love you, but God, you're dumb." She should have given it to me right off, and we could have avoided most of this, assuming it wasn't her summer swimsuit pictures, but I doubted that.

"Del," I grunted again, trying to get air. "Give me your phone, and hand me my wallet from the bag over there."

Del did as I asked, and I pulled out the card I was looking for, dialing the number on the plain white card stock emblazoned with the FBI logo.

Walters answered in typical law enforcement fashion with a crisp, "Special Agent Walters."

I wheezed a little, then, swallowing, I spoke as clearly as I could. "Agent Walters, this is Sarah Rogers. I know where Miranda Reichert is, and I'll make you a deal."

"I'm listening," he said. His voice was impassive, but I detected just a hint of interest.

When I hung up forty minutes later, Delbert was sitting on the edge of the bed. "Are you nuts?" He asked, incredulous at the conversation.

"No, Del. If I'd known I had this," I held up the SD card, "I would have called him straight away. This is our ticket out of trouble. In any event, I need your help with a few things."

Del looked at me. "What is it? That thing we talked about at Jester's?"

I nodded. "Yeah, that. And I need you to go get me some clean clothes from the cabin—it doesn't matter what, just something comfortable. Grab the spare vest in the gun safe, too. It's under the floorboards in the guest room. There's a trapdoor-style panel that just lifts out, so don't go nuts. The combination is Mamaw's birthday."

"There's a gun safe at the Cabin?" He asked, eyes wide.

"Yeah, it's papaw's. There are two rifles in there, including your .308, but I just need my vest."

"You know, Sarah. I haven't shot since the war."

I could see the pain in his eyes. He really didn't want to do what I was asking, and I was asking a lot. A constant life of vigilance and killing in the war is what had sent him to the bottom of a bottle in the first place.

"Del, you don't have to if it's too—"

"No," he interrupted. "I just hope I'm up to it."

I nodded solemnly. "Are you sure?"

He scoffed. "What good is therapy and AA if I can't do what's needed for family when I need to? I'll keep you alive. I promise."

"Okay," I said. As he stood to leave, I quickly added, "And Del —thanks."

He just gave me a curt nod and left.

I lay on the bed for a long time. I put the SD card back in the locket, snapped the picture back in place, and waited. It would be a couple of hours before Special Agent Walters arrived, so I made the best of it and rested.

Del came back over an hour later with my vest. He was also carrying a .308 hunting rifle with a scope. "So, the jig is up. Leeland knows you're not dead. His guys were crawling the cabin, and I had to wait for them to leave."

I sighed. That was something I'd been afraid of.

CHAPTER THIRTY-FIVE
Miranda

Leeland punched me in the face a third time. "You're gonna tell me everything you know! You got that missy?"

I spat blood to the ground and watched a molar drop, but I just laughed. "You hit like a girl, Honeycutt. My husband hit me harder than that. Why don't you do something besides these love taps."

"No one's coming for you, Miranda," he growled. "Just tell us what we want to know, and you can leave. Everyone knows by now that you had your husband murdered."

I tried to roll my eyes, but my left one was swelling shut. "That's not going to fly, and you know it. As soon as they examine Mitchell's computer, the FBI's going to be coming for the whole fucking lot of you."

Honeycutt started to laugh. "Gina wiped it the day after you left. Mitchell made sure no one would see what was there. You must think we're amateurs."

I smirked at him. "Well then, I guess you have nothing to worry about. Of course, there's the backup I made of the hard drive before I left. It took forever, but I'm pretty sure I got everything."

Honeycutt's leering grin vanished, and his face flushed with rage. "Where the fuck is it? Where's this so-called backup."

"It's in a safe place, Leeland," I answered as sweetly as the pain would let me. "You won't have to worry about it for long."

He knelt on his haunches in front of me and put his hand under my chin. I jerked it away, but he gripped it tightly, sending a lance of pain through my jaw, probably fractured. I closed my eyes. I was so tired of all of this. I started wishing the bullet had hit me instead of Mitchell. Then Sarah would've been safe, and my problems would be over.

"Miranda, she's dead. She's not coming to rescue you, so you can stop wasting my time and trying to act tough." Leeland stepped away to a table, whacking his forehead on the lamp hanging from the ceiling, causing it to swing slightly. The pendulum motion of the lamp revealed more of the room. It was small, maybe ten-foot square, with concrete walls and a single door. There were a few file boxes in one corner. If I'd had to guess, I was in a basement, probably in Leeland's home. I wasn't sure since they'd bagged me as soon as they'd put me in the car.

"Show me her body," I spat at him. "Then I'll believe that Sarah's dead and not before."

He just slugged me again, catching me in my temple and rocking my head sideways. Dizziness enveloped my senses for a moment, and I sagged in the chair.

"Give it a rest, Leeland," a voice said from behind me. His accent was thick and Russian. "You can't just beat it out of her like that. Women don't break like that. Besides, we have plenty of time."

Leeland looked over the top of my head. "Fine," he said and stalked out of the room into a darkened hallway, slamming the door behind him.

The man behind me finally moved into my view, coming around and going to one knee in front of me. "That man is a thug," he said, taking a wet cloth and pressing it to my face, wiping away the blood. "But, soon, he's going to ask me to find out where you put the backup, and then, well, I won't be so nice. I used to work for the FSB. You know the FSB?" At my silence, he added, "Of course you do."

I just stared at him through my one good eye, but I could feel the icy spike of fear sinking into my chest. I didn't want this man anywhere near me. Leeland, I could understand. As the man said, he was a thug, but the possibility of a murder rap scared him. But this man in front of me, his eyes were dead, lifeless, the eyes of a killer.

"In the early days, my job was to get information from spies and informants and traitors. I was very good at it. It won't take long before you don't know which way is up, I'm afraid. So give that some thought."

I lowered my head and gave him a whispered "Fuck you."

He finished wiping the blood off my face and left, closing and locking the door behind him.

Time moved in fits and starts. Often, when Mitchell was faced with getting votes for a particularly difficult piece of legislation, I'd dangle the carrot in front of his fellow party members, promising one perk or another in their own legislation. Not directly, of course, just by suggestion. Then I'd let them sit on that for some time, waiting, pushing Mitchell to keep his mouth shut on it until the time was right, then I'd suggest we'd decided not to help them out in their state.

It was extremely effective when looking at things like base closings or other needs they had. Once, we held up aid for Eastern Kentucky flooding for three weeks to push one of Mitchell's bills. Eventually, the party leader in the senate came to us asking for us to back off, offering to bring one of Mitchell's bills to the floor and get it passed. That's what Leeland's little Russian minion was doing now. Making me sweat it out.

He had offered me an olive branch, getting the blood off my face. The stick, in this case, wasn't implied, though. He'd made it clear what would happen if I refused to cooperate. The trick to this type of negotiation was not to let it drag on too long. If that happened, the other party might just give up and move on to something else—or, in my case, just decide they had nothing to lose and eliminate me.

With Sarah dead, no one was coming. I really did have nothing to lose. If I gave up the SD card, which they'd obviously failed to find on Sarah's body, they would just kill me, and Mitch Jr. would probably slide right into his father's spot and become president. I wasn't going to let that happen if for no other reason than spite. They'd taken Sarah. I was going to take this from them.

CHAPTER THIRTY-SIX
Sarah

Six hours later, my phone rang. I let it ring three times before picking it up. I was pretty sure I knew who it was. "Rogers," I said quietly.

"You want your bitch back?" It was Leeland.

"If you've done anything to her, I'll kill you myself," I threatened. I had to make it sound convincing. *Yup, just the hillbilly girl all by herself goin' off.*

"She's a little roughed up, but if you want all of her parts still attached, you'll bring me that locket of yours, unopened, to my home at four o'clock this afternoon—alone."

I took a moment to collect myself. "Fine. I'll be there. But Leeland, this ain't D.C., Louisville, or Lexington. This is the sticks boy, and if you harm a hair on her head, there'll be no end to the world of redneck shit we drop on you. She's family. So don't fuck around. There are two laws out here. One's in your pocket, the other you can't buy."

"Don't you worry? If you bring me that locket, I'll happily let the two of you loose. You have my word."

I rolled my eyes. *Like that was worth something. He'd have one of his goons kill us both.* "Fine. I'll see you there alone at four. But I want to talk to her first."

"No, you don't get to talk to *her* until I get what I want."

"And you don't get what you want until I know she's still alive," I tossed back, voice firm.

"Fine." There was a moment of silence, the sound of a door, and then I heard Leeland say, "Here, your dyke bitch wants to talk to you."

"Sarah?" Miranda's voice was tiny and pained. He'd surely beaten her; there was no way he'd know about the locket otherwise. She wouldn't have given it up and put me in danger. "Sarah, I thought you were dead. Don't do it. Just let me go. I'm not worth—"

A slap. Miranda's pained grunt and then Leeland's voice. I flinched and closed my eyes, my left hand clenching and unclenching. I could take that kind of abuse, but she couldn't, and I knew it. Miranda didn't deserve this. She'd been beaten and abused all her life. I was going to get her out of this in one piece. And maybe protect her a little better.

"Shut up, bitch," Leeland shouted at her. "There, as you can hear, she's still alive. I'll see you at four Rogers, alone. And you know what happens if I get a whiff of the law."

"Yeah, I know. I'll see you there," I growled and hung up.

"Damn," Walters swore, staring at me as I handed back the phone, and he set it aside. "Did we get all that?" he asked his technician.

"Yes, sir," the older man replied, taking a couple of moments to play back the entire conversation for us.

"How do you want to play this?" Walters asked me as he leaned against the wall, a firm scowl on his face.

"He won't kill her," I said. "Leeland's a coward. Even if he's busted, he doesn't want a murder rap. So we do this straight up, breach and rescue. But promise me your men will be careful."

Walters nodded. "You have my word."

My mother brought in fried chicken and mashed potatoes for everyone, and they relaxed and ate while we waited for Walter's guys to come back and tell us what we were facing.

Delbert returned first. "Well, there's a hide out there," he said loudly as he opened the door. Then he spotted Agent Walters and snapped his jaws shut.

I introduced them, brushing past the slip. "Special Agent Walters, this is my brother, Detective Del Rogers."

Walters stood and shook his hand politely, but I could see his eyes narrow. He was likely wondering why an officer of the law hadn't passed on the location of his sister and, more importantly, Miranda, the chief suspect in a murder investigation.

"Give it a rest, Walters," I grumbled, pulling his gaze back to mine. "You should be thankful. You're about to have the biggest bust of your career and stop a bunch of maniacs from turning this country into a fascist state."

"Don't even think about arresting my daughter," Mom snapped at Walters, and I had to hide my snicker when Walters flinched. "You should be thanking your lucky stars she didn't join that bunch of idiots over at Leeland's. She and Miranda could have just hid out for a while and then skated."

Walter's men returned and walked into the dining room, forestalling any response from the chagrined Agent.

"Well?" He said as the three men, Jensen, Pratt, and Anderson, sat down with us, and my mother started putting out plates; God love her.

"There are seven men with semi-automatic rifles patrolling the fenceline and probably a few more inside." One of the men pulled a map of the grounds rough drawn on a legal pad from the bag he'd been carrying. "It's not a fortress, but it won't be an easy breach if we decide to go that route."

Walters shook his head. "We can't have a prolonged standoff. The longer they have to decide they're not getting out of it, the more likely they are to kill Ms. Reichert. And I don't want another Waco or Ruby Ridge if we can avoid it."

Walters reached down, pulled a map from his briefcase, and spread it out. "The property is a hundred acres. How many men out front?"

"Just two," Pratt said, poking a thick finger at the map, indicating the front gate and a low wall. "Here and here. Around the rest is shitty barbed wire."

Delbert jerked his head quickly from behind the men, and I rose painfully, following him into the kitchen. "Are you sure this is the best way to go?" he whispered. "Won't Leeland kill her?"

I shook my head. "No. As far as Leeland knows, he has the upper hand. Even if we show up with a gaggle of Bureau agents, he won't get his hands dirty. He'll want her to die at someone else's hand. That's why I need you out there, Del."

He nodded. "Is he any good?"

I nodded solemnly. "One of the best. But, if you can't—"

He shook his head. "No, sissy. I'll take care of it."

We stepped back into the dining room just as the men were wrapping up. Delbert didn't even say goodbye as he stalked out the front door. I heard his truck fire up and head down the road.

"So, what did you decide?" I asked as if I didn't already know what they'd do.

"Straight in," Walters said. "Fast and hard. Avoid a standoff. The warrant is in. The Louisville SAC will meet us there with a team."

I gave Walters an imploring look. "Don't screw this up."

Walters walked over and put a hand on my shoulder. "I won't. I told you. You have my word."

I strapped on my vest and winced at the pain but nodded and lifted my wrists. Walters placed the cuffs on me.

"Sarah Lou Rogers, you are under arrest on suspicion of murder and obstruction of justice. You have the right to remain silent. If you give up this right, anything you say may be held in court against you. You have the right to an attorney. If you cannot afford an attorney, one will be appointed to you by the court. Do you understand your rights?"

"I do," I said, my voice full of exasperated resignation as my mother sat down and started to cry.

"Mom," I said. "Stop. It'll be fine. And tell Dad to stay calm. This will all be over shortly, I promise. I'll call as soon as I can."

A few minutes later, Walters got a call, and we left.

Pratt and Anderson led me out and placed me in the back of Walter's Suburban. I pushed back the burning in my eyes. Truthfully, this was all a risk. I had no real idea what was on that chip I'd given Walters. And if Miranda didn't survive this, there would be no one to testify as to its authenticity. So many things could go wrong. But Wild West rescues where the hero—or heroine—takes on twenty men and comes out alive and intact never happen. That was only in the movies.

We were banking on the idea that Leeland wouldn't want his home destroyed or to go down for murder. I'd known Leeland for years, and he'd expect he could weasel out of this in court. In his mind, even if convicted, Mitch Jr. would become President this year and pardon him.

CHAPTER THIRTY-SEVEN
Sarah

There was a small army of SUVs, two ambulances, and one armored vehicle camped on the side of the main road just before the turnoff to Leeland's. For a moment, I wondered where they'd picked up the APC. Clearly, they were expecting a lot more trouble than I was.

Another quarter mile up the road, I spotted Del's old Ford sitting empty on the opposite side, where the road butted up against the woods around Leeland's property. I closed my eyes and prayed for him, something I almost never did, for anything. Then I sat perfectly still for a moment, getting the butterflies in check, as we pulled to a stop, and Walters got out, leaving me inside.

A cold spike of anxiety and fear drove through me as I thought about Miranda and what was about to happen. But there was nothing for it. After Ruby Ridge and Waco, the FBI didn't play around. Armed militias were met with overwhelming force in a situation like this, especially when there was a high-profile hostage like Miranda.

But it wasn't Leeland or his goons that worried me. Most of them weren't military, and when confronted with something like what I was seeing here, probably fifty men and an APC, they'd lay down their arms. It was Petrovich.

After a few minutes, Walters got back in the SUV. "Are you ready?" he asked me.

I held up my handcuffed hands. "I guess. Would you mind taking these off? You can trust me not to cause trouble."

"I can't, Ms. Rogers. Sorry," Walters said flatly, shaking his head.

"Come on, Walters. You know we didn't do this. You have to by now."

"Doesn't matter. Officially, you're still a suspect and under arrest."

"You fucking boy scout," I shot back hotly.

"Hey!" Walters snapped. "I brought you along, didn't I? I gave you the option on this, didn't I? That's way off-book. If I were you, I'd be thankful that I called all this in, especially since we don't even know what's on that SD card. It's my ass if either of you is lying."

I snapped my mouth shut. He was right. He'd been more than gracious so far.

"Warrant clean?" I asked after a moment of silence.

"The Warrant's clean. We're leaving in five," Walters said, holding up a folded piece of paper. "No knock, no nonsense. When the shooting starts, keep your head down."

"What's the plan?" I asked, more than a little anxious.

"The plan is that you'll keep quiet and let us do our jobs. You, of all people, should know the drill on this, Rogers."

I nodded. He was right. This was in the hands of the Bureau and a fair few of the Kentucky State Patrol now. I glanced at my watch, practically willing it to move.

Finally, just a few minutes later, the call came over the radio. "All units, in position. Move out."

Following about five cars back from the APC, we drove up the road to Leeland's. The APC didn't even stop at the gate where two men stood, just mowing down the wrought iron as the two militiamen dodged aside. Out of the trees, four men in tactical uniforms, two on each side of the convoy, emerged and jerked the men away from the road, disarming and zip-tying them.

An explosion rocked the APC, and I gasped, but it seemed undamaged as it trundled on and men opened fire from the gun ports. Four other men in camo who'd had the bad luck to be on either side of the APC went down in short order. An old Russian

RPG lay on the ground in front of one of them. *Idiots,* I thought. These men had been so suckered in by Leeland's bullshit that they'd laid down their lives for a criminal—just stupid. Then we were through the gate, and I laid down in the back just as a few rounds whapped against the side of our SUV.

Walters swerved the vehicle to a stop, and he popped out. There were a few more random shots, and then everything went quiet.

I poked my head up. At least a dozen men had thrown down their rifles and were either on their knees or running away, only to be snatched up by men emerging from the surrounding woods. I waited a few minutes more to see if anything else was going to happen. Then, when I figured it was all quiet, I lifted up and opened the passenger-side rear door and got out.

"Rogers! Get back in the car," Walters snapped.

I ignored him and stepped around the SUV. There was a big black mark on the side of the APC, and the center tire was flat, but it was otherwise undamaged. Out on the sprawling lawn of the estate, at least twenty men were all being moved into a line to kneel in the dirt. This was going to make Walter's career, I thought.

I looked at the house. A six-man team was moving up to the front doors with a ram. The doors gave on the first hit, and they funneled inside. There was sporadic gunfire that made my heart skip a beat. But even that didn't last long.

I looked at my watch and couldn't help but chuckle. It was four PM on the dot.

"Well, Leeland," I muttered. "We said four o'clock, and here we are."

The next thirty minutes were the longest of my life as I listened to the radio from just outside the SUV.

"Contact," one man said calmly, then another voice crackled in, "Down. Moving."

"Move," the first man said.

The entire event was surreal. I'd never been on an operation quite like this. The breach team was clearly working with military precision, and the surreal experience of hearing their live communications over the radio was almost indescribable. My heart banged in my chest, and I found myself almost hyperventilating.

"Get down on your knees!" A man shouted through the radio. "Get down on your knees, now!"

Then, it was quiet for several moments, and finally, I heard the words I'd been praying for. "We've got her. She's alive. Coming out. Call in EMS."

Tears sprung from my eyes, and I wiped at them furiously with the back of my cuffed hands. She was okay. She was going to be alright.

I looked around again. One Bureau agent in a suit was holding his arm and being treated with first aid by another. It looked like a bullet graze. Otherwise, everyone was unharmed on our side.

I looked back toward the door again and saw her. "Oh, God!" I gasped.

CHAPTER THIRTY-EIGHT
Miranda

Before the Russian returned—Petrovich, I thought his name was —all holy hell seemed to break loose upstairs. I heard the pop-pop of weapons fire and loud voices. Boots clopped across the floor above me, along with radio chatter. Then, it was suddenly very quiet, and the slow steps of someone moving down the stairs sounded from the hallway outside.

"I'm down here," I squeaked through my parched throat. "Help. Anybody."

"Ms. Reichert?" A man's deep bass called from the other side of the door. "Is anyone in there with you?"

I shook my head in my stunned state, which only made it ache worse. "No," I whimpered. "No. Please get me out." For a moment, I believed this had to be a trick. Some kind of psychological warfare. They were going to pretend to rescue me, only to push me into another place and torture me more.

The door battered open, falling half off its hinges, and several men in fatigues and helmets carrying military-issue rifles swarmed in. One of them used a pair of bolt cutters to snap the chain on my handcuffs, and I sagged forward, almost falling before another of the men caught me. "It's okay, Ms. Reichert. We've got you. You're safe. US Marshals Service." He pulled up his goggles and slid the black gaiter from his face. He had a black beard, a narrow nose, and some of the kindest blue eyes I'd ever seen. "Ms. Rogers is waiting outside."

Relief flooded through me. Despite the brief phone call, I'd had a hard time believing Sarah was really alive. Some irrational part of me, the same one that had conjured up ideas of a fake rescue, had believed it had been a trick. "What about the Russian?" I asked through now furious sobs. "Did you get him?"

"I'm not sure who all we have lined up outside. But let's get you safe." He replaced his gater and picked me up out of the chair as if I weighed nothing, carrying me down a short hallway and up a set of stairs into a large, well-appointed living room. A wide glass picture window showed a large swimming pool and manicured back lawn. The place was in ruins. Various bits of glass and pottery littered the floor from destroyed plants and nicknacks. The floor had several splintered divots from bullet impacts.

Moments later, we reached the grand entrance. Large double doors of solid oak lay akimbo, and I could see sunlight streaming from the outside.

"Put me down," I said finally. "I can walk."

"Are you sure?"

I nodded. I didn't want Sarah to see me being carried out. She'd freak.

Passing through the columned portico, I finally saw light for the first time in three days. My chest burned from the massive cut across it, a scar I'd have forever. I squinted, scanning the line of cars spread across the front lawn of the sprawling estate with my one good eye until it landed on Sarah, who leaned against one of the SUVs with that crooked smile that I loved so much. It didn't reach her eyes where pain and misery sat. She was likely blaming herself, I thought.

I was happy to see she was alive and not dead, but the pain in my abdomen and my swollen right eye dampened my spirit almost as much as the realization of how much risk I'd brought to the Rogers family by my very presence. I realized it would never be over. There would be trials and probably more attempts on my life.

I had to do something. I hadn't really appreciated Sarah's commitment, not fully until this moment. Of course, then I saw she was cuffed. Sarah tried to play it off, gesturing with them and shrugging, but I knew. I had ruined her life. She'd been arrested and would be further detained, maybe even prosecuted for obstruction.

I heard something then; it sounded almost like the buzzing of a bee whizzing past my ear. The crack of a rifle shot sounded, and I looked around. Before I could react, I heard another whizz and a thump as something heavy hit me in the chest and knocked me to the ground, forcing the breath from my lungs. "Jesus," I groaned, realizing that Sarah lay on top of me.

"Sniper!" Someone shouted.

"Stay down," Sarah wheezed. There was a massive hole in her bulletproof vest.

"Oh, God," I shouted. "Help! Help!"

A third rifle report sounded, this time from another direction, and the entire scene grew very quiet.

Men moved around. Binoculars appeared from seemingly nowhere as they scanned the treeline. Then I saw him, Delbert, in a ghillie suit, walking from the woods with a rifle held over his head. I couldn't concentrate on him, though. I just kept rocking Sarah.

"Please be okay! Please be okay! Please, Sarah, I love you. Please be okay."

Slowly, a dim smile spread across her features, and her eyes fluttered open dramatically. "Do you, now? Well, I love you, too."

"Shhh," I said softly. "Don't try to talk?"

The smile grew wider. "I'm okay. Probably a cracked sternum, but my vest stopped it. But that rocking really hurts." She reached up her cuffed hands and tenderly stroked the back of my cheek as the tears started again.

"You bitch," I whispered softly, but there was nothing in it.

I looked around again. I was responsible for all of this: the officer lying in the driveway being treated for a gunshot wound, the hole I could see dead-center of Sarah's shirt, the remains of a bullet peeking through from the vest. She'd come that close to dying. "Jesus," I whispered. "I just can't do this anymore."

"It's over, Miranda. I promise," Sarah said, the backs of her knuckles still brushing my jawline.

"Detective Rogers," A man in a suit greeted as Del walked up.

"You'll find your sniper that way," he pointed into the woods on the far eastern side. "He's dead. Sarah had a hunch they might try to use him as a last resort, so she had me come out here and find him."

Then it hit me. Scout sniper. Del had been a Scout Sniper in the Marine Corps during the war.

He set down the rifle and walked through the dumbfounded men toward us.

"How are you sis? Sorry. I wasn't able to draw a bead on him until the cold shot."

Sarah coughed, and a bit of blood stained her lips. "I know. I'll be fine. How are you?"

Del seemed to consider the question, then gave a soft, serene smile. "I'm okay. I think I'll be fine. This was different. Now, let's get you some help."

As Sarah was loaded into the back of an ambulance, one of the agents gently took my arm and guided me to an SUV. "Ms. Reichert, I'm Special Agent Walters, FBI. Ms. Rogers will be fine, but we need to get you to the hospital, too. Then I'm afraid we have questions for both of you."

CHAPTER THIRTY-NINE
Miranda

Two days later, I woke to find a long line of staples down my chest and one whole side of my face bandaged. Sarah sat next to me, bolt upright and obviously in pain.

"Hey there," she said softly, standing with a grimace and stroking the side of my face. "How are you feeling?"

"What are you doing in here? You're still hurt. I could have gotten you killed."

"I'll be fine. A cracked sternum, that's all. Oh, and I popped my stitches when I fell."

Stroking my jawline, Sarah looked deep into my eyes, and I felt lost in her stunning blue gaze once more. I wanted nothing more than to sink into her and disappear entirely, but I knew I couldn't. She'd really taken a bullet for me this time. If I stayed with her, she would never be safe.

"Why didn't you leave me?" I whispered. "You could have. You should have just let it go."

Sarah scowled at me. "I would never do that. Why would you even—"

"Because I'm not worth all this. Don't you know that?" I turned away, unable to meet her eyes any longer.

Sarah placed her palm against the left side of my face. "What I know is that you've got the sense of a squirrel playing possum in the middle of the road."

I brushed away her hand. There was only one way to get

through to this stubborn woman. I sat as upright as I could manage and looked Sarah in the eye. "I can't do this." My voice was shaky and drug-hazed but firm. "I don't want to do this. I want to get back to my life in D.C. As it is, I have a million things to clean up and an inheritance to fight for. Stop acting as if there's a future for us. There's not."

"What?" Sarah whispered harshly. "But I thought?"

"Thought what? That we'd leave D.C., and I'd just move down to this podunk town in the middle of nowhere and hang out with your redneck family? This isn't the life I want, Sarah. I told you. I wasn't born to live like a pauper. I was born to fight and stand on my own. I've done that all my life. Some of this was nice. But now, it's over." I turned away.

Sarah put her hand on my arm. "Why are you sayin' all this? Is it because I got shot? I made my own choices. I did what I thought was right. That's not your responsibility. It's mine. That's my risk to take."

"It doesn't matter. I don't want this anymore." But I couldn't really decide what that actually meant, even as I said the words. *I don't want this—what was this? My life in D.C. That's what I didn't want, wheeling and dealing in the corridors of power—* But then I stopped myself, stomping on my indecision before I could cave to selfishness. *No. No. I can't stay. I just can't. I've already done enough damage.*

"How can you say that?" Sarah whispered. "I'm in love with you, and you're in love with me. I can see it."

I swallowed hard at those words. "No, Sarah. I'm not. We had a good time, but I need to go back. I can't be here."

"Liar," Sarah whispered, her face angry and accusing as she spun on her heel and walked gingerly from the room, obviously still nursing a more serious wound than she let on.

After another two days of recuperation, Agent Walters collected us.

I sat next to Sarah in absolute silence, me in my wheelchair, her in hers. I could feel her eyes on me, but I steadfastly refused to look at her. But it was so hard, and tears burned at the backs of my eyes. I just wanted to throw myself at her.

Moments later, two typical bureau vehicles pulled around, and

Walters helped me out of the chair. As he cuffed my hands in front of me, he asked, "That's not too tight, is it?"

I shook my head.

He assisted me into the back of a waiting car, and I finally breathed a sigh of relief. I'd been so close to cracking, to giving in. This was for the best.

For just a second, I hazarded a glance out the window and watched as they pushed Sarah into another car and slammed shut the door. Sarah glanced my way, and I tore my gaze away, not just to avoid the pain on Sarah's face but so the woman couldn't see the shame and hurt on my own.

I was doing the right thing. I knew that now. Somehow, I'd get Sarah out of this mess. It wasn't her problem anymore.

A private jet was waiting for us both in Lexington. Apparently, no one was taking any chances, and this was of the highest priority. I sat stoically in the painful, icy silence. Sarah tried several times to get my attention, but I ignored her, looking out the window until she stopped.

I had expected to hear Sarah say something rude, like 'bitch' or 'whore' or any of a dozen other nasty things. She should have, but she didn't. After a while, Sarah finally turned to look out the window on her side, and I took a moment to watch her. All I wanted to do was offer Sarah some kind of comfort. But I didn't dare. Anything I said would open the flood of emotion pent up inside me. If I continued to tell myself that Sarah was just the hired help and treated her that way, they'd leave her alone. It would all land on me, of that I was certain. It was my head they wanted, not Sarah's.

I deserved it. I deserved every heaping of scorn, and every minute I spent in jail over this. I'd been a hypocrite and a horrible human being. I'd helped push a hateful agenda just as I'd been screwing another woman. And most importantly, I'd almost gotten Sarah killed twice. The only saving grace in all of this was that Sarah hadn't died.

I was so lost in my own misery that I didn't realize Sarah had turned to look back at me until she spoke, pinning me with her green eyes and a soft smile. "I am in love with you, Miranda. And when this is all over, you'll know where to find me."

I looked away again, blinking back tears. I turned my head as far as I could and stared out the window once more. I wasn't going to let her see me cry. Finally, after pulling my face back under control, I leaned back and closed my eyes.

'She's dead. She's not coming for you, so you might as well tell us. We'll let you go.' The words rang in my head, and the horror that had filled me—I couldn't go through that again. There were others out there. I would never be safe again, but at least Sarah would be.

After an hour, we landed at Dulles, and as we walked through the Jet Port, I snorted mirthlessly. Right back where we had started, where Sarah had dropped me off that morning. *Had it only been three weeks?*

Somehow, returning to this place seemed fitting, a full circle. But then again, it wasn't. I wasn't the same anymore. A deep, crushing depression filled me, along with a desperate sense that something was very wrong with the world from which I'd come.

This city was a cesspool of corruption and misery from which sprouted a hurricane of madness that engulfed the nation time after time. Constant fighting by politicians who didn't believe a word that came from their lips, at least most of them. And if they did, they were all too ready to compromise their beliefs. *You should know, Miranda,* I thought. *You're one of them.*

This city, I decided, destroyed everyone it touched. And with that grim thought, Sarah and I slid into separate cars as the waiting FBI agents took us away.

CHAPTER FORTY
Miranda

We were escorted to the Hoover Building, the ugly rectangular office building on Pennsylvania Avenue, where I was placed in an interview room. There was an odd irony that we were within spitting distance of the White House, just seven blocks away. I requested no lawyer. Sarah would have probably had kittens about that, but I wanted to get this over with. I honestly hadn't done anything wrong, and the agents were more likely to tell me something about the situation without a lawyer present, although that was a long shot.

Agent Walters and a female agent I didn't recognize entered the room, dropping into the seats on the other side of the table.

"Mrs. Reichert?"

"Danbury." I corrected quietly as I assumed the disguise I'd worn all my life, the aloof Senator's wife and the daughter of an archetypal Connecticut family of means. My hands were still folded in my lap, and my posture was straight, but my legs were crossed at the knee. A protective position, Sarah had said. One which implied that I was uncomfortable, which I was. But I also wanted to portray that. It was important that these agents see me as prim, proper, respectful, and, most of all, cowed by the situation. I'd never noticed these subtle manipulations in my behavior until Sarah had pointed them out.

"I'm sorry, Ms. Danbury," Walters corrected.

"Am I under arrest?"

"No, ma'am," Agent Walters said. "Should you be?"

"You handcuffed both Ms. Rogers and me in Kentucky and kept us that way all the way here. I assumed I was under arrest for something."

"I'm Special Agent Allred," the woman finally said, and I scanned her up and down, taking her measure. She was over five-nine, clearly well-toned, CrossFit if I didn't miss my guess by the muscular body, small breasts, and firm veined hands. Clearly, she was the senior agent between them, just based on the way she held herself, sitting a little behind Walters, letting the young man do the heavy lifting while she watched. "That was a precaution. As of right now, there are several accusations being leveled at you and Ms. Rogers. We're just trying to get to the bottom of them."

"You will find," I stated impatiently, "around Ms. Rogers' neck, a locket. Within is all that you need to understand what happened in Davenport."

Walters gave a slight smile, though it didn't reach his eyes. "We already have the SD card. Ms. Rogers provided it when we arrested her in Kentucky."

I blinked. "She's under arrest? In God's name, why?"

"At this point, there seems to have been some— misunderstanding as to her role in Senator Reichert's death. As Special Agent Allred said, several accusations have been made." Walters then relaxed slightly as I frowned at him. "You're not aware that she's been accused of orchestrating your husband's assassination?"

I raised a cool eyebrow and uncrossed my legs, leaning forward and placing my arms on the table, hands in front of me, but unfolded. My voice was level but full of the barely controlled fury I felt. I spoke slowly and deliberately. "That is preposterous. Sarah had nothing to do with Mitchell's death. She has been my bodyguard for months, and I have found her to be respectful, careful, and conscientious about my safety. Furthermore, she has placed herself in harm's way to protect me without question. As far as I'm concerned, she is above reproach."

There was a twitch at the corner of Allred's lips, and I instantly realized my mistake. I'd said 'Sarah,' not 'Ms. Rogers.'

"Are you saying that because you slept with her?" Allred

asked casually.

I smirked, showing no surprise. Everyone knew that by now, anyway. "No, Agent Allred. It is the truth."

"So you don't deny that you had a sexual relationship with Ms. Rogers."

I tilted my head but never removed the smile from my lips. "No, Agent Allred, why would I? Mitchell and I had been estranged for several years. Why do you think he and his cronies tried to have me killed? It's not my fault it backfired on them. Again, the SD card has everything you need to unravel this." I knew where they were headed, and I decided to cut it off. "Now, if I'm not under arrest, then I'd like to leave. If I am, then I'd like a lawyer."

"Give us just a couple of minutes, please," Allred said, then tapped Walters on the shoulder, and the two of them left.

After they left, I took a long, relieved breath. Then, I was left to my own thoughts for quite a while. It was time alone I didn't relish. My heart was in my stomach, and a lump lay in my throat. "Oh, Sarah. Why didn't you just let it go?" I whispered to myself. "You're just too trusting. No one here works for the people."

After almost an hour, Agent Allred returned with a smile on her face. This time, it was genuine and polite, though not really friendly. "Two agents are taking Ms. Roger's statement as we speak."

I pursed my lips in aggravation. "Will she be released?"

"You should worry about yourself," Allred said. "We're still picking apart the data from that SD card. It takes some time for the forensics guys to go through it, following proper procedures. Can I ask you a personal question?"

"What would you like to know?"

"Ms. Rogers told us that you knew you were going to be assassinated. If that was so, why didn't you contact the authorities?"

I rolled my eyes. "It may seem odd now, three weeks after his death, but you have to remember, Agent Allred, my husband was about to enter the presidential election. Furthermore, with a great deal of help from me, he'd managed to accumulate quite a bit of influence here in Washington. So, no, I wasn't keen on going to the authorities. I didn't know who to trust."

"And when did you see the sniper?" Allred asked out of the blue.

I scowled in irritation at the stupid question. "I never saw the sniper. If Ms. Rogers hadn't been so on the ball, I would have died very publicly and very messily. Instead, Ms. Rogers saved my life. It's unfortunate that Mitchell got in the way, but that, I suppose, is what he deserved."

"And did your husband threaten you at all? Were you in fear for your life?"

I sat bolt upright and lifted my chin. I wasn't going to be cowed by something they certainly already knew. "Yes, frequently. And yes, he was physically abusive on occasion. Why are you asking?"

Allred sat back. "Because I'm trying to figure out if what you and Ms. Rogers say is true or if you arranged to have your husband killed because you were having an affair and, in addition, he was an abusive man."

I stared at Allred and narrowed my eyes. "Are you an idiot, Agent Allred?"

Allred raised an eyebrow, then gave a deep frown. "No."

"Good, then let me remind you that I have already asked to leave, and I have asked for a lawyer, so I'm not obliged to tell you anything. But I'll give you this for free. I was terrified of Mitchell. I'm not sorry he's dead, but I wouldn't know the first place to start to have him killed."

I finally lost my poise, raising my voice as my demeanor crumbled and I burst into tears. "He was a bastard. He beat me senseless on several occasions, all of which are documented. He was constantly gaslighting me, threatening me, and treating me with disdain. *'Bitch'* was often his favored pet name for me. And yes, I hated him. But for the last and final time. I didn't have him killed."

There was a knock at the door, and Agent Allred stepped out.

When she returned, two other agents in tow, her attitude and approach did a one-eighty. "Ms. Reich—sorry, Ms. Danbury, we'd like to take you into protective custody."

"Why?" I asked, my face screwing up, completely puzzled.

"We think it would be best for your safety."

"What about Sarah?" I demanded.

"She's already been released," Agent Allred said. "Now, if you please."

"Are you going to protect her?" I asked, my impatience and anger finally winning out over my despondency.

"She's refused protective custody, but we'll be putting a man at her home. Now, can you please go with these two agents? They will help you get what you need from your home and get you to a safe location."

I nodded, relief flooding my chest. Sarah was going to be okay, and that was all that mattered.

CHAPTER FORTY-ONE
Sarah

I sat quietly watching CNN at Mike's as the talking heads detailed the final day of Thatcher's trial. As luck would have it, the Director had been first on the list of Federal officials to go. It had only been six months, but the special prosecutor assigned by the Justice Department had wasted no time putting several people in jail. I'd been fortunate that I hadn't been called for testimony by either side. Of course, it hadn't been needed; my deposition had been enough, and the defense didn't want me within a thousand yards of the stand. Most of Leeland's men had pled out, taking a deal to testify against him, Wiley, and Branford Cash. Cash, in turn, had cut a deal, shortening his sting to testify against several federal officials. Miranda had been on the stand in every single trial so far, mostly attesting to how the data had been gathered. I'd tried to get through to her again in front of the courthouse one day, but she'd just told me to leave her alone. She hadn't been polite about it either, and a stone still sat in my gut.

"Papa says you have to come out and have hot dogs and get away from the TV," Jessica said, her pretty brown eyes glinting in the light.

"Oh, he did, did he?" I replied with a grin. Jessica was a precocious seventeen sporting a beautiful mix of her parents' black and Latin features. She was definitely a heartbreaker, and Mike was trying desperately to keep her focused on school and not boys.

"He said to tell you that if you don't come out to eat, he'll have to shoot you."

"Well, okay then," I laughed and meandered out to the backyard of Mike's two-story Fairfax County home. The grill was on, and the late afternoon sun felt warm and inviting. Jamal was in the pool, diving for quarters or dimes or something, and I could just make out the star-shaped scar on his back where he'd been shot that awful day. It was just a flesh wound, but my vest had three slugs in its back that would have gone right through Jamal if I hadn't pulled him under me. I still had it as a souvenir of that day, a reminder that sometimes, I do it right.

I stopped in the doorway and watched the boy, reminiscing briefly about the entire event, which had lasted all of about six seconds. I had just come out from escorting the VP's daughter into the building when a man opened up in front of the school with a submachine gun. Maria had been in the car with Jessica, about to pull away. Jamal had been right next to me as I walked out. All I had time to do was to put myself between Jamal and the gunman, but it had been enough. Jamal had survived, and that had been my introduction to the brilliant former Special Forces Operator named Michael Taylor, who now worked for an open-source intelligence non-profit that chased down things like war crimes. He'd traded in his MP5 for a keyboard, but he was no less dedicated to what he did.

I sat down at the outdoor table and took the beer that Mike offered. "He's getting big, you know?"

"Well, his dad isn't a small man—or so I hear," I said, gesturing to his six-foot-four frame with a laugh and grinning.

"No," Mike said, patting the outstretched gut of his ragged 'Legends of Hip-Hop' t-shirt.

"Will you stop doing that," Maria called as she walked out, a tray of carne asada resting on her arms. "Now, I promised Sarah carne asada, and she's going to get carne asada."

Mike and I grinned at each other before he stood and took the tray from Maria, who took his place at the small table.

"So, tell me," she said, her brown eyes bright with curiosity and interest. "Have you heard anything from your lady love?"

I shook my head. "Not a word. Now that the trial's over, I'm hoping she might have a few minutes to talk, but I have no idea how to get in touch with her."

Maria slid a piece of paper across the table from her pocket. "I asked one of our mutual friends for her new number."

I stared at the paper, trying to decide whether to take it. Did Miranda even want to hear from me? Probably not. But I wasn't one to listen to that inner voice that told me something would be a bad idea. It was kind of how I'd gotten here. So, I slid the paper into my pocket with a quiet "Thanks."

After getting the meat on the grill, Mike walked over and picked up his beer. "You know, she probably could use your help right about now. Word is that the IRS has taken everything but her clothes."

I looked up at him, my bottom lip securely wedged under my upper teeth, then I sighed. "Might be so. But, honestly, Mike, this is the second time I've had my heart dashed by some rich girl from Connecticut, you know? Same town even."

"Nope. Not buying it." Mike said with a grin and took a swig of his beer. After a long swallow, he continued. "You're just afraid that will happen. As long as I've known you, at least since the accident, you've avoided any kind of relationship, but trust me, you just need to let her know you're still around. She'll come around, eventually. And if she doesn't, you won't feel any worse for it."

The beer was good, and I glanced at the bottle, avoiding the topic. "I always did like a good lager, though I've never really drunk Moosehead before."

"Sarah," Maria said in a warning tone. "Quit dodging."

I rolled my eyes. "Fine. Look. I'll call her."

With a grin, Mike took out his phone. "She's at the Watergate."

I threw my hands up, nearly spilling my beer. "Okay, okay, I surrender. I'll go see her. Can we talk about something else, please?"

With a crooked smile, Mike went back to the grill, a slight swagger in his step at the tiny victory.

I turned to Maria. "What is it with you two?"

"We just want to see you happy, honey. And Mike and I both know stupid when we see it. She's being stupid, and you know

that. Sometimes, a little persistence is all it takes."
I nodded, but I wasn't so sure.

CHAPTER FORTY-TWO
Miranda

I sat across the table from two attorneys, one of whom, a woman named Carol, was speaking to my parents as if I weren't there. "Okay, so we think we can probably claw back about two million in property and assets from the government. It shouldn't take more than a couple of months to process."

"That's good," My mother said and breathed a sigh of relief.

"Well, it's better than nothing," her father muttered, sitting to her right. "If only Mitchell hadn't died."

My head snapped around as I shrieked at him. "Are you fucking kidding me, Dad? The man was a tyrant! He abused me and tried to have me killed! But then again, you probably gave him pointers!"

The lawyer cleared her throat uncomfortably. "Do you want me to give you three a moment?"

"No," I snapped. "This will only take a second."

My father looked about to pop, his face beat red and flushed with anger. "Miranda, I'm warning you—"

"What? What are you going to do here? In this office, with the attorney sitting right there and a camera in the corner of the conference room? What exactly are you going to do?"

He looked nervously up at the camera and then at the attornies who were eyeing him intently. He sat back down.

I smiled maliciously at him. "That's right. You and your precious reputation. What would people think if they knew that you'd beaten me for half my life? Or that you and Mom auctioned me off to Mitchell like he was the highest bidder in a twisted auction of political clout? Social media is so fickle these days. And regarding Mitchell. He tried to take over the country like some kind of mob boss. Fuck that man. As they say in Kentucky, he was dumber than a squirrel playing possum in the middle of the road! Which, by the way, is why all of his cronies and even his lawyer ended up in jail!"

I realized I was standing and staring down at my father. I sat back down. Then I took a moment to look at them all, the two lawyers and my parents. I reveled in the discomfort written on their faces, looking at me as if I were the crazy one there. "No," I said softly.

"No, what?" My father asked, a bemused expression on his face.

"I don't care to spend another day in this town, nor do I want anything of Mitchell's. The government can have all of his shit and everything I bought with his blood money."

"Ms. Reichert—" the male attorney began. I couldn't even remember his name, James or Jack or something. I'd met so many, and they all ran together at this point. I was tired, tired of this nonsense, tired of this town, and tired mostly of sleepless nights where all I could think of was Sarah.

"For the last time, Mr. Filcher, it's Danbury," I corrected, finally remembering the man's apropos name. Then, slowly, I turned my glare to each of my parents. "Mother, Father, if you'll excuse me, I'm leaving. I need to catch a flight." Then I stood, collected my briefcase, and walked to the door. For a moment, I thought of just leaving them, but that wasn't terribly satisfying, and right now, I wanted to be satisfied. "Oh, one more thing," I said, stopping at the door, turning an icy gaze at my father before launching a final salvo. "Fuck you. I'm going to live with my *cousin*, Sarah Lou Rogers. You know, my *girlfriend!* In *Kentucky!*"

I got great satisfaction in walking away from my parents as my mother gasped scandalously, and my father turned about six shades of red and grabbed his left arm. *Serves you right,* I thought. The nearest hospital was two blocks away. He'd probably survive.

With that, I stood and exited the room, a spring in my step and more than a little anxiety in my breast. I was walking out on everything, leaving just under two thousand dollars after I'd paid off these last two attorneys. Being just a witness in a trial was expensive. But the money was enough. It would get me there.

CHAPTER FORTY-THREE
Miranda

When the bus from Lexington let me out at the stop next to the Walmart, I adjusted my meager plain duffel bag and looked around. The IRS had seized everything of note. My bank account was empty. The house, my Mercedes, my jewelry, the furniture, it was all gone. I could have brought my clothes with me, but I didn't. Instead, I'd packed them all up and put them in storage in Maryland. I had no idea when I might get them, and honestly, it didn't matter. I couldn't bring myself to care about a life that had been one long lie.

I began walking, the waxed canvas bag over one shoulder. I thought about what I might say when I got to the cabin, but absolutely nothing came to mind. I was so far out of my depth. After only a few steps, I stopped, unsure of myself. I could just go back. I had enough cash for a return ticket. I could go through the months-long agony of living with my parents while I waited for the IRS to release the lien on the house in D.C. and let me sell it and refund what they'd taken. I wouldn't have to face Sarah, see the heartbreak on her face.

What if she didn't want me here? I thought in a moment of panic. Did I want Sarah to be with me when I'd been pulled from Leeland's place? Of course I did, more than anything, and I'd been an idiot. But that was me, not Sarah. Maybe Sarah had someone with her. She was pretty, and—I stopped myself. No. The only way to find out is to move forward. I was still Miranda

Soo Danbury, and Danbury's didn't cower in the corner. I would sort this out somehow, even if I had to beg.

"Hey there," a voice called from the road next to me. "Need a ride?"

I turned, ready to give whoever this guy was a brush-off, but it was Delbert. "Hey Del, she home?"

"At the cabin," he answered flatly. "Get in."

I threw my cheap duffel in the back of his truck and climbed into the passenger side, closing the door with a loud creak and the bang of a vehicle that had seen more miles than I had after twelve years as a senator's wife.

As we headed down the road, the rain started up again.

"You gonna break her heart again?"

I sighed. "No, Del. I'm not. I'm just hoping she'll see me."

Del snorted a soft laugh. "Oh, she'll see you, alright. I wouldn't worry too much about that. But if you hurt her again, you'll have me to deal with."

I smiled. "I'll try to remember that."

"So, what brought you down here?" he asked as we turned the corner onto Pine Creek.

"Let's just say I learned what was important."

"Family," Del said as we hit a fat pothole in the road, and I was almost jounced into the ceiling.

I shook my head. "Del, I didn't grow up like you. My family never loved me like you, and yours love you."

"Aw, Miranda, every parent just—"

"Let me stop you right there," I interjected. My tone was probably a little more severe than it needed to be, but he'd struck a nerve. "My father used and abused me. My mother practically slobbered over Mitch even after she knew he was abusing me. So, no, every parent doesn't. Every parent should, though. That being said, I just walked away from two million dollars to come down here and throw myself at your sister's feet and hope. She loves me, and I love her. So I want to see if at least you guys might."

Del pulled off the side of the road and threw the truck in park. "I don't think you have to worry about that either." His voice turned a little choked up. "Dad's been angry but not sure who to be angry at. Mom's been begging Sarah to call you. And Jason and I think you're good for each other. So, we already love you."

Tears burned behind my eyes, and for the first time, I didn't fight them at all. I just let them come. My voice turned thick as I said, "Thanks, Del. You have no idea what that means to me."

"No, don't figure I do, but I know my sister was the happiest I'd ever seen her at that damn barbecue at Jesters. So, what happened with your folks? Wait, did you say you walked away from two million dollars?"

I snorted a laugh and wiped my nose on my sleeve, sniffling. "Yeah. My dad literally had a heart attack, and my mother almost fainted."

He put the truck in gear, shaking his head. "You might want to re-think that."

"Why?" I asked, suddenly feeling a stab of fear in my chest.

"'Cause Sarah ain't worth much more than about twenty cents."

I burst into laughter, loud and full. "No, you're probably right, but what can I do? I'm in love with her, Del."

"You must be," Del snickered, still shaking his head.

The conversation ended there until we pulled up in front of the cabin.

"Well, here you go," Del said, jerking me into a big hug. "Bang on the door if you need to. She's in there."

I hopped out and pulled my duffel from the bed as he backed up and drove away with the squeal of his fan belt following him down the road. Now that I was here, the real anxiety began, but I shook it off. All I could do was throw myself at Sarah's mercy.

"Don't bother knocking," a voice said from behind me. "I'm not in there."

I spun around to see Sarah walking toward me from the garage. As she drew into the light, I realized she was covered in engine grease.

"The Mustang, okay?" I asked shyly, not sure what else to say at the moment.

"Jeep," she said, voice flat as she looked me up and down. "What are you doing here?"

"I came to beg you to take me back," I whispered, almost too quiet for her to hear.

"What about Washington and the money?"

"I didn't take it."

That got her, and she paused. "Why?"

I took a deep breath. *Here goes.* "Because when the moment came, I realized you were more important. I'm in love with you, Sarah, and I want to give this a try," I gestured between us.

"Let me get this straight. You dumped me in D.C. in front of the courthouse, then turned down millions of dollars as if that might win me back when you came crawlin'."

"Uh-huh."

"And I'm just supposed to take you in like some broke stray now and pay for everything."

My eyes went wide until I saw the grin tugging at the corners of her mouth. She was teasing me, but I was so freaked out that I started to cry. "I'm sorry, Sarah. I was scared. Please—mmmph."

I never finished the sentence as she rushed forward and kissed me, stealing my breath and all the words that might have followed. My skin prickled all the way up my back as gooseflesh popped out all over me. I opened my mouth, deepening the kiss, holding her to me until I was breathless and had to stop.

"So," I asked. "Is that a yes?"

"It is," she answered and took my duffel, leading me into the house. "But the first thing we need to do is get you a new phone. Governor Fletcher called me looking for you yesterday. I told him that if I saw you, I'd pass it on."

I gave her a bemused look. "What did he want?"

"I'm guessin' you saw that Senator Smitts died yesterday. I think he wants you to take the job."

"Well, if he calls again, tell him I said no."

Sarah laughed. "You can tell him yourself, darlin'. I ain't your secretary. But you might want to think about it before you say no."

I stopped her in the living room as she dropped my things on the couch. "Would you be with me?"

Sarah shrugged and then cupped my face. "I took a bullet for you. I think I could handle being a Senator's girl." Then she lowered her voice. "But let's not talk about that now." She scooped me up and carried me up to the loft, hitting the switch on the way and dousing the cabin lights.

Epilogue

Sarah

Two years later. . .

"You ready?" I asked, poking my head out from the curtain.

Miranda pressed her lips together. "As ready as I'll ever be. The question is, are you ready?"

"Let's just hope no one is shooting at us this time," I answered glibly.

"These are the people who got us here, pumpkin. We'll be fine."

I chuckled at the nickname. I hated it, but I'd never tell her that. According to our couples counselor, we were supposed to express our feelings, but my dad always told me to pick my battles, and that one sure wasn't worth it.

We'd come so far in the last year. The wedding had been small. Miranda invited her parents, though only her mother showed. Her father, it seemed, didn't want to show his face, which was just as well. Delbert would likely have beaten him to death. As it was, her mother got a chilly reception and was none too comfortable as we said our vows out on the promontory overlooking the gap behind the cabin.

Obviously, Miranda had accepted the appointment to replace Smitts from Governor Fletcher, a Democrat. Apparently, he and the party thought that with her notoriety and, more importantly, the way she'd stood up to her stepson's campaign to discredit her with poise and dignity, she would do well. It had taken some cajoling and phone calls from a half dozen Senators and congresswomen, but Miranda finally accepted. I did point out to her that together, we might be able to undo a lot of the damage Mitch had done—well, the damage that they both had done. She wouldn't let herself off the hook, no matter how much I'd tried to get her to let it go.

In the end, she did well by Kentuckians, helping negotiate some additional funding for green space and tourism conversion for Appalachia. Her crowning achievement, though, hadn't been for the LGBTQ community; her very presence in the Senate had given us all a feeling of representation. No, her jewel had been a multi-billion dollar rural rehabilitation bill that also provided funding for addiction treatment primarily focused on fentanyl and opiate usage.

Not everyone back home had loved the idea of a queer Senator, or a woman Senator for that matter, and we'd had our share of threats. It had taken me quite some time to realize that it wasn't my job to chase things like that and that most of them were cranks.

Now, she'd won re-election by a wide margin, which she owed as much to my mother as anyone. I'd never known my mother could stump so well for a politician, reminding the good people of Kentucky of all they were gaining from her short time in the seat and keeping them focused on Miranda as a woman who did her job.

Miranda's cell phone buzzed while I continued to scan the crowd.

"This is it," Miranda said, pointing to her phone. The call was from Andrew Taylor Johnson, a congressman from Louisville and Miranda's opponent in the race. Frankly, he was an asshole. At every turn, he tried to tear Miranda down personally. He even went after me several times, but nothing seemed to stick, and in the end, he just came off as a prick. It turned out that there weren't quite as many people in Kentucky who liked that kind of ugliness in their politics as we'd all thought.

"Andrew, lovely to hear from you," Miranda answered, the epitome of class and style. After a momentary pause, while she listened to Johnson concede, she said softly, "I appreciate that. I want you to know that I felt you were just as worthy of the seat, and I hope that we'll be able to work together for the future of the state."

They continued on for a moment longer before Miranda let him go, but I wasn't paying attention. I was still watching the crowd that filled the hotel ballroom.

"It's over," Miranda said, tapping me on the shoulder.

A shiver went down my back as I realized this was it. I was now the wife of the Senator-elect from Kentucky. Miranda gave me a kiss on the cheek, and we stepped out and walked up toward the podium, hand in hand.

I stood by, trying not to be too rigid, but the last time I'd done something like this, I'd almost taken a bullet, and Miranda and I had barely survived, so it was hard not to be on edge.

"Good evening, everyone," Miranda began with that broad, dazzling D.C. smile she had.

The crowd responded with massive applause and hoots and hollers.

"I just got off the phone with Congressman Johnson, who congratulated me, my wife, and all of you on a race well run."

More applause.

"Now we look to the future of Kentucky and the future of the United States of America. It is time to begin the hard work of mending this fractured country with decorum and common sense. I am committed to a brighter future for all Kentuckians in the coming years, where I will fight, as promised, to bring in new industries, new jobs, and new education to a state sorely in need of good representation in Washington focused on the people, rather than continually passing along money to the wealthy."

Another round of applause followed. "My wife and I are living proof that this country can be healed of its divides, that the greater numbers of us believe in a future together rather than separate, and that our nation can still stand as the beacon on the hill. I want to thank all of you here who supported me, worked their rear-ends off on the campaign, and gave us this opportunity. You are remembered and loved for your efforts. Especially, though, I want to give thanks to my wife, Sarah Rogers-Danbury, who has supported this effort even when she'd felt her days in

Washington were long behind her. And," she paused for a second and leaned into the microphone in a more intimate fashion. "And, well, I apologize to her for the long nights, missed dinners, and other things we won't be able to do together as we all work for a better, brighter, more colorful future."

That was my cue, so I walked up next to her, held up her hand in triumph, and gave her a whopper right there on the stage to the cheers of the assembled guests. Our campaign manager had advised against it, saying it might turn off prospective support in more conservative districts, but we decided that we had to be who we were as the balloons fell from the ceiling and a few indoor poppers went off in celebration.

We spent a few hours at the party, pressing flesh, graciously thanking people, and accepting congratulatory calls from other senators and congressmen and women who had helped push us forward on the campaign. We even got a call from the President. Then, with a last wave goodbye, we finally left to go back to our suite.

"So," Miranda said, kicking off her heels. "How does it feel?"

I raised a questioning eyebrow. "Which part?"

"Being married to the Junior Senator from Kentucky?"

I snorted a laugh. "I've been married to the Junior Senator from Kentucky for six months now, honey. It feels the same. I've been wondering what it might feel like to be married to the first queer President of the United States, myself."

Miranda's eyes shot up. "Getting a bit ahead of ourselves, aren't we?"

I gave her a crooked smile. "I just wanted to see what you'd say."

"Well," she answered, giving me a glance of mock thoughtfulness. "I'd have to say that I'm not ruling anything out at this point."

I laughed. "Well, I feel like we should celebrate, don't you?"

Miranda turned around, and I unzipped her dress. Then I stripped out of my tuxedo and laid down on the bed, patting the mattress. "Come join me, oh, webspinner of Washington."

"Please don't call me that," she griped as she dropped onto the bed and straddled my hips. "Or you'll get no nookie from me again, like ever."

With a laugh, I grabbed her and pulled her down into a deep, toe-curling kiss.

I'd like to say that we made mad, passionate love that night, but we'd been going for thirty-six hours straight. So, in the end, we just slid beneath the sheets. Miranda put her head on my shoulder, and within minutes, we were both nodding off.

That was until Miranda whispered, "I want a baby."

"What?"

The End.

About the Author

Aoibh Wood lives in Massachusetts with her loving wife of over two decades and their beloved cat, Papaya, who looks suspiciously like an intergalactic gangster of some note.

First on Scene

Howling Sirens: Book 1

In a small town shattered by violent animal attacks, four first responders must confront their pasts and embrace their destinies as they become humanity's last line of defense against a supernatural threat.

In the quiet, quintessential small town of Hudson, Massachusetts, a dedicated group of first responders—Kitty, Zuri, Angell, and Eric—commit themselves to the safety of their community. Kitty, a Southern transplant and new medic, is eager to prove her worth and find her place, not knowing that the woman of her dreams, Zuri, is more than just an EMT. Eric, who struggles in his role as a paramedic, learns to lean on his partner, Angell, a skilled medic with a mysterious, bewitched past.

When a series of violent animal attacks shatters the town's tranquility, it unearths hidden secrets and thrusts these healers onto a warrior's path. As they rush from one medical emergency to another, each pulse-pounding call brings them closer to each other and their destiny. The perils of the paranormal threaten to destroy everything they hold dear, forcing them to confront their pasts to save their future.

In this adrenaline-fueled world of EMS, the lives of Kitty, Zuri, Angell, and Eric intertwine in ways they never expected. Their call to duty transcends the ordinary as they become humanity's last line of defense against a supernatural threat. Every siren heralds a potential showdown, challenging them to redefine what it means to be 'of service.' Follow these warriors on a gripping journey where every heartbeat could signal a supernatural confrontation.

Cait is jetting off to Ireland for a crucial confrontation with the Light Fae in an effort to save her sister, Aoife. En route, an Army Medic, caught in the chaos when Cait and Nastasia escaped Boston, becomes an involuntary tagalong. It's a hostage situation for sure, but our unusual companion is as intrigued by Cait and her powerful duo as she is terrified, and there may be more to her than meets the eye.

Meanwhile, Doyle is undergoing unsettling changes. Her usual fructivorous cravings have shifted to something more carnivorous, leaving everyone baffled and worried for her. Adding to the complexity is the mysterious Rowan, likely the first vampire ever made, whose motives and intentions remain shrouded in secrecy.

Unbeknownst to Cait and her companions, something is amiss on the Emerald Isle. The typically benign Light Fae have taken on a darker, more sinister presence. Amidst this turmoil, Cait grapples with her lingering feelings for Nastasia and a strange echo of her own voice that trails her in her thoughts. Nothing is as it seems, with Fae glamour clouding reality, as they race toward a final confrontation Cait never saw coming.

Prepare for a thrilling journey where every step is fraught with danger, and trust is as elusive as the Fae themselves.

You can find other fine titles published by Carson Press LLC through major book retailers everywhere.

More Titles by Aiobh Wood

The Cait Reagan Series

Blood Rituals

Black Mirror

Green Rath

Dark Sisters (Coming Fall 2024)

www.ingramcontent.com/pod-product-compliance
Lightning Source LLC
Chambersburg PA
CBHW022127310726
48972CB00007B/2232